CW00522591

Fiona Cane graduated from Exeter University with a degree in Philosophy. She worked in film and entertainment PR before moving into sports management and tennis coaching. She lives in Sussex with her husband and her two children. *When the Dove Cried* is her second novel.

When the Dove Cried

FIONA CANE

Caracol Books

For Susie

1

Her brain is buzzing, vibrating in her skull like a wasp in a jar. It drowns out the metronomic sound of her trainers pounding the compacted mud of the bridle path. Her black Lycra crop-top and shorts cling to her sodden skin, sleek as cellophane. Cool droplets of sweat dribble down her forehead, over the razor-fine line of her brows, into her dry, bloodshot eyes. The sting of the salt blinds her momentarily. She pinches the corners of her eyes with her thumb and forefinger, grits her teeth and increases her speed. Her heart is hammering her ribs. Her lungs are burning. The build up of lactic acid in her muscles is fast approaching unbearable. She knows she's reached her physical limit.

She slows to a jog, unclenches her jaw and gulps mouthfuls of spring-fresh, evening air until her pulse begins to settle. And then, bam. There it is again. The pathetic image of her boyfriend slumped against the bath, a discarded syringe by his side. She can hear her terrified wail flying towards her from the woods, as though the awful noise she made when she found him has grown wings and followed her. She tried to rouse him. She shook him, shouted at him, screamed. But Liam's head was nodding like that stupid Churchill dog, his dilated pupils fixed on the carpet. He'd been gone a while. His mind displaced in a chemical euphoria. That's how it is. She knows the drill. She's nursed enough addicts at the hospital. Within twenty-four hours Liam would go looking for his next fix. It was either that or suffer withdrawal. She's seen that too. The waking horrors as the junkies try to kick their habit, stinking of rotting corpses, every minute of their misery an hour of mental torture.

Coke used to be Liam's drug of choice. She knew that when they met and she didn't mind. Not really. Everyone is into it these days. A couple of pints down the pub, a snort in the toilets. It's sociable, harmless. But she doesn't know why or when he swapped his lines of white for a shot of brown. Not until this afternoon. Liam didn't bother to tell her. And his betrayal hurts like mad.

The alarm on her pink and black sport's watch bleeps. Frowning, she glances at the numbers flashing on the screen. She's run the last mile in five minutes flat. A personal best. She should be elated. But she isn't. She doesn't feel anything. She is totally numb. It's ludicrous to think she can run her fears away.

'You okay?'

At the sound of the voice she jumps and turns around. A tall, dark-haired man is scrutinising her. Even though he's comically dressed in a pair of baggy white shorts and a black-and-gold striped rugby shirt, cut off at the shoulders, she can see he's buff. She recognises him immediately as the bloke she passed most Friday evenings last autumn as she finished her run and he started out on his. They'd taken to acknowledging one another – a nod of the head, slight wave of the hand – but so far this year, since it's been light enough to run by the river, she hasn't clapped eyes on him.

'Yeah. I'm fine. Thanks for asking,' she says. Despite his ready smile and easy manner she feels his eyes appraising her fit, toned body. She wishes she wasn't wearing her crop-top. She's not as slim as she should be, thanks to all the curries she's been eating lately. She covers her belly with the flat of one hand and fiddles self-consciously with her ponytail.

'Are you sure? You look as if you're about to burst into tears.'

His voice is pure public school. She isn't sure why she's surprised. She clocked his car in the pub car park. A BMW M5, its silver paintwork polished to a mirror-like finish. She assumed he was rich rather than a toff. Not that it matters. They are hardly likely to become friends. He's only stopped to talk to her because he's concerned. It touches her. She isn't used to blokes being kind.

'You're out early,' she says.

The man nods and stretches his mouth into a dazzling white smile, the Hollywood A-list kind she's more used to seeing in glossy magazines. She feels the prickle of goose bumps on her skin.

'It's the wife's thirtieth. We're having a bit of a do. I'm under strict instructions to be back by seven-thirty.'

'Oh! Great. Have fun,' she says. She doesn't mean it. His scant description of marital bliss has rubbed salt in her already raw wound.

'Thanks.' He smiles again and plugs his headphones into his ears. 'See you,' he adds and winks.

'I guess,' she says, blushing like a schoolgirl.

He turns away and eases his legs into a strong athletic stride, his expensive trainers kicking up the dust as he speeds towards The Star Inn. Nice fella but not a care in the world, she thinks enviously as she sets off in the opposite direction.

Dusk arrives all of a sudden, catching her unawares. She can see the lights of the pub in the distance, the bushes to her left and the dark water of the river to her right, but not a lot else. Her foot catches on a broken branch and she almost falls but doesn't, righting herself at the last minute. She slows to a walk. She's competing in a half-marathon on Saturday and can't afford to get injured. The race means everything to her. Running is all she has left. Outside of her job, it's the only credible part of her life. And this time she wants to win. Victory will give her fractured world some meaning. If she does she'll move out. Split with Liam. It's not as if he needs her anymore. Not now he's filling his veins with smack. She's become the third person in the relationship. She doesn't need that kind of shit. She'll make a clean break. Move away from here. Start over. Find a job at another hospital. Brighton maybe.

A tear trickles down her cheek. Don't think about him, she tells herself. He's not worth it.

A twig snaps in the bushy undergrowth. She hears the rustle of branches and the crunch of dry leaves. Posh boy having a piss after a pint? she wonders, straining her eyes. Mustering some courage, she calls out to the gathering gloom, 'Hello.'

Silence.

Probably a fox, or a rabbit, maybe a deer, she thinks. She breaks into a jog but is aware of thudding footsteps not far behind. Is someone following me? she wonders. Her pulse quickening, she sprints away but the darkness makes it impossible to seek out a safe path and she is running blind. She trips on a stone and falls to her knees. She hears a rasping breath. Whoever it is, is gaining on her. Panting, she scrabbles to her feet and hurries on but then the ground seems to give way. Her right foot sinks awkwardly into a hole. There's a loud crack and her ankle buckles. She gasps and yanks herself free and hobbles forward, ignoring the searing pain shooting up her leg. The lights of the pub glow like an invitation in the distance. Not far now. You can do it, she urges herself. But it's no good. No matter how hard she wills herself on, her ankle simply cannot support her weight. Running out of options, she begins to hop.

The leaden-footed thump is close now, the ragged breathing louder. Her blood speeds down her arteries, hammering at her eardrums. Fat tears roll down her cheeks. She tries her injured leg again and staggers forward moaning in agony until a tug on her ponytail wrenches her head backwards. Hands flailing, she falls to the ground landing sharply on her buttocks. Something cold and thin is slipped around her neck. She screams and clutches at the wire with her fingers and tries to pull it over her head. But the ligature tightens around her throat. Gasping for breath, she tugs at it, her body twisting and writhing as she fights for air.

Suspended in a vacuum somewhere between living and dying, she hears the rip of elastic as her shorts are torn from her body.

Please don't. Not that. Please, she screams, but the words get lost somewhere between her brain and her lips. A warm trickle of urine courses down the inside of her thigh before what little light is left in her world goes out.

2

Lily hurries down the stairs as fast as her sheath-like dress will allow. The catering company delivered the food an hour ago. The starters have been plated up; the main course is in the oven, the desert in the fridge, the champagne on ice. She glances at her wristwatch. Seven-thirty. Great. Adam will be back from his run any minute. Taking tiny steps she skims, Geisha-like, across the quarry tiles to the dining room. She catches sight of herself in the gilt mirror and stops to admire her new haircut. She thinks the layers have added more body. Or perhaps the highlights have given it extra vitality. She smiles and continues to the dining room. The polished mahogany table is strewn with cut-glass crystal, gleaming silver, white-bone china, yellow linen napkins, skilfully folded, and a floral centrepiece studded with candles. And the best thing is, she's played no part in the preparation. Didn't even know about it. She thought Adam was taking her out to dinner to celebrate, as he did every year. But in bed this morning, after they made love, Adam sprung his surprise.

Where is he? She checks her watch again. Seven thirty-seven. He's probably stopped for his usual pint in the pub. Still, he's cutting it fine. If he isn't back soon, their guests will arrive before him.

A burst of fresh air envelopes her as the front door swings open. Adam, hot and sweaty from his run, a grey towel draped around his neck, steps into the hall.

He sees her and smiles. 'Wow. You look hot. Love the new haircut. And the dress. Red really does suit you.'

'It's not too short?'

'No, and not too tight.' He takes her arm, pulls her towards him and slides his hands over her bum.

She screws up her nose and pushes him away. 'Ew! You better take a shower.'

He ogles her with heavy lidded eyes. 'Fancy joining me?'

'No time,' she says, laughing, shooing him towards the stairs.

He bounds up them, two at a time, as fit now as he was when they met at university. Not for the first time she thanks God she's naturally slim. She can't imagine Adam with a fat wife. Not that she's any reason to worry. They've been together just over ten years, five of them in married bliss. They're best friends as well as lovers. They share the same interests; good food, rugby, rock music, films. Theirs is a perfect marriage.

Well almost.

For the past two years they've been trying for a baby. The first few months were fun with Adam insisting on *practising* continuously and spontaneously. They've had sex on the kitchen table, under the kitchen table. They've tried doing it al fresco, in the garden, in the wood, and on one memorable occasion, the toilets of an Italian restaurant, another regrettable one, the back seat of his car, ruining the upholstery. Six months excitement however, was superseded by exhaustion, her monthly period accompanied by an aching disappointment that consumed her for days. Emotionally wrung out, she was ready to quit but Adam refused to be defeated. Holding her in his arms one night, he suggested they adopt a more scientific approach.

'There are things you can do,' he said.

'Like what?'

'Work out when you're ovulating. Take your temperature. Change your diet. That kind of thing.'

She smiled and kissed him. 'Still full of surprises, Mr Hutchinson. That's what I love about you.'

'So you'll give it a go?'

'Just try and stop me.'

But time wore on and although she didn't let on to Adam, she felt an increasing sense of doom with every monthly bleed. Fate, she felt, had mapped out her future and it didn't include children. She wasn't meant to be a mother.

'You're too thin,' Adam said. 'We need to fatten you up.'

'It's my fault, isn't it? Something's wrong with me. That's what you really mean.'

'Lily, I was joking.'

'But it's possible, just as it's possible something might be wrong with you.'

'Nonsense. You're perfect,' he said, kissing her on the top of the head.

She fell silent then and, in the weeks that followed, although she often wanted to, she never referred to the subject again.

Her childlessness is the reason the last five weeks have dragged. Adam has been in Milan, working on a takeover with a team from the Mergers and Acquisitions department of Goldbergs, the City-based Investment Bank where he works. Something big, was all he could tell her, which was little compensation for his absence. The weeks seemed endless, the house larger, their bed emptier. It's the loneliest Lily can remember being in the two years since they relocated to Sussex and the sleepy village of Adlington, tucked away at the foot of the South Downs.

It had been Miles Spencer, Adam's oldest friend, who sold them both the house and the rural dream. He trained as a surveyor in London after graduating, then turned his back on the big smoke four years ago, without a backward glance, and headed to the affluent south. He got a job at the Steers and Parsons estate agency in Lewes and bought a two-bedroom semi on the high street, a three-minute walk away from his office.

She'd never forget the first time Miles showed them Orchard House. It was a beautiful summer's evening. The faded sky was tinged with pink as the dying sun sank behind the Downs. Birds were singing in the bushes, lambs bleating in the surrounding fields and the house, covered with gnarled ropes of wisteria, was dripping with grape-like bunches of dusty-blue flowers. Immaculate lawns at the front and the back, a rose garden to the side, an orchard of plum and apple trees at the bottom and an enormous horse chestnut tree weighted with cream candles out front, capped off with stunning views of the Downs.

'I've stepped into a fairy tale,' she said.

Adam laughed and rubbed his hands together, unable to contain his delight. 'When shall we move in?'

'Can we afford it?'

'Just about.'

Through the open front door, she caught sight of Miles tactfully admiring the horse chestnut tree, while they deliberated in the cavernous hall.

'We'll need a pretty big mortgage but factor in my annual bonus and we should be able to pay it off within three years.'

'Sounds a tad over-optimistic.'

'Trust me, Lily. It's a golden opportunity.'

She bit her lip. 'I'm not sure.'

'It'll make us money in the long-term.'

They were standing at the foot of the grand oak staircase, slightly to the right of centre of the hall, which rose steeply before curving to the left and disappearing from view. Beyond them was the vast kitchen, recently renovated and with a wall of glass the full length of one side of the room, which slid open onto the back garden. Kitted out in brand new white-gloss cupboards, shiny granite surfaces and with a gleaming beige tiled floor, it was every young bride's dream.

'It's lovely, of course it is. I'm just not sure I want to leave London. What about my job? Your job?'

'You'll be too busy to work.'

'But I like it at the agency. It's small but it's on the up. I don't want to be a housewife. Besides, you'll have to commute.'

'I mean you'll be too busy looking after our three children.' He clasped her arms. 'Think about it, Lily. What a fabulous place to grow up in; a big house with two acres of garden, the sea nearby, the Downs to explore. Fresh air on tap and no more London fumes.'

Put like that it was impossible to resist.

Within a month they'd sold up and moved to Sussex. Initially, she was excited about swapping her hectic London life for the peace of the countryside. A handful of houses, a dozen cottages, two pubs, a village store, a church, a river, two farms, endless fields, and acres of dense, verdant woodland, that's all there was to Adlington. But reality didn't live up to the ideal. Weekends were great but commuting exhausted her and, after almost a year of trying, she still wasn't pregnant.

'You're too tired,' Adam said. 'You should give up your job.'

She was inclined to agree, so she took his advice and handed in her notice.

Another year passed and still no baby.

For an unemployed, childless city-dweller, whose commuter husband worked long days, time crawled. Most of the villagers were elderly couples who'd lived in Adlington all their lives. They made friends with a young couple, Mark and Steff Macdonald, but eight months ago Mark had been posted abroad and had taken his wife with him. She got on well with Paul and Sally Pearton but he was busy on the farm and she was heavily pregnant with their third child. She lunched with Miles occasionally but one of his recent girlfriends, Jules perhaps, or Isla, no, Alice, didn't like it so she stopped. She joined a gym in nearby Lewes and made friends with a couple of the ladies from her Pilates class, but both were busy mothers with young children and very little free time on their hands to go shopping, visit art galleries or sit around chatting in cafés.

'I miss my friends,' she told Adam.

'Then go visit them. London's only sixty miles away.'

'They have jobs,' she said. 'Like normal people.'

'You don't need to work. We don't need the money.'

'Yes but I want to.'

'Why, when we're going to have a baby?'

She sighed and shook her head. 'Am I?'

'Yes, Lily, *we* are.'

Buoyed by Adam's unwavering optimism and with nothing else to do, she has spent the last five weeks in her pyjamas, scouring the internet for information about IVF treatment. If she can't conceive naturally, it's the obvious next step and the best thirtieth birthday present Adam could give her. It's expensive though. She hopes they can afford it. I'll ask him now, she thinks. Before the guests arrive.

'You haven't moved,' says Adam, creeping up behind her.

She turns around. Adam is cradling an enormous bouquet of red roses, a broad grin stretched across his face.

'One for each year of your life,' he says.

Lily's childlessness is temporarily forgotten. Seated around the table are the six people she cares about most in the world. Friends she and Adam made at university and Susie's boyfriend, Fabian Stephens, who works with Adam and Rose and who is very much part of the gang.

'You're glowing,' says Miles. 'Being thirty suits you.'

Lily smiles. 'I don't know about that but it is great to have Adam home.'

'You two make an unbeatable advert for marriage. Don't you think so, Rose?'

'What's that?' asks Rose, who is sitting on the opposite side of the table next to Adam, who's seated at the head, and Nat. Rose is wearing her straight, raven hair loose tonight, which highlights the angles of her thin face.

'Ignore him,' says Lily. 'He's talking nonsense as usual. I'm much more interested in hearing about little George. Why didn't you bring him with you? We'd love to have seen him. It's been a while.'

Rose shrugs. 'Honestly? I fancied the night off. It's hard work being a mum.'

Lily winces. Miles notices and makes a face at Rose.

'I'm sorry, Lily,' says Rose. 'I meant being a single mum. It won't be like that for you.'

'No, it won't,' says Miles.

Lily bats the air with her hand. They all know she and Adam are trying for a baby. Only, since they've failed to produce so spectacularly, she wishes they hadn't told them. She forces a smile. 'Don't be silly. How is he? Is he enjoying school? He must be in year three now.'

'He's doing well.'

'So he's bright then. Like his father?' Miles asks, raising his eyebrows.

A little insensitively, Lily thinks. Somehow the infamous skiing trip always comes up, although it's usually Nat who resurrects it. As if anyone still needs reminding of Rose's brief but life-altering fumble in a cramped broom cupboard with a virile French waiter. He was left-handed, apparently. It's the only detail Rose remembers. She was off her face drunk that night. We all were. It was New Year's Eve. She glances at Rose who has turned a deep red.

'Miles!' she says, and nudges him in the ribs. She wonders who's looking after the child. Is he at home with Nanny Lizzie or has Rose farmed him out to her parents again? His grandparents have always seen far more of little George than his mother.

'I know it's a bit schmaltzy, making speeches about your wife,' says Adam, clinking a glass with a spoon as he rises to his feet.

Nat groans. 'Must you? I'm still eating.'

Lily blushes and motions to him to sit down. On the other side of Nat and looking gorgeous in a blue velvet corset, which sets off her fabulous breasts, Susie catches her eye and winks.

'Yes I must,' says Adam.

Nat rolls his eyes and shovels another spoonful of crème brûlée into his mouth.

It's been tough for Lily recently. I've been away a lot. But she never complains.'

'She's a saint, your wife. You're lucky to have her,' interrupts Miles good-humouredly.

Fabian, sitting on her right, laughs. 'Nonsense. She's only after your money. Isn't that right, Lily?'

'Absolutely!'

'Get on with it,' says Nat, dropping his spoon in his bowl and reaching for his champagne.

Lily frowns at him. Nat comes in two flavours: sweet and sober and pissed and poisonous. It's a shame Angela is on one of her yoga courses this weekend. He usually behaves himself when she's around, although how or why she puts up with his drinking is anyone's guess.

'I will if I can get a word in.'

'Shush. Let the poor man speak.'

'Thank you, Rose,' says Adam and, delving into the pocket of his jacket that's hanging on the back of his chair, he turns to Lily. 'I love you, darling. Thank you for everything.'

Lily is not sure why but she cringes.

'Bollocks!' mutters Nat, swinging his legs out from under the table and crossing them, exposing the dirty-white Converse trainers he's paired with his over-the-top dinner jacket and bowtie.

Susie glares at him and thumps him on the arm.

Nat glowers. 'Gerroff.'

Ignoring them, Adam walks behind Miles and hands a small, blue velvet box to Lily. 'Your birthday present.'

She lifts the lid. A pair of diamond earrings the size of marbles glint in the candlelight.

'How appropriate. Ice for the ice-maiden,' mutters Nat.

Her cheeks burning, she stares at them unable to speak. She wanted a baby but has been given diamonds. Her heart sinks. Does that make her selfish or just plain ungrateful?

'Don't you like them?' asks Adam.

She swallows the lump in her throat and lifts her eyes, smiling.

'Darling, they're perfect. Thank you.'

Susie and Fabian are lingering in the dining room. Susie is sitting on her boyfriend's lap, admiring his face. He should have been a model, not a banker, she thinks, he's that pretty. Perfect, symmetrical cheekbones rising in two sleek angular lines on either side his slender nose, and those dark brown, bed-me eyes of his, with the long, thick lashes. The first time I met him, I was convinced he was wearing mascara. Not unreasonable, given his androgynous looks.

They'd met the Christmas Eve before last, at a drink's party in Rose's Fulham flat. Susie didn't want to go. She hated hobnobbing with Rose and Adam's Goldbergs colleagues; insufferably dull men in grey suits and high-maintenance, opinionated career women in red lipstick and stilettos. Lily and Adam were holidaying in Barbados, which meant she wouldn't know a soul. Despite her prejudices, imbued with festive spirit, and slim for the first time in ages, her curvaceous body squeezed into a low-cut, skin-tight, emerald dress, she was on red-hot form. She'd attracted the eyes of most of the men by the time Fabian, prowling the room like a panther as he tried to summon the nerve to speak to this *vision in green* (his words not hers), finally made his strike. It was love at first sight. They left the party and headed to a candlelit bar and sat in a corner, talking until the small hours of Christmas morning.

Susie absently runs her hands through Fabian's mop of almost-black hair and turns her mind to Adam.

Handsome, well-mannered, oozing with confidence, Adam is and always has been the epitome of unrehearsed cool. Even his bang-on clothes are a defining part of his character. Crisply ironed, white cotton shirt + black designer jacket + Diesel jeans = Adam. Then there's his walk: one hand in his pocket, deliberate, exacting with long measured strides. But it's his walk, she thinks, affected, manufactured as though he's practiced it in front of a mirror for weeks, which gives him away. He never used to walk like that and he was never given to grand gestures. What had that been about? Why did he suddenly feel the need to show off? Look at me everyone. I'm successful and rich. And I can prove it. Here you go, darling. Some over-the-top diamonds. I know you'll love them. It isn't like him, she thinks. He's trying too hard. He's not as self-assured as he used to be. Beneath the surface of his calm exterior, she's sure she can detect an inward struggle, as though he's fighting something, an emotion perhaps, which he can't control.

But what it is, she can't quite put her finger on.

'You're very quiet,' Fabian says, tracing his fingers over the exposed, pale flesh of her breasts.

'I'm worried about Lily,' she says, lowering her voice.

'Go on.'

She considers expounding her theory about Adam but decides against it. Fabian wouldn't like it. He adores Adam. 'She's lonely.'

'Really? She looks pretty happy tonight.'

Susie frowns. 'Don't be naïve. You know she rings me nearly every evening for a chat even though she's got absolutely nothing to say.'

'She misses you. And who can blame her,' he says, wrapping his arms around her. He squeezes her gently, leans forward and nibbles her ear.

She groans and pushes him away. 'I'm serious.'

Fabian sighs. 'I know.'

'She gave up her job to move down here because they wanted to start a family. But two years later and still no baby.

15

She must be bored to tears. And then there's this house. It's vast. Lily must rattle around in it when Adam's away.'

'True.'

'Something's wrong.'

Fabian strokes his smooth, hairless chin and scrunches up his eyes. 'Maybe Adam's sperm aren't up to the job. He can't be brilliant at everything.'

'Exactly, so you'd think Lily would want to talk about it. Trying and failing to get pregnant must be heartbreaking.'

'Maybe you should try broaching the subject with her.'

'I hoped you'd say that. Honestly, Fabian I don't know how I ever managed without you.'

Fabian smiles and runs the back of his hand over her cheek. 'And with as much sensitivity as possible. If she still doesn't open up then forget about it. But right now my legs are numb. I think it's time we joined the others,' he says and levers Susie off his lap.

'Is that your way of telling me I've put on weight?' she asks, thumping him on the arm.

Ignoring her, he takes her hand and leads her out of the room. Susie follows, admiring his slender hips and pert buttocks as they cross the hallway. When they reach the half-closed door of the sitting room, they stop and turn to look at one another in surprise. Adam, speaking in a loud whisper, is angrily berating someone. Susie has never known him lose his temper. Intrigued to know who's got him riled, she places a finger to her lips and moves closer to the door.

'I'm *not* drunk. And you know I'm right.'

My God, thinks Susie. Rose. Adam's number one disciple. What has Little Miss Meek and Mild done?

'Then you're lying,' says Adam through gritted teeth.

'It's the truth. I swear.'

'Jesus Christ, Rose, what's wrong with you? Telling me this, today of all days.'

'I had no choice.'

'Are you out of your tiny mind? I'm warning you, Rose, if you breathe a word of this to Lily, I'll ... I'll ...'

'What Adam? What will you do?'

Beside her, Fabian's leg twitches. Susie prods him and glares at him but it's too late. Fabian loses his balance. His foot nudges the bottom of the door and it inches open, squeaking on its hinges. In an effort to make the action appear spontaneous he saunters into the room, dragging Susie after him. At the sight of them, Rose flushes crimson.

'Fabian, Susie. What can I get you?' Adam asks, his voice cool and collected, as though he's been talking about the weather. 'Whisky? A little Port? Baileys?'

'A whisky sounds good,' says Fabian.

'Susie?'

Susie shakes her head. 'Nothing for me.'

'Sure I can't tempt you?' asks Adam.

'Sure.'

Adam smiles and makes for the door. 'Back in a mo.'

Susie waits until she is sure he's out of earshot then turns to Rose. 'What was all that about?'

'All what?' asks Rose, whose complexion has regained its milky pallor.

'Don't play the innocent. Adam sounded furious. He accused you of lying.'

'We couldn't help but overhear,' explains Fabian.

Rose frowns and looks away.

'It's obviously something pretty serious because he told you not to tell Lily. What have you done, Rose?' asks Susie.

'Nothing,' mutters Rose.

'It didn't sound like nothing,' persists Susie.

Rose spins round, eyes flashing. 'Don't shove your nose in where it isn't wanted.'

Susie throws open her arms. 'Unbelievable!'

'Girls!' exclaims Fabian. He turns to Rose, who's glaring at Susie through narrowed eyes. 'It didn't sound good,' he explains reasonably.

Rose sighs and juts out her chin. 'It's a work matter.'

'Oh really. Something I should know about?' asks Fabian.

The loud knocking on the thick oak front door brings an end to the conversation.

'Who on earth makes house calls at one in the morning?' asks Rose, glancing at her watch. Without waiting for an answer, she brushes past Fabian and marches into the hall.

Lily is alone in the kitchen making coffee when Miles joins her. He looks a little uneasy, his mud-brown eyes darting this way and that behind the glass of his spectacles, like a mole caught in a sunbeam.

'I've bought you a little present. I hope you don't mind me giving it to you here,' he says and hands her a small gift wrapped in purple paper, tied with white ribbon.

'Oh, Miles. How sweet of you. You really shouldn't have.'

He smiles awkwardly. Apart from a few fine lines around his eyes and mouth, and his shorter hair, he looks exactly like the twenty-year-old boy she first met.

'I knew you'd say that,' he says.

'Am I that transparent?'

'Go on, open it.'

Slowly, carefully, Lily unties the ribbon and removes the wrapping paper to reveal an old tan leather jewellery box. She stares at it awkwardly.

'Well go on then.'

She flips back the lid on its tiny brass hinges and gasps at the silver bangle studded with tiny diamonds.

'It belonged to my grandmother. Do you like it?'

'It's beautiful, Miles, but I can't accept it. You should keep it. Save it for someone special. It's too precious to give to me.'

Miles takes off his spectacles and rubs his eyes with the back of his hand. 'It's not worth a great deal. I thought it would suit you.'

Lily smiles, leans forward and kisses him on the cheek. 'Thank you. I'll cherish it.'

The door opens with such force it crashes into the wall and swings back hitting Nat, who has kicked it open, on the side of his head. He pulls a face, rubs his temple then runs his freckled hand through his coarse, ginger hair.

'Gotcha!' He staggers forward and, tripping over the untied lace of one of his trainers, lunges at Lily, draping his arm around her to stop himself falling. She recoils and levers him off her. Undeterred, Nat leans forward until their noses touch. His breath reeks of whisky. 'Ssso you two having a fling?' he slurs.

'Go away, Nat. You're pissed,' says Miles.

Nat peels back his top lip in an attempt at a smile. 'I'm not sure Adam would be best pleased to hear about this,' he says, running his tongue over his chipped tooth.

'Hear about what?' asks Adam, marching into the room, his forehead furrowed.

'Miles has given me a present,' explains Lily quickly, holding up the bangle.

Adam takes it from her and studies it for a moment. His face relaxes and he nods his head. 'Very stylish, Miles.' He grins, strides over to Miles and pats him on the back. 'Now where did I put the whisky?'

'It's in the larder, I think,' says Lily.

The sound of someone hammering on the front door makes her jump. She looks at Adam who shrugs his shoulders then checks his watch.

Disorientated, Nat loosens his bowtie and squints at the large numbers on the clock on the wall.

'Adam, the police are here to see you,' says Rose, rushing into the kitchen followed by two men; one tall, with light brown hair dressed in a crumpled navy jacket and fawn jeans, the other smaller and stouter, wearing a brown pinstripe suit.

The taller man holds up his ID. 'Detective Chief Inspector Marshall and Detective Sergeant Harry Mills.'

Nat rubs his hands together and grins. 'Marvellous. The strippers. 'Bout bloody time.'

Lily cringes.

'Which one of you is Adam Hutchinson?' asks Marshall.

'I am,' says Adam, raising his hand.

'I'm here to talk to you about the murder of Carly Stoner.'

'Murder!' gasps Lily.

'Fuck!' says Nat.

'Carly who?' asks Adam, frowning at the detective.

'A local girl. Trainee nurse. She was found strangled to death on the bridle path by the river near The Star Inn at seven-thirty this evening. I believe you were the last person to see her alive.'

3

The group are huddled around the kitchen table, silently nursing cups of coffee and tumblers of whisky, apart from Nat who's slumped at one end, his head tipped sideways at an awkward angle, when Adam and the two detectives return to the kitchen. Lily glances at the stainless steel clock on the wall. It's nearing one-thirty. She springs out of her chair and rushes over to her husband, who is pale and solemn but otherwise calm.

'Mrs Hutchinson?' Marshall asks, running his hand through his light brown hair.

Lily's heart seems to grow to twice its usual size. Her tongue, like sandpaper, sticks to the roof of her mouth. She nods.

'Time is marching on so I'll cut to the chase. What time did your husband return home from his run?'

The bluntness of the question stuns her momentarily. Why did he ask that? 'Seven thirty-seven,' she replies in a flash.

'You're very precise.'

'I remember looking at my watch as he came in,' she says.

'If only everyone was as efficient,' he says with a wry smile, jotting it down in his notepad.

Lily smiles at him nervously then glances at Adam. He flinches almost imperceptibly. Why? she wonders. What has she said?

It's early Saturday evening when Adam returns. Lily hears the car pull up in the drive and dashes out of the kitchen where they've been waiting, drinking tea. Adam's face, she notices

21

as he closes the front door behind him, is pale, his eyes ringed by deep black shadows. He greets her with a wan smile, opening his arms. She runs into them without hesitation and hugs him, slipping her head in the concave well beneath his shoulder.

'You all right?' Miles asks, poking his head out of the kitchen.

Adam lets her go and nods. 'Fine, although I could murder a drink.'

Lily cringes at his choice of words. She drops her head so Adam won't notice but when she looks up he's already halfway towards the kitchen. She hurries after him and sits down beside him as he pours a stiff measure from the bottle of whisky, still on the table from the night before. He raises the crystal tumbler to his lips. Dark ovals smudge the tips of his fingers. She frowns but says nothing.

'What did they want?' Nat asks.

'I would've thought that was obvious,' Adam replies, rubbing his eyes with a fisted hand. Lily holds her breath. 'I'm a witness. I was helping them with their inquiries.'

'Man, I thought you were going to say you've been released on bail,' says Nat, slapping his forehead.

Fabian frowns. 'For God's sake, Nat.'

Lily, sitting still as stone, closes her eyes and recovers her breath. She is relieved. She was thinking the same. Why else would they have fingerprinted him? I'll ask him later, she thinks. When the others have left.

'Did you see her, then? The girl? Carly whatever her name was?' asks Susie.

Adam takes another swig. 'Yes, I did as it turns out.'

'Who found her?' asks Fabian.

'Ian Venables, the landlord of The Star, and some local guy who heard her screams when he was parking his car. He told Ian, who grabbed a torch. They found Carly's body on the bridle path about three hundred metres from the pub. She'd been strangled with some wire and her shorts had been removed.'

The description of the girl's violated body, though sketchy, makes Lily nauseous. She winces and glances at Susie who is pulling a face like she's been sucking a lemon. She feels Adam's hand reaching for hers. He squeezes it and she looks at him and smiles reassuringly.

Adam gulps another mouthful of whisky. 'I knew her. Well, kind of. Not by name. We jogged past each other most Fridays last autumn. I'd never spoken to her until yesterday and I only did because she'd stopped running and looked upset.'

'Upset?' Lily asks.

'She looked like she was about to cry. Her eyes were red. Her face blotchy. I asked her if she was okay. That's all. She said she was fine. She was one hell of an athlete, far quicker than me. The darkness must have done for her. She'd have outstripped anyone had it been light. I was running earlier last night. If I'd been out at my usual time she may never have been killed.'

Lily touches him on the arm. 'You mustn't think like that. It's not your fault.'

'I strongly advise you girls never to go jogging on your own at night,' he says.

Susie snorts. 'As if.'

'I tend to keep to well-lit pavements,' says Rose.

'Joggers are vulnerable,' continues Adam. 'Carly's killer probably watched her for weeks, checking out where she ran and at what time.'

'It would never occur to me!' says Susie.

Rose groans. 'That's because you don't run. '

'No. I mean it would never occur to me that someone was watching my every move. All those times I've travelled back late on the tube. It's quite a long walk from the station to my flat.'

'You're a creature of habit yourself, Adam. You should be careful too,' says Miles.

'It's different for a man. We're not such sitting ducks.'

Fabian shakes his head. 'All the same. I'd think about changing your route.'

4

Outwardly, Adam seems unaffected by what has happened. But like a swan gliding through the water, Lily guesses that beneath the surface, he's making a great deal of effort in appearing so.

'Why did they fingerprint you?' she asks him as they lie in bed that night.

It's a while before he answers. 'It's police procedure.'

'Do you want to talk about it?'

But Adam is seeking out her mouth with his, his hand reaching down between her thighs. She assumes it's his coping mechanism kicking in and she has no objections. With the growing numbers of hours spent apart, she can't get enough of Adam.

On Monday morning, the police arrive in droves with sniffer dogs on leads and metres of blue and white police tape.

'The vicar told me they've erected a tent on the bridle path where the young nurse died,' Mrs Jessup the postmistress tells Lily when she ventures into the village to buy some stamps.

To add to the furore the press pitch up, armed with photographers and television crews. At ten o'clock an eager young reporter from the *Mirror* bangs on the door of Orchard House and asks to speak to Adam. He has greasy hair and reeks of cheap aftershave.

'He's in Italy,' Lily lies through clenched teeth.

'I doubt that,' he says, thrusting his Dictaphone at her. 'Suspects aren't allowed to leave the country.'

'Well he has, so what does that tell you?'

Besides, she tells herself as he drives away, if Adam were in trouble, the police would want to speak to him too.

On Tuesday, Adam leaves a message on her mobile while she's weeding the rose garden. She listens to it when she comes in for lunch.

Darling, I'm up to my eyes in work. I'm going to have to stay in London for a few nights.

She's not sure if she's more upset or angry.

That wasn't part of the deal, she thinks, flinging down the phone.

By Thursday, Lily is convinced she is going crazy with boredom. Too scared to go into the village in case she's accosted by a news-starved journalist or worse, one of the gossip-hungry villagers, she feels like a prisoner in her own home.

I can't go on like this, she thinks as she searches the fridge for something to eat. If I can't have children then I'm going to have to get a job. If only Adam could see how cut-off I am down here. It may be his genetically inherited dream but it's not mine. I'm not like his mother. I don't want to immerse myself in charity work and golf and Bridge, and only see my husband at weekends. Country life does not inspire me. I employ Pietr to see to the garden three hours a week because I hate gardening. I have no desire to make jam, arrange flowers or learn the art of bell ringing.

'You could enrol on a course,' Susie suggested when Lily, having handed in her notice, complained that all she did was walk, watch DVDs and read. 'It's what people who don't work do.'

Lily shivered. It sounded like a death sentence.

I'm not part of anything anymore, she thinks, snatching the cherry yoghurt hidden behind a jar of onion chutney at the back of the bottom shelf. Most of the villagers don't even like us. Adam might have found it hilarious when he heard one of them in the pub refer to us as Yuppies. But

I didn't. And now the gossip in the village is all about Adam and the murder.

'Two old guys are talking about Adam and Carly in The Star last night,' Pietr told her yesterday.

'It doesn't surprise me. They're all so narrow-minded and outdated,' She replied.

'They do not like me either. They think I illegal Polish immigrant.'

She slams the fridge door shut, picks up the telephone handset from the table and wanders into the sitting room. It's far too large and grand for one person to sit in but she fancies a change from the kitchen. Adam's thirty red roses are wilting in the cut glass vase on the coffee table. She sighs and flops dejectedly onto one of the two cream sofas that flank the stone fireplace, and glances at the large oil painting of a foxhunt and the two gloomy portraits of bearded old men, hanging from the walls. Priceless heirlooms handed down through generations of Hutchinsons, apparently. She sniffs. Unwanted art that needed a home, more like. Her gaze wanders to the walnut display cabinet stuffed full of antique silver, and the grand piano at the far end of the room that neither of them can play. I'd be far happier living in London and working. We could rent a flat. If he can buy me enormous diamonds, we can clearly afford it. We could live there during the week and spend the weekends here. If by some miracle I manage to conceive, we could move back down. It's the perfect solution. Once Adam realises how unhappy I am, I know he'll agree. If only he were here, we could discuss it.

She checks her watch. A mere twenty minutes have passed since she last looked. Nine fifty-five and Adam still hasn't telephoned. It isn't like him not to call. She's rung him at least three times today and left a couple of messages. To ring again is a bit desperate, she thinks. What a pathetic existence. Waiting, hoping, longing for Adam, that's all she seems to do these days. Pressing her lips together she picks up the remote and turns on the flat screen television. The news is on. She peels back the lid of her yoghurt and settles back in the chair to listen to the headlines. Third up, the latest news on Carly Stoner's death.

'Police have today been questioning Carly Stoner's boyfriend, Liam Smith, a heroin addict who claims to have been high the night of her death.'

With zero desire for any more idle press conjecture, she switches the telly off. She plonks her bare feet on the coffee table and finishes her yoghurt. I used to be feisty and independent, she thinks miserably. How have I ended up like this? I've got a degree in English and yet I'm up a bored, frustrated housewife, soon-to-be-basket case. If I'm not careful, I'll lose Adam too.

That thought has her squirming on the scatter cushions. Adam means everything to her. He's like the favourite book she knows in such detail she can recite huge chunks off-by-heart. Life without him doesn't bear thinking about. But he fell for the laid-back girl from Singapore with the sunny disposition, not this whining, jobless, childless waste of space whose brains have turned to mush.

I'll talk to him about the flat the moment he gets back, she decides. Before I let things slide any further.

Placing the empty yoghurt carton on the coffee table, she throws herself back against the cushions, closes her eyes and casts her mind back ten and a half years to the day she arrived at Exeter University. It seemed a far cry from Singapore where she'd lived with her brother and their academic parents for six years. She'd been happy there, carefree. Her parents were too engrossed in the minutiae of their own lives to pay too much attention to hers, although it didn't stop them grumbling when she got into trouble.

'Can't you at least try to control yourself?' her mother asked, when another teacher had rung to complain about her behaviour. She'd met Niall Preston by then. A bright-eyed expatriate's son, who'd introduced her to the joy of sex. 'You're far too clever to be a teenage parent.'

Ironic, really, she thinks, considering the way things turned out.

She can still recall, with vivid clarity, stepping off the Cathay Pacific flight on to the glistening wet tarmac of London's Heathrow Airport, drowning under a charcoal cloud spewing rain. She was tired and hungover from a stifling summer of endless partying spent mainly in the arms of Niall Preston. Staring out the window of the Intercity Express train, homesick and forlorn, her summer of love blown away by the chilly autumn air, she'd thought she'd made a terrible decision. By the time the taxi had dropped her at her hall of residence, the ironically named Hope Hall, she was on the verge of doing a swift three-sixty and heading back home. Clutching the handle of her trunk in one hand, her umbrella in the other, she'd staggered towards the main building.

'Oh look. It's Mary Poppins!'

Glancing over her shoulder she saw a tall youth with unkempt, ginger hair and freckles. Nathaniel Tyler. The first person she met in her first hour on campus. 'Convent Totty! Don't be shy. Come and say hello.'

'I'm sorry,' said a dark haired boy, rushing over.

'Don't worry about it,' she said, watching the back of the ginger youth as he swaggered away.

'I'm Miles by the way. Miles Spencer,' he said, removing his spectacles and wiping the lenses with his sleeve.

'Please to meet you, Miles. I'm Lily, short for Eliza, Green. An unremarkable nineteen-year-old with an unremarkable name.'

He replaced his spectacles and smiled shyly. 'Oh. I don't know about that.'

'You in this Hall?' she asked conversationally.

'We're second years actually. We live out. It was Nat's idea to come here and check the Freshers out. I kinda came along to keep him out of trouble.'

'Does he make a habit of insulting people?'

His eyes blinked rapidly. 'He's pissed. I'm sorry. It's inexcusable really. Better go just in case he's insulting someone else. See you around.'

Things picked up dramatically when Susie Ashton pranced into her room. She had messy, dark-blonde hair, bright blue eyes, a nose stud and three earrings, two in the conventional place and one in the top of her right ear.

'We're going to have a blast,' she said, once she'd introduced herself.

Her room, to the left of Lily's, was a treasure trove of make-up and jewellery, with a wallpaper of posters of singers and film stars – all tousled hair, shiny muscled bodies and pouts. She sat Lily on the bed and poured her a large vodka and orange, whilst Lily relayed to her the less-than-perfect details of her arrival.

'I'm reading drama,' Susie said. 'You?'

'English.'

'Cool. By the way, you have the hugest, strangest, most wide-apart eyes I've ever seen.'

Lily laughed. 'My brother tells me I look like a bush-baby.'

'He's lying. You're totally stunning. Blonde and slim, lucky you. I'm going to be your guardian angel. You're going to need somebody to protect you from all the horny undergraduates. By the way, do you like the tattoo?' she asked, changing the subject suddenly and dropping her skin-tight jeans to reveal a g-string and a tiny butterfly embossed on her left bum cheek.

Rose de Lisle had the room on the other side of Lily's. Whereas Susie was wild, adventurous and loud, Rose was quiet, calm and diligent, her dark brown hair scraped off her face in a ponytail, which she sometimes tied with red ribbon. Opposites attract and this was certainly true of Rose and Susie, with Lily the filling that glued their sandwich together.

They were in the second year when Rose fell pregnant on the skiing holiday. She was a straight-A student, reading maths and nothing, not even an unplanned, gorgeous baby boy, was going to get in the way of her ambition. She gave birth in early October and, four weeks later, returned to university to complete her third and final year while her parents took care of George. She gained the first class degree she craved, got a job in Goldbergs and hired a nanny to look after her little boy.

I just wish she'd appreciate George more, or at least pretend to, thinks Lily. I know it's been tough but George is eight now and a lovely little boy. A joy. She must realise how envious I am. Strange the way life works. She doesn't want what I can't have.

The telephone on the cushion beside her starts to ring. Lily snatches the handset. 'Adam?'

'Oh good. You're alone.'

Lily's heart shrivels. 'What now, Nat?'

'Don't be like that. You know you want me.'

'Actually, Nat, I don't. And I don't think Angela would be impressed to hear you keep calling me either.'

'Angela who?'

So another one's seen the light, thinks Lily, rolling her eyes.

'You'll be begging for me when Adam leaves you,' he says.

'Shut up, Nat. You're drunk.'

'It will happen, Lily and you know it. You're punching way above your weight.'

Why am I having this conversation? she wonders angrily. Why don't I just tell him to get lost?

'You'll be very grateful for me one day. Just you wait.'

There's a *click,* and the line goes dead. Nat has hung up. On her! She growls in frustration and hammers the floor with her bare feet, a reaction she knows would delight Nat. I need a drink, she thinks. She springs up and marches into the dark hallway towards the kitchen, not bothering to turn on the lamp. Two cylindrical beams of light sweep across the walls, blinding her momentarily, before angling away. She freezes.

Who on earth is visiting me at this time of night? It can't be Miles. He always telephones before dropping by. Perhaps it's Nat. Perhaps he called me from his car. Don't be ridiculous, she tells herself. Even Nat wouldn't be that stupid.

The car door slams. She feels an icy shiver as the hairs on the back of her neck stand on end. She thinks it might be Carly Stoner's killer. Perhaps he's been watching the house these past few days, seen that I'm on my own and has come to rape and strangle me.

The crunch of gravel underfoot signals the visitor's approach. She keeps her eyes glued to the large, oak front door. The handle turns slowly.

It's unlocked, she thinks panicking.

Barely able to breathe, she tiptoes backwards towards the staircase, sits down and inches up the stairs on her behind, holding her breath. The door edges soundlessly open and a tall figure, swathed in darkness, enters the house. She opens her mouth and screams so loudly her eardrums rattle with the force.

The intruder covers his ears.

'My husband's upstairs with a gun,' she yells.

'Bloody hell, your husband's here, you idiot!' says Adam, running towards her and taking hold of both her wrists. 'My God, you scared me.'

Lily wriggles free and lands a well-aimed punch in Adam's solar plexus. She can't work out whether she's angry or in shock or both.

'Ouch! That hurt.'

'I thought you were going to kill me. I thought you were the murderer.'

Cupping Lily's face in his hands, he kisses her gently on the lips. 'I'm sorry, darling. I didn't mean to scare you.'

Terrified one moment, gloriously happy the next, Lily is not yet fully in control of her emotions. And out it comes. Just like that. Bam!

'I'm sorry, I'm not myself. It's these calls from Nat. He's taken to ringing me when he knows you're away. He says you'll leave me and that—'

Adam steps back, frowning. 'Whoa! Hang on a minute. What did you say?'

'It's true. He rang tonight. Just now.'

'Really? Nat?'

'Yes,' she says, stamping her foot. 'Why would I lie?'

'The bastard,' he snarls.

Lily is thrilled by his response but her delight is fleeting and soon turns to dismay when Adam stomps upstairs ashen-faced, his balled fist hitting the walls as he goes. She rushes after him, into their bedroom where Adam is undressing, tearing the clothes off his body, throwing them roughly to the floor.

'How many times?' he asks, his back to her.

'What?'

Adam raises his voice but doesn't turn around. 'How many times has he called?'

'Half a dozen. Maybe more.'

She picks up Adam's clothes and places them neatly on the cream slipper chair. On one hand she's relieved to have it out in the open. Adam will confront Nat and she won't have to suffer the indignity of his inebriated cynicism any longer. But the flip side is, she's made him angry. She's never seen him this cross. She's annoyed with herself because she wants to ask him about renting a flat.

He yanks back the duvet, climbs into bed and lies on his back, staring at the ceiling. She slips off her clothes and creeps in beside him.

'I'm sorry. I shouldn't have told you,' she says.

'Of course you should.' He clenches his lips together in a tight line, as though her words have wounded him some more. Dejected, she reaches over and switches off the light. As she lies down Adam rolls on to his side.

If only she'd kept her mouth shut they'd probably be making love by now. She snuggles up to him and lies there, staring at his back, aching with regret.

It isn't until the dawn breaks that she falls asleep.

When she wakes up four hours later, he is gone.

By the time Lily returns from shopping in the town later that day, Adam has returned, his sports car parked in the drive. Sighing with relief, she charges into the house.

'Adam? I'm home.'

She stands in the hall waiting for a response but there's no answer so she hurries into the kitchen. She pulls up when she sees him. He is staring out the wall of windows, his back to her, but even so she can see that his usually immaculate hair is dishevelled, his clothes crumpled.

She runs to him, thinking he's hurt, desperate to hug him. Comfort him. Whatever he needs. 'What's the matter?'

He laughs then but it's a cold ironic sound, totally lacking in humour. 'You don't have a clue do you?'

'I can see you're upset. What's happened? Did you talk to Nat? Did he upset you?'

He twists round and grabs her arms, holding them by the biceps in an iron grip. She gasps and looks into his eyes. They were dull, she remembers later, the pupils dilated. And there was no sparkle to them either. Only cold intransigent anger.

'You're so fucking perfect,' he says.

And then he shakes her as if she is a rag doll, this way and that, her head lolling painfully from side to side.

'What have I done?' she asks sobbing.

But Adam says nothing. With a look of intense loathing, he flings her roughly to the floor.

Like a petrified mouse dropped from the jaws of a cat waiting panic-stricken for the next strike, Lily cowers on the cold tiles until he walks away. Each stride he takes more painful than a steel-capped boot to her head.

5

The telephone handset on the kitchen table, beside her bowl of parsnip soup, starts to ring. Lily pounces on it. 'Adam. Is that you?'

But there's no response. No sound at all. Just silence.

'Nat?' she asks, her voice cracking.

She hears a click and the line goes dead. Without hesitating, Lily dials 1471.

'You were called today at four twenty-six pm. The caller withheld their number,' the dispassionate voice informs her.

She drops the handset and buries her head in her hands. She's been waiting all day, praying Adam will call, willing him to. At midday, unable to stand it any longer, she called him. Since then she's called at least a dozen times more, although she is so strung out with worrying she can't be sure.

Gathering herself, she gets up from the table, tips the unfinished soup into the sink, rinses the bowl under the running tap, pours herself a glass of water, picks up the handset and heads for the sitting room. She's spent the entire day like this, wandering aimlessly from room to room with the phone, intermittently attempting to eat, while trying to make sense of the last couple of days. She wonders if Adam was angry because Nat made up some cock-and-bull story about the calls that placed the blame firmly on her. But if he had, why didn't Adam accuse her of anything?

He's more likely to believe me anyway, she reasons. He knows what Nat's like, particularly when he's been drinking, which is happening more and more these days.

36

Yes but what if he's angry about something else? she wonders. What if the police do suspect him of Carly Stoner's murder?

Call Nat, her conscience urges. Ask him what happened.

What's the point? He'll probably be drunk and lie.

She groans. She has a thumping headache. Letting out an anguished sigh she collapses on the sofa. If only I knew what had triggered it. Adam has never so much as raised his voice to me before. It's completely out of character. She rolls up the sleeve of her T-shirt to glance at the circular bruising, the tattoo of Adam's rage.

It's just not like him, she thinks for the millionth time.

The phone rings shattering the stillness.

'Adam!'

The silence on the other end is absolute.

'Adam? Hi. Can you hear me?'

She strains her ears for something. But there's nothing. No background noise. Not even the faintest sound of someone breathing.

Click! The line goes dead. She pauses for a moment before dialling 1471 but the voice on the other end repeats the same message.

It's probably an unfortunate coincidence, she reasons. One of those market research companies with the automated dialling systems the newspapers have been writing about. She shakes her head and reaches for the remote. I'm becoming paranoid, she tells herself, turning on the television. He's stayed away and he isn't calling because he's embarrassed by his behaviour. He'll be home soon. Everything is going to be fine.

It's past midnight. Lily is huddled under the duvet, attempting to sleep, when the phone on the bedside table rings again. This time she hesitates before answering.

'Hello?' Her voice is quiet, timid.

Nothing.

'Nat? I know it's you.'

Silence for a moment then the all-too familiar click. With a trembling finger, she dials 1471.

'You were called today at twelve-twenty-one pm. The caller withheld—'

She slams the handset down. Three anonymous calls in one day is surely no coincidence. Disconcerted, she creeps down the stairs and checks she's bolted the front and back doors. Thinking it might be wise to have something on hand just in case she needs to protect herself, she fetches the cricket bat from the study. She slips it into bed beside her, in the space where Adam should be. Silently castigating herself for being such a wuss, she covers the phone with a pillow and turns out the light.

Susie is worried. Lily hasn't called in over a week and it isn't like her. She thinks she'd want to discuss the murder if nothing else. The police whisking Adam off to the station had freaked them all out, but Lily most of all. Idling the days away in that ridiculously large house with a murderer on the loose, must be scaring her shitless. Which makes it all the more weird she hasn't called.

It isn't the only thing bothering Susie. The mysterious conversation she and Fabian interrupted between Rose and Adam is niggling away. Adam sounded properly angry with Rose. And whatever she said must have been bad because he warned her not to tell Lily. And freakier still, Rose had answered back. She'd never heard Rose argue before. Not at a social gathering, anyway. She may behave entirely differently at work. Given how successful she is, it's entirely likely. She doesn't know. As far as she is aware, in the last ten years Rose has only deviated once from the straight and narrow – the insane hour she spent in the broom cupboard with the horny waiter. Poor love hasn't lived. She is, and always has been, squeaky clean and sensible. Little Miss Orderly and Precise, her life is like an exquisitely wrapped gift, tied up with one of her daft red ribbons, a pretty bow on top.

What has Rose been up to? Or was she telling us the truth when she said it was a work matter? Fabian believed her.

'And I'm pissed off because as part of the team they really should have included me,' he said.

Susie has been busy. Too busy to call Lily herself. She's just finished filming her small part as a dying patient in *Holby City* and a two-day shoot for a tissue commercial. Not very glamorous but work nonetheless.

'If you need money you only have to ask,' Fabian said, when she told him.

Susie rolled her eyes in exasperation. 'I'm not a charity case.'

Six months earlier, he'd asked her to move in with him. She was more than happy to stay at his house in Notting Hill for days, sometimes weeks on end, but she'd declined the offer and continued renting her one-bedroom flat in Clapham.

'I'll be homeless when it all goes wrong,' she said.

'*When*? Is there something you're not telling me?'

'Ugh! I just don't want to tempt fate.' She'd done that once too often in her life.

Caution wasn't something Fabian associated with Susie. He'd been unable to hide his amusement and had given her a key anyway.

'I hope you'll see this underlines my commitment,' he said.

It's Saturday morning and they are sitting at the breakfast bar in Fabian's modern kitchen, with its red gloss cabinets and polished, black granite surfaces. Fabian is reading the paper while Susie, restless and preoccupied, sits on a stool, drumming her fingers.

'Something is wrong,' she says. 'I can feel it in my bones.'

Fabian peers at her over top of the *Financial Times*. 'If you apply your logic, shouldn't you be less worried about her than when she was calling you every night?'

'It's been two weeks.'

'Adam's on leave. They've probably gone away somewhere.'

Susie screws up her nose. 'Really. Why didn't you say?'

'I must have forgot,' he says, ducking behind his paper.

'But she tells me everything. There you are, you see. Something's wrong.'

'Stop deliberating then and call her, you nutcase.'

'That's precisely what I was about to do.'

She picks up her mobile and wanders out of the kitchen, down the chequer-board tiles of the hallway, to the sitting room at the front of the house. Lily answers after three rings. She sounds nervous and edgy.

'Are you okay?' Susie asks.

'I'm fine. Just a bit tired that's all.'

'Let me guess. Too much sex?'

Instead of the laugh she's expecting, there's a pause on the other end of the line. 'Adam's away.'

'Oh really? Where's he gone?'

Another pause. 'Milan. How's the work going by the way?' Lily asks, changing the subject. 'Has Brad Pitt been on the phone with an offer too irresistible to refuse?'

They chat for another five minutes about Susie's work. The conversation over, she wanders back into the kitchen.

'That was quick,' says Fabian, lowering the newspaper. 'How was she?'

'Adam's away.'

'I know. I told you, remember?'

'Yes but you didn't tell me he'd gone to Milan.'

'Milan?'

'That's what Lily said.'

Fabian frowns. 'I was told he'd taken annual leave.'

Susie climbs on to the stool and sits down with a thump. 'Shit. You don't think Lily's lying for him?'

'Now you've lost me.'

'That girl. The jogging nurse.'

'What about her?'

'Maybe Milan's a cover-up.'

Fabian shakes his head 'Nope. Still not with you.'

'Maybe Adam's been arrested.'

Lily is growing increasingly paranoid. The endless days are wearing on and still no word from Adam. Too embarrassed to tell her friends, she can feel herself withdrawing from the world, her confidence shot to pieces.

The crank calls aren't helping. She knows it can't be Adam. He isn't the type to play games. That's more Nat's thing. And given she's squealed to Adam about Nat's night-time telephonic antics, what better way to get back at her than to frighten her with anonymous calls? And after a second day of them, it's working.

Of course it's also possible the caller isn't Nat, she reasons. They're too frequent to be from a call centre but I might be the target of some sad pervert. That kind of thing goes on all the time. Or maybe the caller wants to speak to Adam, not me. That would make sense too.

She wonders if she should contact the police. But something is holding her back. A question begging to be answered, which she can't confront.

On the sixth day, miserable and exhausted, Lily realises she has to do something. One avenue is still open to her. She takes a deep breath and dials Janice White.

'Alex Delaney's office.' Janice's tone is singsong, robotic.

Lily takes a deep breath and asks to speak to Adam Hutchinson, disguising her voice as best she can.

'Who's speaking please?' asks Janice

Lily wonders whether to come clean. She decides against it and introduces herself as an old university friend who's organising a reunion.

'Sounds fun but I'm afraid Adam's away at the moment. He's on holiday. Can I take a message?' Janice asks, the tone of her voice less clinical now.

'Er ... no. It's fine. I'll call again. Thank you.'

Lily replaces the handset. Her hands, she notices, are shaking. Almost immediately, the phone rings again, echoing through the high-ceilinged hall like a death knoll. She picks it up and answers it.

'Who is it?'

Nothing.

'For God's sake why are you doing this?' she shouts.

The connection is broken and the line goes dead.

In a last ditch attempt to preserve what is left of her sanity, Lily unplugs the phone.

6

Rose stares glumly at her empty diary. It's Friday evening. The weekend will be upon her in a matter of minutes. And all she has to look forward to is a prep-school cricket match. She wishes she hadn't promised George she'd go. He was very excited when she said she would and couldn't stop talking about how they were going to win, the runs he'd score, all the wickets he'd take.

'I'm really good at bowling, Mummy,' he said, eyes gleaming.

Sadly his enthusiasm for the game hasn't rubbed off on her. It takes such a long time and the rules are beyond her.

I'd rather stick pins in my eyes than sit in a deckchair on the boundary exchanging pleasantries with happily married parents for an entire afternoon, she thinks miserably, picking up the framed black and white photo of her eight-year-old son. She smiles as she does every time she looks at it. He's such a gorgeous little boy with his big blue eyes, cheeky grin and dark unruly curls. She runs a finger over the smattering of freckles on his nose then groans. I should be working this weekend. I'm overloaded at the moment, with Adam away. If I come in tomorrow, I'd have the whole of the fourth floor to myself and I could deal with the backlog. I'll ask Mum and Dad if they'll look after him. Dad likes cricket. He'll go and watch the match. George would love that. She puts down the frame and leans forward to rest her head on the table.

How dare Adam just take off like that? On holiday, of all things. Why did Delaney allow it? We've never been so busy. Worse still, Adam didn't even bother to tell me. He's been avoiding me, the bastard. Hasn't spoken to me since the party. I knew what I had to say would piss him off. I had to tell him. I didn't have a choice.

'Lily will find out sooner or later,' she'd said, raising her voice. It wasn't her fault after all.

'Shut up, Rose. Please. You're drunk.'

'I'm *not* drunk. And you know I'm right.'

'Then you're lying.'

But she wasn't lying and she wasn't going to shut up. She was on a roll and wouldn't stop, and Adam on the point of erupting, when Fabian and Susie toppled into the room.

I hate him, she thinks. I really hate him. She slaps the desk with her hands and lifts her head. How much did they hear? she wonders. Not that it matters. They'll all find out soon enough. She sighs and closes her diary. She slips it into her handbag then starts to tidy her desk, straightening the pens in a neat line, the pile of papers in the corner into a perfect rectangle. Fabian has been noticeably cool towards me since then but, ever the gentleman, hasn't referred to it. He says hello, smiles if we pass on the stairs or in the corridor, but he hasn't dropped by my office for a chat or taken me to lunch as he usually does at least once a fortnight.

She hates to admit it but she misses him. He's one of the few real friends she's made at Goldbergs. Now it seems she's blown it.

And all because of that arrogant bastard. You've got it coming to you, Adam, she thinks, leaning on her elbows and cupping her head in her hands. I'll get my own back. Just you wait.

'Hey, Rose. You got a minute?'

Rose starts and looks up at Fabian, standing in the doorway. 'I was just thinking about you,' she says.

'I'd take that as a compliment if it wasn't for your body language.'

'Oh. No. I wasn't … I mean …'

'I was joking,' he says but he isn't smiling.

'What's up?' she asks tentatively.

Fabian shifts his weight. 'It's a bit awkward actually.'

'Oh!' she says. She knows what's coming.

'Something's been bothering me for a while.'

It's the moment she's been dreading. 'Fire away.'

Fabian seems to expand with relief. 'Lily told Susie that Adam's in Milan. Why would she do that?'

'What? Really?' She's shocked but at the same time, relieved. This blows all her theories out of the water. Maybe things aren't so wonderful between Lily and Adam after all. Sweet revenge. Inside she's dancing but she has to be careful not to let on to Fabian, who's biting the inside of his cheek as he paces the carpet tiles in front of her desk.

He stops suddenly, frowning. 'Rose, what exactly were you and Adam arguing about that night?'

7

Lily is scanning the calendar that hangs on the larder door. It's Tuesday, which means Adam has been gone ten days. And now the police are after him. The third time Marshall calls her mobile Lily, fraught and tense, finally snaps. 'I don't know where he is. We had an argument. I haven't seen him since.'

'Were you arguing about the murder?' Marshall asks.

'What? No!'

'We need to speak to him, Mrs Hutchinson. He's not answering his phones. Please ask him to call us the moment he gets home.'

She puts down the phone, trembling. Why did the detective ask her that? Why does he need to speak to Adam? What has he done? She hasn't forgotten him wincing when she told the police what time he'd arrived home after his run. Was that because he lied to them? Is that why they'd taken him to the police station, why they'd taken his fingerprints? Questioned him? He told her he was a witness. Had he lied to her too?

She tells herself not to be so stupid. It's nonsense. Adam wouldn't hurt a fly.

He hurt you, her conscience goads.

Yes but he was angry.

He was, wasn't he? But you still don't know the reasons why? Maybe he was angry with Carly Stoner too.

He didn't know her, she thinks shivering.

She feels strangely detached, as though she's watching her life not living it. Unplugging the house phone has helped to some degree but she's still consumed with anxiety. She unlocks the windowed door and wanders outside, clutching her mobile. It has never bothered her before that it only works in the garden. But it is maddening now it's her only source of communication with the outside world – with Adam.

It's a warm spring day. The sun is out. Small cotton-wool clouds scud across the forget-me-knot sky. Birds sing at the tops of their shrill little voices. Leaves unfurl as trees drop their blossom. The sweet smell of wisteria hangs in the air. She breathes in deeply, savouring the aroma as though it's an expensive perfume, and walks across the freshly cut grass to the end of the garden. There's a spot here, where the tailored lawn meets the long grass of the orchard, where she and Susie like to sit on the weekends she comes to stay. On the stone bench, beneath the overhanging branches of the old apple tree, they indulge in the type of girlie conversations that would bore Adam senseless.

Lily sighs and plonks herself down on the cool stone seat beneath the apple tree, blushing like a bride in its spring apparel of pink-tinted blossom. The bees, greedy for nectar, buzz noisily and busily around its flowers and the bluebells in the orchard, pollen clinging to their fuzzy coats. Susie comes down far less often these days, she thinks sadly. Strange really, given that Adam and Fabian are such good friends too.

The mobile bleeps suddenly making her jump. Nervous, she opens the message.

Haven't seen u 4 weeks. Fancy dropping by for coffee? Finn x

She lets out another frustrated sigh and closes her eyes. Where are you Adam? she wonders for the trillionth time. And why won't you phone?

She opens her eyes and rereads the message. She thinks she should text him back and arrange to meet up. Apart from Miles, Finn is the only person down here she can call a close friend. They met about a year ago when she was shopping in Lewes. Somebody in the street handed her a leaflet advertising an art exhibition at the Star Gallery. With endless time on her hands she decided to check it out.

A handful of people were milling around, chatting in respectful, hushed tones as if the pitch of normal conversation would sully the works on show. On a table in the centre of the room, a display of white-stone sculptures caught her attention. She walked over for a closer look. The largest piece was a naked man cupping a naked woman's face in his hands. The sculptor had managed to convey a lover's glance, the man's stone eyes radiating desire for the woman he held. She found herself blushing at the sensuality of it and focused her attention on the piece next to it; a semi-naked man lying on his back, his arms folded behind his head, smiling as he gazed up at something, a woman perhaps, a discernible twinkle in his sculpted eye. She picked it up and turned it over. The sumptuously smooth feel of the cream stone, criss-crossed with gold-coloured veins, felt cold to the touch.

'They call it the stone that enchanted the light.'

Startled, Lily turned round. A man with wavy, shoulder-length, brown hair was grinning at her. He was dressed in a close-fitting, grey, long-sleeved T-shirt that accentuated his lean frame, an assortment of African bracelets on his wrist.

'Do you like it?' he asked, in his Irish lilt.

'Very much. In fact I was hoping to buy it. If it's not too expensive that is.'

Beneath two bushy brows his eyes, the colour of well-polished army boots, sparkled mischievously. 'Well let's see then, how much would you be prepared to pay for it?'

Lily laughed. 'How much is it worth?'

'Well that depends on how much you want it?'

'You're the artist,' she said, blushing. 'Sorry.'

'Sorry I'm the artist, or sorry you've changed your mind.'

'Neither. I meant ...'

'Shall we begin again?'

Lily nodded.

'Okay. How much money do you have on you, if that's not too personal a question?'

'Fifty pounds or so but I've got my cheque book with me.'

'Fifty quid it is then. I'll just wrap it for you.'

'Thanks.' Lily smiled and handed him the sculpture then followed him to the table by the door. The man placed it on its side and began to roll it up in bubble wrap. 'So where is your studio?' she asked politely.

The man looked up at her and stretched his Mick Jagger lips into a huge grin. 'At home. An old farmhouse just outside Lewes. I give the odd demonstration too. I've got one next week as it happens. You should come. That way you can see how it's done. Here. I'll give you my card er …?'

'Lily,' she said.

'Finn Costello.' He handed her the parcel and winked. 'Enjoy him, Lily.'

Back home she put the sculpture in a shoebox and stowed it in the back of the wardrobe, not sure how she'd explain it to Adam. She'd no intention of taking Finn up on his offer. But boredom took its toll and, the day before the demonstration, she changed her mind, picked up the phone and called to register her name.

'Lily Green. We met in Lewes last week.'

'Great. I'll book you in,' he said. 'See you tomorrow, Lily Green.'

She was surprised when she arrived at his house the next day to find she was the only person there. 'You should have told me you had no takers,' she said.

'Well at least this way I'll be able to give you my undivided attention.'

She thought she should have left then but she didn't. At last she had something to do.

Finn's home was a quaint half-brick, half-tile-hung old farmhouse that was crumbling at the edges. He led her through the hallway into the kitchen at the back of the house and made her a mug of freshly ground coffee with hot frothy milk. Coarsely tied bunches of dried hops hung from the ceiling, bowls of fruit, jars of jam, flagons of beer littered the work surfaces, and an untidy row of shoes and boots lined the edge of the stone-flagged floor.

'First of all I must introduce you to my doves,' he said. 'I inherited them with the house. It was one of the reasons I fell in love with the place.'

Through the open back door Lily could see the old, round flint-and-brick dovecote with a tiled conical roof, the dove escapes peppering the walls under its eaves. There was a loud fluttering of wings and a white dove alighted the ledge in front of one of the holes. It glanced around briefly before it disappeared inside.

'In the summer that area beyond the lawn is a wilderness of flowers.' Finn pointed proudly to the surrounding woodland opposite, where the trees, bare of leaves, stood tall, like ghostly sentries guarding the landscape. 'You'll love it.'

It was a throwaway comment but loaded with inference. And why not? she reasoned later. I'm desperately short of friends.

Finn motioned to a cardboard box beside the Aga. 'I'm tending a sick bird at the moment. I found it comatose in the garden this morning. I thought it was dead but actually I think it's exhausted. With some persistent coaxing, I've managed to get it to drink some water.'

Lily walked over and knelt down beside the box. A grey-brown bird with black spotting on its wings, a bluish crown and purple-pink patches on its neck, was cowering in the hay.

'It's a dove but I'm not sure what species,' he said.

'What happened to it?'

'I expect he got separated from his mate.'

'Poor little thing.'

'I intend to spoil the wee fella while he's here. I've named him Archie. I'm pretty sure it's a boy.'

He led Lily outside and across the flagstones to the circular dovecote. A dozen or so doves were cooing as they strutted around, pecking the ground for food.

'I inherited the white ones with the farm. Those brown-grey doves, with the pinkish-buff coloured breasts and the black and white band around their necks, are Collared Doves.'

'They look like wood pigeons,' said Lily, 'but smaller and prettier.'

Finn laughed. 'They're wild but they like it here so much they've set up home in the conifer trees.'

'Not in the dovecote?'

'No. They don't go into holes.'

'They seem very peaceful.'

'Actually, they're nervous creatures and fearful, particularly at night. They hate sudden noises.' He grinned. 'Here's an interesting fact. Doves mate for life. The male spends hours, even days courting his chosen one. He paces about in front of her, cooing, his crop full of air, lowering his head, fanning his tail and turning circles.' Finn doubled over, folded his arms beneath his armpits and acted out the ritual. 'Any rivals he gets rid of by pushing them away. Suddenly the moment is right. The female approaches her mate and the love-birds smooth each other's feathers before billing.'

'Billing?'

'Kissing to you and me. He feeds her a few regurgitated seeds and POW! – they mate. The female struts off proudly. Then with a loud clapping of wings they fly off to begin their life together. Romantic, isn't it? We humans could learn a lot from their behaviour.'

Lily wasn't sure why but she blushed.

'But not all doves are so sweet,' he continued. 'The Collared Doves can be a little sly and bully the others out of food.'

'So a lot like humans then.'

Finn looked at her warily. 'Next time I'll show you the nesting boxes.'

'Why not today?'

'Because it really stinks in there. The floor is covered in their mess. I've been meaning to clean it out but I haven't got round to it. Anyway I promised I'd show you my workplace. Come and see my studio.'

Now her sightless eyes are fixed on her mobile. It would do me good to see him, she thinks. He's a free spirit, upbeat and positive. Some time spent in his company could be just what I need right now.

She types her answer. *Yes please. I'd love too.*

Her mobile beeps again. *Gr8 cu l8er.*

Feeling brighter than she has for days, Lily runs back to the house, plonks her mobile on the kitchen table then dashes upstairs. After a shower she changes into some clean clothes. The white cropped trousers she chooses hang loosely from her hips, so she digs a tan leather belt out of a drawer and fastens it tight, then slips a yellow T-shirt over her head.

She bounds down the stairs but a gentle knocking at the front door halts her in her tracks. She glances at her watch. Ten past nine. Please God not the police, she thinks as she trudges down the last few stairs. Reluctantly, she opens the door.

A slim, elegant woman, in fashionably large, black sunglasses, is standing on the doorstep. She is dressed in a beige pencil skirt, a white blouse, with a wide, black patent-leather belt around her tiny waist, her hair obscured by a pale blue headscarf.

Her lip-glossed mouth flickers into the briefest of smiles. 'Hello.'

'Hi,' says Lily, feeling shabby and parochial.

'Honor Vincente. An old friend of Adam's.' She speaks softly with an Italian accent and holds out a slender, manicured hand.

Lily shakes it bemused. Old and long forgotten, she thinks. Adam's never mentioned anyone called Honor before. She needs this like a hole in the head. 'I'm afraid

Adam's not at home. He's away on business. Milan actually. I'll tell him you stopped by. Why don't you leave me your number?'

The woman stares at Lily behind her dark glasses. Not being able to see her eyes makes Lily uncomfortable.

'I won't but thank you.'

She turns, folds herself gracefully into her silver Porsche and drives off as suddenly and quietly as she arrived.

8

It's warm and still, with barely a breath of wind. The smell of freshly mown grass lingers in the rural air. The sap is rising in the Sussex flora and Finn's doves are cooing and billing as they strut over the flagstones in front of the dovecote. West Coast Jazz blares loudly from the speakers of his studio, a converted flint barn half-hidden by a large lime tree at the bottom of the garden. Lily stands there for a moment, on the periphery of Finn's world, comforted that his life, at least, continues as usual.

Smiling to herself, she walks over to the door and knocks.

'It's open,' he says. 'Come in.'

The door creaks on its antiquated hinges as she prises it wider. It's deceptively large inside with a fireplace in the far wall, a small white corner sink and a pile of stones on the dusty floor waiting to be carved. Clay figures sit side by side on one of the robust, wooden shelves, goggles, a dust mask and a CD player on another.

Finn adds his chisel to the lethal-looking row of tools on the table beside the lump of marble he's working on, pulls off his goggles, bounds over and wraps his arms round her.

'It's good to see you,' he says, squeezing her tight. 'I thought I'd upset you. I haven't seen you since we celebrated your birthday.'

Lily bites her lip, embarrassed. She'd come round to his farmhouse three days before she turned thirty. Finn had insisted on celebrating.

'I'm going to take you star-gazing,' he said.

She laughed. 'Star-gazing?'

'You'll love it.'

'I'm sure I would but I can't.'

'Why not? Mr Green is away.'

She flinched. She was used to him using her maiden name, which he did, often, even if she wasn't sure why she'd given it to him in the first place. But she was certain she hadn't mentioned Adam being away.

'How on earth did you know?'

'I didn't know, I guessed. Well, what do you say?'

It had been cool on the downs that night as the dew came down and Lily had been grateful for Finn's fleece. They lay on his rug, staring at the heavens, sipping champagne from plastic cups.

'There's Ursa Major. Ursa Minor next to it.'

'Naturally!'

'Orion, Gemini, Leo, Sirius the Dog Star and over there is Cassiopeia.'

Lily listened intently as Finn rattled off the names of the constellations. Later, after another cup of champagne, he produced a telescope from out of his battered, khaki Land Rover.

She whistled. 'Impressive.'

'Don't worry I know what you mean.'

'Idiot,' she said, thumping him.

'And now, Mrs Green, I'm going to attempt to show you the rings of Saturn and the moons of Jupiter,' he said, fiddling with the focus. 'Eureka! Take another look.'

He backed away and Lily looked down the lens. 'Wow! What was that?' she shrieked.

'Judging by your reaction, Jupiter.'

'Flying through the sky?'

'Hmm. Strange that. Scientists have insisted for years that the world is spinning.'

She groaned at him then clapped her hands. 'What else can you show me?'

'The jewel of the sky.'

She stepped away while Finn located Venus then looked again and saw the planet burning like a white flame. 'Incredible. It seems so close. How do you know all this?'

'I was an unruly yet inquisitive child.'

She spun the scope round. 'Do you think I could see my house from here?'

'Depends where you live.'

'Orchard House in Adlington.'

'I'm sure you could if it was light.'

That had been four weeks ago but Lily hadn't even sent a text to thank him. She feels awful. He must think I'm a spoilt, ungrateful bitch.

'I had the best time,' she says, wriggling free of his embrace and brushing off the grey-white dust that's clinging to her yellow T-shirt. 'I've been busy, that's all. And before you tease me about being a bored housewife, let me tell you I've bought lunch.'

He holds up his hands. 'Would I?'

Finn is busy preparing for an exhibition. An influential dealer that an art agent friend of his introduced him to has invited him to show his work in his London gallery. Lily has whiled away many an hour watching him work. Sometimes, like a pianist practicing scales, he takes a blob of clay and, working it with his fingers, shapes into a temporary face or body. When he's ready to start, he first of all roughs out the stone with an angle-grinder. The noise is awful so she tends to wait until he's working with the point chisel, which is when the stone begins to take shape. He refines the piece with the claw chisel, and with the riffler, his favourite tool, he smoothes out the chisel marks and carves the final detail; the expression and the sense of real emotion that characterises his sculptures. He files them before sanding, the job he likes the least. Then he polishes them, seals them and occasionally mounts them.

The first few days that he works on a new figure, Finn sculpts from models. Once, Lily turned up at his studio to find a dark-haired woman lying naked on the floor in a highly provocative position, leaning on her elbows, her legs splayed. Her firm, improbably large breasts only heightened Lily's embarrassment. Feeling like a voyeur, blushing, Lily made her excuses and left.

'What's this one called?' she asks, walking over to his workbench.

'*The Secret*. Do you like it?'

She takes in the girl's huge, terror-stricken eyes, her hands tightly clasped behind her back. She seems to be bravely facing both the world and her fears. Lily screws up her nose, unsure. 'She looks scared.'

'It's her secret which frightens her,' he says, catching her eye.

'Oh right. Of course,' she says, feeling stupid.

He smiles and picks up his riffler. 'I'll be done in twenty minutes. Why not sit in the sunshine,' he says, refocusing on his figure.

'I thought I might check Archie out.'

'Grand idea. I can't believe he's been here a year. I think I'm stuck with the wee fella.'

'You saved his life. He feels safe here.'

'He's a long way from home more like.'

Lily wanders back towards the house. Archie is taking a bath in the metal bowl on the flagstones beneath the dovecote. He's easy enough to identify, being a little smaller than the other birds, with his distinctive pink belly and the purple patches on his neck. After extensive research on the internet, Finn had reached the conclusion Archie was a Mourning Dove.

'They're native to America,' he had told her when she'd visited one day. 'If I'm right we could be witnessing history.'

'Why do you think he came here?'

'He probably lost his mate. In many parts of the States these birds are hunted for game.'

'The name's a bit morbid.'

'He's named after his song. It's beautiful but mournful.'

Lily watches Archie hop out of the bowl and nod his head, throwing it back quickly and obliquely. As his head comes down, his tail shoots up before it sinks slowly to its original level. Standing stock still, he tenses. Lily holds her breath. She knows what's going to happen. Archie is about to sing.

The song slurs up then down, remaining on the same pitch for about three notes, like a call to a long lost friend. As she listens she finds herself thinking of Adam.

'Sad eyes,' says Finn.

Lily starts out of her trance. 'What?'

'You have sad eyes today, Lily Green.'

Lily manages a weak smile that gets nowhere near her eyes but finds she can't hold it for long. Her lips waver and for an awful moment she thinks she might cry.

'I don't suppose there's any point in me trying to raise a laugh?'

Lily shrugs.

'Murphy's Law!'

'Murphy's what?'

'Nothing is as easy as it looks. Everything takes longer than you expect. And if anything *can* go wrong it *will*, at the worst possible moment.'

She stares at him blankly.

'I'm joking.' He pulls a face. 'What's up, Lily?'

Lily squints and shades her eyes with her hand and looks at Finn but can only see the shaggy silhouette of his hair. Seeing her discomfort, he moves out of the sun. Concern is etched in fine lines around his eyes. He has grey smears of clay on his cheeks. Combined with his unruly hair he looks comical, clown-like. Lily can't help but smile. The effect is instantaneous. The heavy hand of gloom releases its vice-like grip on her heart.

'Ah ha!' he says triumphantly.

'Well, you should look at yourself.'

He inclines his head gently to the left like a curious cat. 'You know you can talk to me. I'm here for you, Lily. You know that don't you?'

Lily is tempted. The timing is perfect. Life doesn't throw up such clear-cut opportunities all that often. But something prevents her. Fear, perhaps or guilt. She can see no sense in discussing her problems. It's not what they do. They've talked for hours, swapping stories about his wild upbringing in Dublin, his misspent youth with his reprobate friends, his exhibitionist mother, his escape to London to study at the London Art School, and Lily's unorthodox childhood in Singapore, her three years at university, the death of her parents in a plane crash six years ago, and her job as a copyrighter that she gave up last year.

'We planned to start a family,' was all she said.

In all that time she's never once referred to Adam by name. Finn hasn't asked her about him either, or why after so long trying, there is no baby. She assumes it's out of tact.

Finn walks over to the doves and deftly picks up a white one. He takes it in the palm of his right hand, his third and fourth fingers around its legs, and the index finger and thumb holding the wing feathers. The dove looks comfortable and coos appreciatively as Finn strokes its head.

'Have you ever heard a dove cry?' she asks, absently fingering her diamond engagement ring.

Finn doesn't laugh as she expects. 'No, Lily. I haven't,' he says, letting go of the dove.

She watches it flutter prettily to the ground.

Susie has no idea where she's going to put this latest batch of complimentary tissues and toilet paper. Freebies are a perk of her job but this is ridiculous. The growing mountain of boxes, a lifetime's supply surely, is taking over her flat. I could build a small house with them, she thinks. She sighs. She'd set her sights a lot higher than this when she graduated from drama school. Still, the company pays well and money is something she never has enough of, no matter how frugally she tries to live.

The sound of Jesse J singing *Price Tag* brings an end to her thoughts. She takes a last look at the mess before hurrying to the kitchen to answer her mobile.

'I'm glad I've caught you,' says Fabian.

'You sound tense. What's up?'

'There's been a bit of trouble at the office.'

'Oh?'

'Adam's back.'

'Did you find out where he's been?'

'No but he was in a foul mood. He stormed in and manhandled Delaney into his office and slammed the door. We could hear them shouting and swearing at one another then there was an almighty crash as something went flying through the window. Ten minutes later, the door swung open and Adam marched out. A few minutes after that, Delaney emerged with a bloody lip and a black eye. He screamed at everyone to get back to work then left the building.'

Susie whistles. 'Blimey!'

'Rose told me she thought Delaney was involved in something dodgy. Seems she was right. Talk at work is all about insider trading.'

Little Miss Know-It-All, thought Susie. She'd been convinced Rose had lied about the argument they'd overhead. Her explanation just didn't ring true. But now she wasn't so sure.

'But that's not why I'm calling,' continues Fabian. 'I've got to go to Milan.'

'How long for?' she asks, swallowing her annoyance

'I don't know but I'll call you. I've got to go now. Bye.'

She stares at the phone in disbelief. Bloody cheek, she thinks. Still, I'll bet Lily's delighted Adam's back. I'll give her a call.

She dials Orchard House first. The phone rings for ages, but there's no reply and, unusually, the answer phone doesn't kick in. She tries her mobile. Lily doesn't pick up, so she leaves a message asking her to call. Disgruntled, she trudges back to her living room and lands a well-aimed kick at the tower of boxes.

After lunch, Finn returns to work and Lily sits on a steamer chair in his garden, soaking up the warmth of the sun. More relaxed than she's felt since Adam's disappearance, she falls asleep. At six-fifteen, Finn wakes her and hands her a glass of chilled white wine.

'My sister is arriving in half an hour,' he says, wriggling out of his dust-covered shirt. 'Why not stay for supper?'

'Thanks but I ought to get back,' she says, trying to look anywhere but at his tanned, hairless chest.

'Your husband must be mad leaving you at home at the mercy of a mad Irish sculptor every day.'

Taken aback, Lily shifts uneasily in her chair and spills some wine.

'I may be speaking out of turn but I sense all is not right between you two.'

The bruises, thinks Lily, pulling on her short cap sleeves. He's seen them.

Finn squats down beside her and picks up her hand. 'Surely you know by now your secrets are safe with me.'

Lily's heart begins to pound. And just as involuntarily, out it pours. 'Actually, I am worried. Adam has sort of … He's gone … I mean, I don't know where he is. He's not returning my calls.'

'Is this unusual?'

'Yes.'

'Have you called his work, his friends?'

'I've spoken to his PA but not his friends. I didn't want to worry them,' she explains clumsily. She wonders how Finn could begin to understand. He knows nothing about her life, her world. Nothing.

'Well my advice to you would be to phone either his work again or his friends. Only I sense that perhaps we're skirting deeper issues.'

What am I doing? She wonders. Why am I discussing my private life with Finn? Baffled by her stupidity, she leaps to her feet. 'I'd better be going. I expect tonight will be the night he comes home.'

Finn springs up and studies her for a moment then tucks some stray strands of hair, which have fallen in front of her face, behind her ears. 'Stay, Lily. Talk to me,'

It's an intimate gesture. She feels awkward. 'I'm fine. And anyway, your sister will be here soon.'

'She'd love to meet you.'

She responds with a strange, shallow laugh, and bats the air self-consciously. 'I really ought to get going.'

But she doesn't resist when Finn reaches out and gathers her in his arms. She knows she should but it feels good to be held. She rests her cheek on the smooth skin of his chest, warmed by the sun, and breathes in the scent of him. She is surprised when a rogue tear escapes her eye and trickles down his sternum. She's not the crying sort.

'It's okay,' he whispers.

Lily remains where she is for a moment then gently eases away.

9

Lily has been to Tesco. She thinks it's important to carry on as normal. More than anything, it gives her fractured life some meaning. She's bought far too much food. Either she's being over-optimistic or she hasn't got used to shopping for one.

She's unloading the bags from the boot of her yellow Mini, when a metallic-blue car rolls up the drive. She remains where she is, clutching the heavy bags, as the driver and his female passenger get out of the car. She recognises DCI Marshall immediately. Her instinct is to put down the bags and run, but common sense advises her to stay put.

'Hello, Mrs Hutchinson,' says Marshall approaching her. She takes in his tired, blue eyes and his forehead grooved with four concentric lines and puts his age at somewhere in his late thirties.

'Inspector,' she says with a slight nod.

He runs his hand through his thinning hair, which she notices he wears swept back off his forehead to hide the beginnings of a bald patch. 'This is Detective Sergeant Day, a Family Liaison Officer,' he says, jerking his head at the small, shorthaired woman.

'May we come in?' she asks smiling, her tiny eyes disappearing into the flesh of her cheeks. Her voice is higher than Lily expects from a woman who looks to be in her early thirties, childlike, cartoonish, like Lisa Simpson but with an English accent.

'Of course,' Lily says, suppressing the urge to giggle as she leads them into the kitchen. She puts the bags on the floor by the fridge.

'Why don't I make us some tea?' says DS Day.

Isn't that my job, thinks Lily, staring at her dumbly.

Marshall pulls out a chair. 'Please sit down, Mrs Hutchinson.'

She notices he smells of limes. Trumper's Extract of West Indian limes in fact, the aftershave her father used to wear.

He strides around to the other side of the table and sits down opposite. 'We're here about your husband.'

'Have you found him?' she asks, vaguely aware of a stirring sensation in her lower gut.

The detective clears his throat and shifts awkwardly in his seat. 'Yes, we think we have.'

The stirring in her gut is more noticeable as she glances from one detective to the other. 'What do you mean, you think? Where is he?'

'Mrs Hutchinson, I'm afraid we have some bad news. There is no easy way to say this but we believe your husband is dead.' Marshall speaks slowly, pronouncing every word with care.

Well that explains his humourless expression. Feeling strangely detached from the situation, she looks at the large circular stainless steel clock on the wall above the detective's head. It is ten-fifteen.

'A body has been found on the bridle path by the river, half a mile from the place where Carly Stoner was killed,' he continues gently. 'We believe it is your husband.'

DS Day sets a mug of tea in front or her.

'But Adam is away, has been for the last eleven days.' It isn't that she hasn't heard his words, just that her brain can't compute them.

'Where has he been, Mrs Hutchinson?' the detective asks.

'A business trip.' Given that she's been asking herself the same question, over and over, her confidence surprises her.

'Really? Where?'

'Er ... Italy. He ... er ... He ...' Lily stutters. 'Milan I think. I'm not sure, but he's still away.'

'On the business trip?'

'Yes,' she replies conclusively, pleased that she's managed to clarify things. She slurps the hot tea. It has sugar in it, which she isn't expecting.

'And you're sure of that?'

Lily hesitates. Marshall stares at her intently as if her pupils are a well to some deeper source of understanding. It must be transparently obvious she has no idea where Adam is.

'He hasn't been home,' she says eventually.

Marshall rises to his feet. The metallic click of his heels as he paces the beige tiles echo round the kitchen. 'You told me you'd had an argument. Do you think that's why Adam disappeared?'

He stops beside her and lowers his gaze. She feels his eyes scanning the exposed bruises on her upper arms. They have turned yellow but are still visible. She crosses her arms and covers them with her hands, suddenly self-conscious. What is this? Why are they interrogating her?

'We think he's been murdered,' he says, when she doesn't reply.

She hears him this time. Loud and clear. Her guts are spinning now. She clutches her belly. 'Murdered?'

'The body on the bridle path. We think it's Adam.'

'But you're not absolutely sure?'

'No,' he says kindly and with a half-smile.

Something washes over her. Relief perhaps? Hope? 'Well there you are then!'

'We'd like you to identify the body.' The comic sound of DS Day's voice is completely at odds with the seriousness of her words. Lily's guts heave. Trembling, she tries to swallow but her mouth is dry and she gags instead.

'Are you okay?' asks DS Day, placing a reassuring hand on her arm.

Lily nods, eyes wide with shock. 'I'm fine.'

'Where were you yesterday at six o'clock in the evening?' asks Marshall, pulling out a notebook from the inside pocket of his jacket.

'Here.' Lily's voice is as small as the frightened child she has become.

Marshall produces a fountain pen from the same pocket. Slowly he unscrews the lid. 'But obviously not when Adam returned.'

'Returned?'

'Where were you?' he asks, ignoring her question.

'I was in Lewes.'

'Where exactly?' he asks, pen poised.

She pauses. 'Er ... Waitrose.'

'You appear to be a fan of supermarkets,' he says, gesticulating at the bags of shopping.

Lily nods foolishly.

'What time did you return home?'

'Er ... around seven I think.'

And now Marshall starts to write. 'Was Adam's jogging kit missing?'

'Jogging kit?'

'T-shirt, tennis shorts, trainers. That sort of thing.'

Her guts churn unpleasantly. She thinks she might have to leave the room. 'I ... I don't know.'

'And the clothes he'd been wearing, a suit perhaps, a shirt? Was it on a chair?'

'If he'd been home, he'd have hung it up. He's obsessively tidy.'

'Could you show us your bedroom?' asks DS Day kindly.

Adam's jogging kit is missing but that doesn't prove anything. Lily thinks he's probably taken it with him. She can't remember. Adam does his own packing. His favourite suit is hanging in the wardrobe. Has it been there since he disappeared? Lily has no idea. But it is the white shirt DCI Marshall finds in the laundry basket in the en suite bathroom that sets her teeth chattering. It's lying on the top of her pile of dirty washing. Without speaking, the detective pulls on a pair of blue latex gloves, picks it up with his thumb and forefinger and places it in a clear plastic bag.

Lily watches him with a growing sense of foreboding. She has no idea how or when the shirt came to be there.

10

'This isn't usual police procedure.' Marshall's voice is kind, lacking the abrasiveness of earlier. 'We would normally ask a relative to view the body through a glass screen but, due to the nature of the injuries and because the post mortem has yet to be performed, we will be taking you into the post mortem room.'

Lily breathes in a hefty lungful of air, screws up her nose and half-closes her eyes. She's listening intently but nothing Marshall has said since they found Adam's shirt has made any sense. She nods dumbly.

'This is highly irregular,' says DS Day, her brows knitted together in a tight frown. 'If you don't want to do it, just say.'

A door swings open and a tall, blonde woman, strides into the room. She is kitted out in a blue surgical gown, green plastic apron, purple latex gloves and white Wellingtons.

'Dr Frazer is the forensic pathologist assigned to this case,' explains Marshall.

'I want to warn you,' says Dr Frazer. 'What you are about to do is tough for even the bravest person. If at any point you want to stop just let me know and we'll leave the room immediately.' She hands Lily a white suit, mask, hat, gloves and overshoes. 'To prevent cross contamination,' she explains.

Lily fumbles with the suit and gloves but loses her balance when she tries to slip on the overshoes and has to be helped into them by DS Day. She puts on the hat and secures the elastic mask. Time seems to have slowed down. The multi-coloured images that pass before her eyes are totally out of sync with the protracted sounds they produce, like a record played at a slower speed.

DS Day scrutinises her, her tiny porcine eyes twitching nervously over the top of her mask. 'Are you ready?'

No, she thinks. I'm not. I could never be ready for something like this. But she nods anyway.

Dr Joanne Frazer loops a mask over her head and leads the group into the post mortem room. It is large and windowless and reeks of disinfectant and is almost entirely constructed of stainless steel. The sluices and work surfaces along one tiled wall gleaming in the fluorescent light, the tables in the centre of the room with the integrated sinks, the rows of floor-to-ceiling double-door refrigerating units, buzzing with electricity along another tiled wall, and behind the glass-fronted cupboards, row upon row of shiny steel instruments.

And the trolley bearing the body, covered in a sheet.

Panic hits Lily hard, a punch to her lower abdomen. Her stomach, intestines and colon twist in a nervous dance. Certain she's going to throw up but frozen with fear, she watches Dr Frazer peel back the top part of the sheet to reveal the head of the corpse.

Waxy. Cold. Dead.

So this is what a dead body looks like.

A dead man.

Adam?

Lily's heart starts to thump as the awful truth hammers her brain. He is unrecognisable from the handsome man she knows. This man's dark hair is matted, plastered to his skull. His grey, hollowed face is a ragged patchwork of skin, lacerated by several short slashes, his features out of place; one eye punctured and misty, the other staring, terror-crazed.

'No,' she says suddenly unsure. It isn't Adam. It doesn't look like him.

'Are you sure?' Marshall asks, his voice muffled by the mask.

She takes a step closer. 'I ... I ... I don't think it's him.'

Dr Frazer eyes the Chief Inspector warily.

'Does Adam have any distinguishing features? A birthmark for example?' he asks.

'Yes,' she whispers. 'A birthmark on his left hip.'

'Lily, it's not police procedure to ask the next of kin to view any part of the corpse other than the head,' explains DS Day. 'Are you sure you're up to it?'

Lily stares straight ahead. 'I'm fine. Go ahead.'

Without further debate the mortician peels back the sheet to reveal the naked torso. Lily reels back in horror, stamping on Marshall's foot. He steadies her and says something she doesn't hear, deaf to the world around her. Terror is beating a furious rhythm on her eardrums. Hypnotised by fear, she's unable to focus on anything other than the ghastly apparition in front of her. The once perfect body is a mass of stab wounds, as if it has been sliced and hacked by a recalcitrant medic's scalpel. The skin is thick and leathery, scored like a joint of pork. The deeper cuts to his abdomen gape open, exposing muscle and the silver-grey strands of tendons that glisten in the intense light. Spilling out of a yawning gash beneath his ribs is a twisted snake-like coil; Adam's guts, frayed and disintegrating like a worn out cable. The wonderfully smooth toned body that Lily has held in her arms so often is gone. This tacky, bruised and pulverised carcass is all that's left. Carved up like the Sunday roast. There is dirt under his nails and dried blood on his hands, she notices as she stares at the birthmark just above his left hip.

She struggles to compute the information her brain is receiving at point blank range. The dissected body lying naked in front of her, stripped of all dignity, is, without doubt, her husband, Adam.

Dead.

Murdered.

She tries to scream. But her voice gets lost, strangled in her throat. She can't move, can barely breathe. A dragging sensation in her stomach and the bitter sting of bile in her throat serves as a warning. She has to get out of here before she empties her guts in this impossibly clean room.

'It's him. It's Adam,' she cries, recalling the point of this macabre visit. Her task complete, she runs towards the steel-framed door, yanks it open, shedding her mask and hat as she flees to the nearest toilet.

11

Lily is sitting on the edge of a chair on the opposite side of the desk to Marshall. Three telephones, a box of tissues and a buff envelope labelled *personal effects* lie between them. Adam's personal effects, Lily presumes. There must be a better word, she thinks. He's not a person anymore just a body. Every inch of him, dead. She believes it now she's seen it. She hugs her arms around her and clamps her teeth together to stop them chattering.

'Let me get you a blanket,' Marshall says.

'I'm fine but thank you.' She lets her limbs drop. The taste of acid lingers in her mouth. Remnants of bile sting the back of her throat. Marshall watches her intently. Remembering the bruises, Lily replaces her arms.

'Your husband died a violent death,' says Marshall, absently poking the envelope. Nerves, Lily supposes. It would be difficult for even those with the hardest hearts not to have been affected by Adam's corpse. 'It seems his killer slashed at him, causing a number of superficial cuts to his face, arms and hands as he tried to defend himself, before stabbing him repeatedly in his abdomen. At least three of these stab wounds could have proved fatal. The killer appears to have continued with his frenzied attack, perhaps unaware of his victim's death.'

Lily rocks backwards and forwards on her chair, clutching her arms. Beneath her cold, clammy skin, her nerve endings prickle uncomfortably. 'Thank you. Thank you for telling me. I ... I'm sorry I didn't believe you earlier.'

'It's okay, Lily. May I call you that?' Marshall takes off his navy jacket and places it over her shoulders.

'Yes and thanks,' she says, grateful for his persistence.

The door swings open behind her. Her senses on red alert, Lily cranes her neck. DS Day offers an encouraging smile as she walks into the office, carrying a chair. She places it in the corner of the room, sits down and folds her hands in her lap.

Marshall prods the buff-coloured envelope with his forefinger. She notices the nail is bitten ragged. 'His gold signet ring and his watch are in here. His car keys, iPod and the clothes and trainers he was wearing will be sent off to forensics. They'll examine the suit, shirt and tie he was wearing yesterday before he went jogging as well.'

'Thank you,' she mumbles, staring at the floor.

'And his car, of course. We found that in the car park of The Star Inn. We found his wallet locked in the glove compartment. We'll be going through that too.' Marshall flicks some invisible fluff off his crumpled, navy jacket then leans back in his chair.

'What will happen to Adam? His body, I mean. What will they … what will Dr Frazer do?'

'Before Joanne does anything, a Home Office pathologist will examine it. They'll take swabs of Adam's blood and scrapings from under his nails for analysis. To ascertain the type of knife used, the pathologist will measure the depth and length of each stab wound.'

She looks up, shocked. 'But Adam has hundreds of stab wounds.'

'I'm afraid it may take some time. The pathologist will work on the body until every single scrap of evidence has been preserved and documented. It may be that his killer left behind his DNA calling card: some blood, a hair, saliva. If he has, the pathologist will find it.'

Lily shudders. Somehow she has to divorce the Adam she knew and loved from the decimated corpse next door. A belief in some kind of god would probably be of help right now, she thinks, wrapping the jacket tight around her. At least then I'd have the comfort of knowing he was in a better place.

'The press tend to be a bit insensitive when researching a murder,' continues Marshall. 'As I mentioned before DS Bella Day is a Family Liaison Officer. She'll stay with you for as long as necessary to offer support and to field enquiries from the media. You'll probably also want support from your family or friends.'

'My parents are dead,' she says flatly. 'And my brother lives in Singapore.'

'Friends then. It's not a good idea to isolate yourself.'

She nods mechanically.

'The pathologist called to the crime scene believes Adam's death occurred between seven and eleven last night.'

'Last night? When was his body discovered?'

'At ten past seven this morning.'

'So he lay there all night, on his own?'

DS Day straightens up then quickly crosses her legs. Marshall frowns and clears his throat. 'What time did you say you got home?' he asks.

Why all the questions? Why won't he let up? She glances at DS Day who nods reassuringly. She is aware that her right leg is jiggling. She takes a deep breath. 'Around seven.'

Marshall laces his fingers together, his eyes fixed on hers. 'And you saw no sign of Adam or evidence to suggest that he'd been there?'

'No!'

'And you'd been shopping in Lewes?' he asks, raising an eyebrow.

Lily bites her lip and nods, too upset to alter her story now, both legs jiggling rapidly beneath the table.

'What did you do last night?'

It's one question too far. 'Why are you interrogating me?' she asks, raising her voice.

Marshall sucks his teeth before answering. 'Because roughly seventy per cent of all murders are committed by someone known to the victim.'

Lily leaps to her feet, her cheeks burning and Marshall's jacket falls to the floor. 'Do you think I did it? Do you think I killed Adam?'

DS Day frowns and clears her throat.

'No. I'm just doing my job,' he says, picking up his jacket. He offers it to her but she shakes her head vigorously. 'The sooner we eliminate you from our enquiries, the quicker we can proceed with the investigation. Please, Lily, sit down.'

A tear rolls down Lily's cheek as she collapses back down on the chair. 'I loved Adam, why would I kill him?'

Marshall places his jacket on the desk, pulls a tissue out of the box on the table and hands it to her. Lily snatches it and dabs at her face angrily.

'I know how tough this is. And I'm sorry to put you through this but I have to ask,' he says.

Her shoulders sag. 'I had supper, watched a bit of TV, had an early night.'

'Was yours a happy marriage?'

Lily's legs start jiggling again. She balls her fists. 'Yes, very happy.'

'But not recently.'

'Yes. No. I don't know. We'd never fought before.'

'Fought? Did Adam hit you, Mrs Hutchinson?'

'I meant argued,' she replies irritably. 'We never argued.'

Marshall coughs throatily. A smoker's cough? Was he hankering for a cigarette? she wonders. She isn't a smoker. Never has been. But right now if Marshall was to offer her one, she would accept eagerly. She glances at the detective's fingers, at his bitten nails, but there are no nicotine stains that she can see.

Marshall shifts in his seat. 'I want to talk to you about the bruising on your arms.'

He says it as if he's her doctor not a police officer investigating a murder. She squirms and covers her biceps involuntarily.

'Did Adam do that?'

Lily lowers her head, closes her eyes but says nothing.

'If he did, I need to know. It's important because it will help me construct an accurate profile of your husband. The bruises on your arms, although they've faded, are quite substantial.'

Lily is mortified at the thought of having to discuss her private life with this man. He may as well be asking her to strip for him. But what choice does she have? She wants his killer caught. 'Yes,' she whispers, clasping her hands together.

'Was it common for him to get angry?'

'No. Not at all. He was easy-going. Gentle. Kind.'

'So you were a loving couple?'

'Yes, very.'

'Was he angry about something you'd done?'

She glances at DS Day who, like Marshall, is eyeing her questioningly. She doesn't want to tell them about Nat. It would sound like an accusation. But she realises she has no option.

'And Adam was angry when you told him about these conversations?' coaxes DS Day when she's finished.

'Yes, and the following morning he left without waking me. When he came back later he was in a worse mood.' She stops, not wanting to divulge anymore.

'And that's when he hurt you,' prompts Marshall.

Lily lowers her eyes. She can recall the scene in vivid detail, how he squeezed her arms, the anger in his eyes, the way he threw her to the ground, as though she was a piece of rubbish he wanted to dispose of. She nods her head.

'And this happened eleven days ago. The day he disappeared?'

'Yes.'

'Has he ever hurt you before?'

'No. Never.'

Marshall stands up and starts to pace the small office. 'Can you think of anything you may have done to provoke this outburst?'

'No, unless Nat managed to turn him against me. That's possible I suppose.'

Marshall continues pacing, backwards and forwards, his fingers laced together behind his back. Eventually he stops in front of her. 'Lily, I have to ask you something as part of the investigation.'

Her legs start jiggling again. 'Okay.'

He leans forward until his eyes are inches from hers. 'Were you having an affair?'

Bang! Just like that! No skirting the issue. Straight to the point. Lily stares back incredulously. 'No!'

Marshall backs away, out of her space. 'Does anyone apart from you have access to the house? A cleaner for example?'

She sucks in air, her shoulders heaving up and down. Questions are coming at her from all angles, making her dizzy. She shakes her head. 'Can I go home now? Please.'

Marshall clears his throat. 'I'm afraid that won't be possible. A SOCO team has been dispatched to the house.'

'But he wasn't murdered at home. It's not a crime scene.'

'No, but they may find something of significance to lead us to his killer. We have to be prepared to disprove any story whoever murdered him might come up with. They'll be dusting for prints, looking through his personal belongings, brief case, computer files and so on. It should only take a day or so.'

'But it's my home. I have nowhere else to go.'

'Is there a friend you could call? A neighbour, perhaps?'

'I want to go home. My husband's been murdered. I want to go home,' she pleads, her breathing rapid.

Marshall leans over and presses her hand but she pulls it away. He sighs. 'Lily, we want to find the person who killed your husband. I wouldn't ask you to do this if I didn't feel it absolutely necessary. I'm sure you have friends who would be only too happy to help you'

She nods.

Marshall runs his hand through his hair and frowns.

Oh God, there's more, she thinks, hugging her arms around her body.

'Given the press coverage, I'm sure you're aware Carly Stoner's murder remains unsolved, just as I am sure you're aware Adam was helping us with our enquiries.'

Lily tenses. 'What do you mean?'

'Precisely what I said.'

'Sir,' DS Day springs to her feet. 'I really don't—'

Marshall holds up his hand to silence her. 'He must have told you we questioned him.'

He told me he was a witness. He told all of us, she thinks. She can feel her world rocking. She isn't sure of anything anymore. She juts out her chin. 'If you're saying you suspect him then that's crazy. Whoever killed Carly Stoner must have killed Adam.'

'They were killed in the same place but the MOs are entirely different, as, I believe, are the motives. I think we're looking for two killers.'

Lily stares at him horrified. 'So what was *Adam's* motive?'

DS Day touches him on the arm. 'Sir, please. I don't think this is the right—'

'Rape,' says Marshall.

She feels herself redden. 'No. You've got it wrong.'

His eyes lock on to hers. 'Adam knew exactly when Carly Stoner went out running, and where. He'd seen her every Friday last autumn. The evening of 18 April he stopped and talked to her. Maybe he tried to kiss her. She said no so he lost his temper and tried to rape her anyway. There was no semen in her vagina and no injuries consistent with a sexual attack, which infers her attacker was disturbed. She screamed when she was attacked. They were close to the pub. He would have panicked. He strangled her and then ran away.'

'Adam is not a rapist. He wouldn't hurt a fly.'

'He hurt you.'

'No. You have no proof.' She is on her feet now, stamping her foot. 'No fingerprints. No DNA.'

'DCI Marshall, I insist!' says DS Day sharply.

'Adam lied to us about the time he returned home.'

His words slice through her. 'He probably couldn't remember.'

Marshall laces his fingers together and stretches them back until the joints crack. 'It's interesting, isn't it, that he didn't tell you we questioned him. Was he in the habit of lying to you?'

She clenches her teeth. 'No. He never lied.'

'I see.'

What? What did he see? Her overloaded brain begins to pound. She clasps a hand to her forehead and lowers her eyes as the room starts to sway.

12

It's late afternoon and Lily, dazed and disorientated, is slumped in the back of DS Day's car. They are on the way to Orchard House to pick up a few of her things before she moves in with Miles. That much she knows. The present. It's all she can deal with right now. The past and the future are incomprehensible.

Coaxed by DS Day, she managed to telephone Miles at his estate agency from the mortuary. She heard herself speaking to him in a voice devoid of emotion as though she were listening to the conversation.

'Adam's been murdered,' she said. No preamble. No explanation. Just raw fact. It was insensitive but under the circumstances it had been an achievement just to string three words together.

'Sorry. What did you say?' Miles asked.

'Adam's dead. Murdered.'

'No. No, he can't be.'

'He's dead, Miles. I've seen his body. He was killed on the bridle path by the river,' she says, all in a rush.

'Shit. What was he doing there?'

'Jogging.'

'But that girl. I warned him—'

'He's dead, Miles. Adam's dead.'

'Lily, I'm so sorry. I ... I ... can't believe. Shit.' Miles's words tailed off.

'Oh God, I'm sorry. It's just – it's awful – his body – Miles, I don't know what to do – the police – they want to search the house – they want to question all of you ...'

She heard Miles sniffing on the other end of the line, a strangled sob as he tried to bring his emotions under control. 'Can I stay with you?' she asked.

'Of course you can,' he said, his voice hoarse.

Through the open window of the car, Lily stares blindly at the Downs rising out of the earth like the rolling backbone of some giant, sleeping animal. Oilseed rape glows gold in the sunshine, while in the neighbouring fields, ewes and lambs bleat loudly. Nature seems at odds with the brutal reality of her day, the cloudless sky too blue, the sun too bright, the carpet of bluebells in the woodlands too vivid.

DS Day turns into the drive and parks between a marked police car and a large van. Lily stares at the house she left this morning now tied up with blue and white tape. Men and women in white overalls and gloves, hooded and masked, walk in and out of the open front door, like astronauts working on the moon.

DS Day digs inside a large black bag and hands Lily a packet of blue overshoes and blue gloves. 'I'll wait for you here. I can't go in.'

Lily frowns and rips open the sealed packets. She slips on the overshoes, pulls on the gloves then shuffles across the gravel into the house. A SOCO officer, carrying an object in a clear plastic bag, stands back to let her pass as she climbs the stairs. In their bedroom, at the front of the house, another suited member of the SOCO team is dusting the surface of her dressing table.

He stops when Lily enters. 'I've finished in here but could you stay out of the bathroom?'

She nods. 'Is it okay to use the phone?'

'Go ahead. I'll leave you to it.'

Alone at last, Lily flops on the bed and stares at the ceiling. She's worn out, drained, as though she's done eight rounds in a boxing ring. The image of Adam's body flashes in front of her eyes, bloodied, broken and disfigured. It takes all of her willpower not to scream. She clutches her hands to her head. You must have been scared, my darling, she thinks. Terrified.

She'd seen him frightened before, the day he was admitted to hospital with a burst appendix. He was in agony but it wasn't the pain that bothered him, or the surgeon's scalpel. It was the anaesthetic.

'Don't leave me, Lily, he said, clutching her hand as the porters wheeled him down to the operating theatre. 'Promise me you won't leave me.'

She hated seeing him so upset. It wasn't like him. 'I'll be right here waiting for you when you wake up.'

He sat up then and started shouting. 'No. No, I can't do this. I can't go through with the operation. I've changed my mind.'

His face was pinched with pain, his forehead laced with sweat but he was adamant he wasn't going to theatre. The nurse accompanying him did her best to calm him, but Adam was working himself up into a state and wouldn't be placated. 'What if I don't wake up?'

'If you don't have the operation you won't,' said the unsympathetic nurse. 'Come on now. You're not going to feel a thing.'

That wasn't the point, of course. It was the thought of handing control of his life over to someone else that bothered him. She understood, but it took all her powers of persuasion before the nurse consented to let her hold his hand while the anaesthetist administered the drugs.

The surgeon saved his life only for him to be murdered by a knife-wielding maniac, she thinks miserably.

Spreading her arms out wide, she clutches the soft, down duvet with her gloved hands, rolls over and wraps herself up in its warm, comforting folds. She breathes in long and hard. But Adam has been away too long. No trace of his scent remains, only the fabric conditioner she used a few days ago when she washed the bedclothes. Reality inches ever closer. Adam is dead. His smell, his smile, his voice, his touch, his pale grey eyes, his brilliant smile, all the emotions which make up Adam, are gone. And all that's left is a mutilated corpse lying on a tray in a mortuary fridge. His body. A pile of bones that will, eventually, turn to dust. The good times, the bad, the shared dreams, the love, reduced to memories. She clutches her heart. Pain, like a piece of shrapnel, has lodged itself there. An atrocious pain, searing and sharp, haemorrhaging despair, denial and grief indiscriminately as it strangles forever any glimmer of hope. She buries her head in her pillow and cries, her body juddering with the force of her grief.

She isn't sure how long she lies there sobbing but the pillowcase is soaking wet, her face swollen, when DS Day's ludicrous voice drifts up from the drive through the open window.

'Lily! Are you ready to go?'

Lily extracts herself from the duvet and stands up, a simple action that suddenly requires monumental effort. Her limbs have turned to lead. Or tin, that probably describes it better. She feels as hollow as the Tin Man, apart from the fact that she has a heart, and it hurts like hell.

What I would tell that humanised piece of waste metal if I had the chance, she thinks, dragging her body to the window. What's so bad about an empty alloy body? At least you're naturally armour-plated. No chance of being knifed to death. And no heart equals no pain.

Ignoring the fine dust on the frame, Lily leans out of the window. 'I'm just going to make a call.'

DS Day nods.

She goes back to the bed, sits down and picks up the handset from the bedside table, where she left it this morning. It feels heavy. Foreign. Useless. She stares at it and wonders whether now is the right time to call Susie. She shakes her head. There is *no* right time. Besides, Susie is the one person she can really talk to. With trembling fingers she taps in the number. The phone rings nine times before switching to answerphone. She dials Susie's mobile. It's switched off. She leaves a desperate message, throws down the phone and dives face down on the bed and cries again.

DS Day calls up to her. 'Lily? Are you okay?'

'Go away,' says Lily, her voice muffled by the duvet she's drumming with her fists.

'Lily?'

Mouthing profanities, Lily sniffs, wipes away her tears and sits up. 'I'm fine. One minute,' she calls out, picking up the handset. Susie isn't available, so I'll call Rose. She pulls out the tan, leather-bound address book from the drawer of the bedside table and finds Rose's office number. She answers after three rings.

'Lily! Hi! Listen, I'm a bit busy at the moment. Can I call you back tonight?'

'No! No you can't.' Lily's voice is shrill, almost a shriek. She needs to keep Rose on the phone.

'What on earth's the matter?'

'Adam's dead,' she says, charging straight to the point. 'He was murdered while he was jogging, like that girl.'

'Oh my God. No. Adam?'

'Rose, the police are all over the house. I'm going to stay with Miles. Could you come down? I could really use all my friends at the moment and I can't get hold of Susie.'

'I ... I ...'

'Rose?'

'You know I'd drop everything for you.'

'Yeah. I know. Thanks, Rose. I really, really appreciate it.'

'Normally I would, I mean. Oh God. This is so awful. Awful. I can't believe it but ... I'll come down as soon as I can.'

'What do you mean?'

'There's a crisis. Our boss, Delaney ...' she hesitates. 'I'm very, very sorry but I can't leave. It's impossible. I have to deal with this ... problem. There's no one else. I'll be right down, I promise.'

Lily listens in disbelief. Does Rose understand what she is saying? Does she realise that Adam has been murdered? That he is dead? 'His body was carved up by a maniac. I've seen it and it was terrible. But don't worry, Rose. Work is far more important.'

'Lily. I'm sorry. I didn't mean—'

But it's too late. Pricked by Rose's thorns Lily slams down the handset, tears of self-pity coursing down her cheeks. Seconds later, the phone rings. She takes a deep breath to compose herself then answers it. 'Hello.'

Nothing.

'Hello? Rose? Susie?'

Silence.

'For God's sake say something,' she screams.

Click! The connection is broken. The line goes dead.

'Go away!' she yells down the receiver to the buzzing line. 'Leave me alone.'

13

Susie knows she should be in the mood for celebrating. She's spent the past hour with her terminally enthusiastic agent, Mary Truman, in her Poland Street office, an airy, sparsely-furnished room, with bleached wooden floorboards and white walls covered in framed black and white ten-by-eights of her clients, including a flatteringly airbrushed one of Susie. She's been on Mary's books since leaving drama school six years ago and can't fault her efforts in trying to further her career. She's been seen by some of the country's finest directors – Richard Eyre, Michael Boyd, Trevor Nunn – and has been called back for second, occasionally third auditions. Her biggest regret was losing out to a LAMDA colleague last year for the lead part in a Stephen Poliakoff television drama. The disappointment hit her hard. Her career would have skyrocketed, doors would have opened, scripts would have arrived by the lorry-load. Disillusioned, she threatened to chuck in the towel but Mary, with much cajoling and gentle entreating, persuaded her to stick at it.

'All you need is the one big break to hurl you into the spotlight,' she reminded her, 'and the offers will come tumbling in. You have to be patient, darling.'

The job Mary has negotiated today, while not exactly earth-shattering, is at least high profile. A two-month contract for a job on *EastEnders*. It's a juicy part, the mistress of one of the central characters. Filming isn't due to start for three weeks but when it does, Susie knows she'll be working ten, maybe twelve-hour days. But she doesn't mind one little bit.

I'd be quaffing champagne in some Soho bar if Fabian was around, she thinks, switching on her mobile, eager to share her news with him. After a minute, the phone beeps. He's remembered, she thinks happily as she glances at the screen. One missed call, she reads. But it isn't Fabian who's tried to contact her, it's Lily and she's left a message. Susie smiles, pleased she's got in touch. She's still no idea what's going on with her and Adam.

I'll call her the moment I've spoken to Fabian, she thinks, dialling his number. But there's no answer. And no international ring code. Which means that unless Fabian has forgotten to take his mobile with him when he left for Milan yesterday, he's still in London today. Without deliberating further and with mounting irritation, she dials his office.

'Alex Delaney's office.' The instantly recognisable voice of Janice White does nothing to improve her mood.

'Is Fabian there, Janice?'

'Susie? No, he's out of the office for the next few days. How are you? Are we going to be seeing you on television soon?'

Janice's ever-so-slightly patronising tone grates on her nerves. 'Is he in Milan?'

'I don't think so.'

Ultra-efficient busybody, thinks Susie. 'Where is he then?'

Janice clears her throat. 'He didn't tell me his exact movements, only that he wouldn't be in the office for the next couple of days.' She pauses, waiting for a response. But Susie, who's silently fuming, says nothing. 'Shall I take a message?'

'Yes please, Janice. When he turns up, tell him Susie says, Fuck Off.'

'Oh!'

She's done it. She's shocked Janice. She smiles. 'Goodbye Janice. You take care now.'

The triumph Susie feels as she breaks the connection is fleeting. She's furious Fabian's PA knows more about his *movements* than she does.

'Movements,' she mutters, glowering at the mobile. 'I wasn't asking about his bloody bowels.'

Her iPhone beeps again as she turns left into Great Marlborough Street, a reminder for her answer phone message. Pleased that she'll have someone to share her success with, she holds the phone to her ear and listens, her stride slackening with every word Lily utters.

14

Rose is sitting alone in her office, her head propped in her hands, staring into space. She's been in a trance since Lily called. She covers her face. Tears squeeze their way through the gaps between her fingers and dribble down her wrists to the pristine, pinstriped cuffs of her shirt. She presses the heels of her hands in the sockets, trying to stem the flow, but she can't stop.

Oh God. It's such a mess. One huge gigantic mess.

She rolls herself back up into a sitting position and wipes away her tears with her already sodden sleeves, and squints with stinging, narrowed eyes at the photo of George. Her son has started asking questions about his father. He wants to know his name. He wants to know if he will ever meet him.

As if she doesn't have enough to deal with.

The situation she finds herself in is diabolical. That's why she did it. She had to do something. Besides, Adam deserved it. He'd provoked her. Insider trading is a serious offence. Most of the broadsheets have already picked up on it and are covering the ominous-looking shift in the market. She couldn't sit back and watch him get away with it.

She prides herself on being a hard worker, competent, reliable and trustworthy. But she also likes to keep things in order. Everybody knows that. But the office is in chaos. The FSA are crawling over them like maggots through carrion. There is no method to her tidy world anymore. Everything is in disarray. And she is stuck in the middle of it all, a lone figure caught in a vortex that threatens to drag her under.

She is losing control. George is growing up. And Adam. Adam is dead.

He should have listened to me, she thinks. If he had then maybe it wouldn't have come to this.

He got what he deserved.

She shivers.

Soon the police would be here asking questions.

15

'I remember the first time I met him. It was on the stairs of the Queen's Building. I was a Fresher but I still knew who he was. Everyone knew Adam Hutchinson. Anyway, he stopped when he saw me. *Hey, It's Eliza isn't it?* he said. *I've been dying to meet you.*

'I almost collapsed in shock. *Him*, dying to meet *me*. I smiled stupidly, too nervous to speak. Adam speaking to me. He was inches away, close enough for me to see how handsome he actually was. His face was completely flawless, no freckles, moles, scars or any other imperfection. He was perfect. I was so over-awed I had to cling to the banisters. *I heard about your exploits last night, Eliza*, he said. *Very impressive.*

'Do you remember, Miles? It was Rag Week and Nat and some of the other second years stormed Hope Hall and kidnapped half a dozen of us girls. It was the middle of the night when they forced their way into our rooms and dragged us, kicking and screaming, into their waiting cars. The joke was to drive us to the edge of Dartmoor and leave us there. It was winter, it was freezing cold, we were dressed for bed and they were going to abandon us in the middle of nowhere. Rose and two of the other girls became hysterical, which was their objective, of course. I remember wishing Susie was with us. She was always brilliant in those situations. But she was out clubbing.

'Anyway, just as they were about to leave us by the side of the road, Rose crying and the others screaming, I snatched the keys from Nat, bundled Rose into the back, jumped behind the wheel and drove away.

'I smiled at Adam and explained I preferred to be called Lily and then I apologised about hurting Nat. I knew they were good friends. *Well what did the idiot expect, leaping on the roof and peering in the windscreen?* he said laughing. I was frightened when I saw his face, upside down. It's not what you expect, I explained. That's why I braked. Nat shot across the bonnet of the car, flipped over in a near-perfect somersault, before skidding across the road for about ten feet on his behind. *He can barely walk his arse is so bruised. You've got guts, Eliza. Sorry, Lily.*

'I think I replied *thank you*, like an idiot. Next thing I knew he'd leant over and kissed me on the cheek. I almost fell over when he moved his lips to my ear but instead of another kiss he whispered, *meet me at the Clock Tower tomorrow night at eight. Wrap up warm.* That's how we met. Do you remember, Miles?'

'He took me to the beach that night, at Dawlish, in his clapped-out MG. He always was a sucker for sports cars. The first thing he did was produce the cold box he'd stashed behind my seat. He opened it and offered me an ice-cold beer. It was February and it was freezing but I took one anyway. I figured it would calm my nerves. Excited nerves, mind you. I was on a date with Adam Hutchinson. I had to pinch myself several times that night. He opened the small boot. I remember being surprised it was crammed full of logs. He dug a hole in the sand with a toy spade that he'd brought with him and made a fire in the centre. He had sausages in his cold box. He gave me a long fork and we sat on the sand roasting them in the flames, then later marshmallows. I'll never forget it. They were the best sausages I've ever tasted, the sweetest marshmallows. You see, it was the first properly romantic evening I'd ever had. It was unforgettable.'

Miles leans over and buries his face in her hair, his cheeks dewy with tears. He puts his arm around her and draws her to him and they cry, locked together, until DS Day returns with the tea.

The unmelodious ring of DS Day's mobile punctuates the evening. Eventually, she apologises and tactfully retreats to the spare bedroom on the first floor to deal with the enquiries.

When she's sure she's out of earshot, Lily turns to Miles. 'You know Adam's still a suspect in the Carly Stoner murder.'

Miles looks at her not comprehending.

'My thoughts exactly,' says Lily. 'How can he be when he's dead?'

'I thought he was a witness.'

'Yeah, well, turns out he wasn't. He told them he'd arrived back at our house earlier than I did but really, either of us could have got the time wrong. Jesus, Miles, I had the most awful time this afternoon. Marshall is a brute. He just kept on and on at me. It's crazy. There's no way Adam could have killed her. He wouldn't have been so relaxed at the party if he had.'

Miles's mobile rings. He checks the screen. 'It's Susie,' he says, handing Lily the phone.

'I'm so glad I've finally got through to you,' she says. 'I've been calling your mobile for ages. Where are you?'

'I'm at Miles's. The police are all over Orchard House.'

'My poor love. Are you all right? No, of course you're not. I'm on the train. I'll get off at Lewes. I should be with you in less than an hour.'

It's the most encouraging news Lily has had in a while. Susie is the best person to have around in a crisis. She's practical and strong. And I have so much to tell her, she thinks. All the stuff I've been keeping to myself – Adam's inexplicable anger, his weird disappearing act, the crank calls.

She turns to Miles. 'There's something you should know.'

He stares at her expectantly.

93

'I told Adam about Nat's calls.' Lily lowers her gaze and fiddles with the bottom of her T-shirt, rolling it into a tight coil. 'I know you advised me not to. I know it was a stupid thing to do but I couldn't stand it anymore. Nat scared me. I was upset. I had to tell Adam.'

She raises her head, letting go of the shirt. Miles is pulling a face, his eyes scrunched, his nostrils flared as though he's just smelled something horrible. He takes off his spectacles, rubs his eyes with his thumbs then relaxes his face.

'What did he say?'

'He was angry. Called Nat a bastard. Then the next day he left. I assumed he went to have it out with Nat. When he came home he was angry. I tried to talk to him but he wouldn't speak to me. It wasn't like him. That was the last time I saw him alive.'

Miles replaces his spectacles. 'Why didn't you call me?'

'I was embarrassed. I thought you'd say, *I told you so.*'

'You know me better than that.' He puts his arm round her again and strokes her hair affectionately.

I know and I wish I had, thinks Lily ruefully, leaning into him. 'When did you last speak to Adam?'

'About a fortnight ago, I think.' Miles pauses and presses his lips together for a moment. 'He tried calling me the day he died though.'

'Really?' Lily's heart judders. Why didn't he call her? Then she remembers she'd unplugged the landline. Perhaps he tried to call her but couldn't get through. But why didn't he call her on her mobile? Or did he? Come to think of it, she hasn't seen it for a while.

'I was having a hell of a day at work,' says Miles, interrupting her thoughts. 'I'd switched my mobile off but when I turned it back on after my last meeting at about nine in the evening, there were a couple of messages he'd left asking me to call him. I tried but there was no answer.'

'He might have been dead by then.' Lily sucks in a mouthful of air, fighting back the tears. 'What did he say in the messages?'

'Nothing really. Just that he needed to talk.'

'Needed?'

'Yeah. I think so.'

'Did you keep them?' she asks hopefully.

He shakes his head. 'I only wish I had.'

'Since he disappeared I've been getting a lot of anonymous phone calls,' continues Lily. 'I had one this afternoon when I went back to the house.'

'Have you told the police?'

'I told DS Day on my way over.'

'And?'

'She said they'd trace the calls.'

'But did she think it was the murderer?'

'She said they might be connected.'

There's a gentle knock on the door and DS Day appears, her mobile pressed against her jacket. 'I'm sorry to disturb you both, but I've got Adam's father on the line. Detective Sergeant Mills has just arrived at his house to break the news of his son's death. Understandably, he's a bit raw,' she warns, with a sympathetic smile.

Adam's parents, Ursula and Henry Hutchinson, live near Faversham; a market town nestled between the Downs and the sweeping flatlands of the north Kent marshes. It's an hour and three quarters' drive away, a journey she and Adam made four times a year. It's my duty, he assured Lily, which just about summed up the relationship. She'd been appalled when he told her his mother never hugged him as a child. What with the lack of parental warmth and physical affection, the boarding school upbringing, it was a miracle that he turned out the way he had. But for all that and despite their two daughters, Adam was their golden boy. They adored their son in their cold, Victorian way. Their son's choice of bride, however, fell short of their expectations. They were too polite to actually come out and say it but their body language gave it away.

Lily has never felt comfortable in their presence. And right now, she has no idea what she's going to say.

'I'll talk to them if you like,' says Miles.

'No. It's okay,' she says. Trembling, she takes the phone. 'Hello, Henry. I believe you've heard—'

'Yes. Yes. I know what's happened.' His voice is gruff, irritable.

'I'm very sorry, Henry. You must be—'

'Good God, girl, I'm in pieces. Adam meant the world to me.'

'He meant the world to me too, Henry.'

There's a pause. 'Are you being taken care of? Would you like Ursula and me to come and stay? Sort out the estate. That sort of thing.'

'No. Thank you, Henry. That's very kind of you. I'm staying with Miles Spencer at the moment while the police are in the house. But thank you. That's unbelievably kind.'

Silence on the other end of the line is followed by an audible sob. She's shocked. She didn't think him capable of tears.

'Henry? Are you all right?'

But Henry Hutchinson is no longer there.

DS Day is drinking tea again. Lily wonders if she ever gets sick of the stuff. So far she's only experienced one day of excessive tea drinking and the taste was palling by mid-afternoon.

DS Day puts down her mug and flicks through her notebook. 'I have some news for you. Ian Venables, the publican of The Star Inn, saw Adam talking on his mobile last night before he went for his jog.' She scans a couple of pages. 'At around seven-fifteen.'

'Do you know who he was talking to?' Miles asks.

'No we don't. Adam's phone is missing.'

'Do you think it was his killer?' asks Lily.

'We try not to make assumptions but it's possible. We're searching the area for his mobile. The killer might have kept it or disposed of it, although it's also entirely possible it was lost in the tussle. Can you tell me the name of his service provider so we can trace the call?'

'Vodafone,' says Lily.

DS Day writes it down. 'Has anything else out of the ordinary occurred these last few days? Anything at all?'

'No. Nothing,' Lily replies evenly, as the cogs of her brain tick over. 'That is if you discount yesterday's visitor,' she adds, recalling the expensive-looking woman who'd rocked up looking for Adam.

DS Day's ears prick up like an eager dog. 'Visitor?'

'She introduced herself as an old acquaintance of Adam. It was strange because I'd never heard him mention anyone called Honor before. It's not a name you would forget though, is it? There can't be all that many Honors around. And she was Italian, I think. I mean, she sounded Italian. She called around nine-fifteen on Tuesday morning and yet she seemed surprised he wasn't home.'

'Honor who?'

'I can't remember. Something Italian. Er, Vettori. No, Villetti. Vincente. Yes, that's right. Honor Vincente.'

'Could you describe her?'

'Yes. Attractive, slim, tall, quietly spoken. Refined, definitely.'

'What about hair colour, eyes?'

'She was wearing a pale blue scarf over her head and a large pair of black sunglasses. Sorry.'

'And you say she introduced herself as an old friend?'

'Yes. She asked when I expected Adam home. I told her he was away on business and I wasn't sure when he'd be back. I said I'd tell him she'd called and suggested she leave her phone number. But she just thanked me, got into her car, a silver Porsche I think it was, and drove away.'

'Okay. We'll follow it up.' DS Day stops scribbling. 'One more thing. The press are now aware of the murder.

They're attracted to yards of blue and white tape and plain-clothed detectives, like moths to a flame, I'm afraid. The murder was featured on the lunchtime news in response to a press release we issued. Adam's name wasn't included in that information. Anyway, now that you've formally identified Adam, we'll be issuing another press release detailing his name and occupation. It'll feature on the ten o'clock news. Unfortunately, you will consequently be of great interest to the press.'

Lily buries her head in her hands overwhelmed with dread. It's obvious really. She's watched enough appeals, read enough newspaper articles over the years to know what to expect.

'We've asked them to respect your privacy, which means very little in actual fact, although it's highly unlikely they'll find you while you're here. I'll continue to liaise with DCI Marshall and the police press office and field the calls. Then tomorrow morning at nine, DCI Marshall will front a television appeal. He'll issue a photograph of Adam to jog the memory of potential witnesses.'

16

Lily's face is the colour of old, milky tea. And she's lost weight, Susie thinks as she gives her a hug. She can feel her shoulder blades, bony and raised, beneath her T-shirt. She's thin. Too thin. Like a coat-hanger. Her clothes, falling off her.

Whispering words of encouragement, Susie tries to soothe her. 'I'll stay as long as you need me. I'm your guardian angel, remember?'

'Rose—was—too—busy,' says Lily between sobs.

What is that girl playing at? Susie wonders, horrified.

'I thought she was my friend.'

Some friend, thinks Susie. She's about to offer her opinion on the subject when she remembers what Fabian told her before he disappeared. 'Actually, Lily, there has been a spot of bother at work. I'm sure she'll be down as soon as she can.'

This seems to comfort Lily. She stops crying and wipes away the tears gathering in a pool beneath her eyes.

'Let's go outside,' Susie says, seizing the initiative. She picks up her large, stripy, canvas overnight bag and takes Lily by the hand, leading her through Miles's L-shaped living room and out the French windows into the small flint-walled courtyard garden, to the teak table at the far end of the paved area, beside a raised bed full of shrubs. 'First things first,' she says, producing a screw-top bottle of Pinot Grigio and two plastic wine glasses from her bag. She pours the wine and hands a glass to Lily. 'Here, get this down your neck. Nothing like a bit of wine therapy to ease the pain.'

A small smile plays on Lily's lips. Well that's a start, thinks Susie. She pours herself a glass and has a sip.

'I can't believe he's dead,' Lily says, tipping her head onto Susie's shoulder.

Susie puts her arm round her and kisses her hair. 'It must have been horrific. I can only imagine what you've been through.'

She feels Lily's body shuddering. 'Oh, Susie, it was awful. I can't get rid of the image of his body in the mortuary. It didn't look like Adam at all, he was a mess.'

Susie takes a large swig of wine. She's never had the stomach for corpses.

'At first I thought they were joking. The police that is,' continues Lily.

'It's such a shock.'

Lily nods and has a sip of wine. 'Then DCI Marshall bombarded me with questions. He wouldn't let up. Apparently most murders are committed by someone the victim knows, so they suspect me.'

Susie's jaw drops open. 'You? That's ridiculous. Total crap.'

'So you don't think I did it then?'

'Don't joke, Lily. Not at a time like this. It's too awful.'

They drink their wine for a moment in silence, listening to the cars driving along the road beyond the garden. Behind the mound of the Downs the dying sun sinks slowly, its face freckled with birds flying home to nest.

'Why did you tell me Adam was in Milan?' asks Susie.

Lily sighs and shrugs. 'I didn't know where he was. It seemed easier to lie.'

'So where was he?'

'I've no idea but I do know he'd taken the time off as holiday. I haven't seen him since I told him about Nat's late night calls.'

'Nat?'

It doesn't take long for Lily to explain what happened; the calls, Adam's inexplicable rage, his disappearance.

Susie can't believe what she's hearing. She isn't sure if she's more shocked by the series of events, or that Lily's kept them to herself. 'I didn't think you two argued.'

'We don't. I mean didn't. Not really. Not like that. It was just that one time and it was more of a fight than an argument.'

'Has Rose said anything to you?'

'I've already told you. She's too—'

'Yes, yes of course. Sorry, I forgot.'

Lily's shoulders droop. She looks as though she's about to start crying again.

Susie thinks it would be better if she tried to focus on the positives. 'Think of all the good times you had together,' she says. 'Your Caribbean wedding. I was so envious. All those amazing holidays he took you on, the wonderful surprise party he threw for your thirtieth birthday. The beautiful diamond earrings he gave you.'

What little colour there is left drains from Lily's face. 'Yes but if everything was so great, why did he disappear these last eleven days? Where did he go? Because I've got no idea. Where did he go, Susie? Where did he go?'

She sighs and shakes her head, baffled. 'Honey, I don't know. But you know what? We are going to find out. He didn't just disappear. Someone will know,' she says, although she's not sure if she's referring to Adam, now, or Fabian.

Susie manages to coax Lily to her feet. Supporting her by the arm like an elderly aunt, she leads her across the garden, through the back door and into the kitchen. Miles is slumped over the table, his right hand pulling at his left index finger. He looks up when they enter. His face is flushed and his brown eyes, red-rimmed and tired.

'DS Day has gone home,' he says.

Susie encourages Lily into a seat and turns her attention to Miles. 'A drink. That's what you need.' She finds a glass, fills it with wine and places it in front of him.

A tormented frown creases his forehead. 'I'm sorry. It's all so raw and all those questions. I thought DS Day would never stop.'

Lily reaches over the table and touches him lightly on the arm.

On the dresser behind Miles's head, Susie catches sight of a framed picture of him and Adam dressed in school uniform. She walks over to it and picks it up. Adam must have been around sixteen, she thinks as she studies it. He's immaculately turned out, his tie in a small tight knot, his blazer freshly pressed. She imagines him breezing his way down a corridor, handsome, arrogant but charming with it, files under one arm, a group of boys in tow, hanging on his every word.

'What was Adam like at school?' she asks Miles.

'Pretty cool. A bit of a dude. He broke all the rules but he managed to charm the prefects and masters, so he never really got into trouble. Everybody looked up to him, even some of the teachers. He was Head of House. A school prefect.'

So Adam was idolised even then, she thinks, putting the picture down.

'You've been friends a long time,' says Lily.

Miles's eyes glisten with unshed tears.

'I'll never forget when Nat bet him he wouldn't strip to his boxers and ski that red run on the famous skiing holiday,' says Susie, eager to lighten the mood. 'That's the bravest, stupidest thing I think I've ever seen anyone do. I mean, imagine the looks he must have got on the chairlift. Epic.'

'It was a fun trip,' says Lily.

'Bonkers more like,' says Susie. 'I don't think I've ever drunk so much alcohol in one week. Neither had poor old Rose. I've always meant to ask her if she lost her virginity to that waiter. Pretty rough to pop your cherry and get knocked up all in one go.'

'Well if you do, I doubt she'll tell you,' says Miles. 'You know what she's like.'

'Nat was rubbish. Do you remember? Every time he snowploughed he managed to swivel round and ended up skiing downhill backwards,' continues Susie. 'And Rose wasn't much better.'

'Adam was a brilliant skier,' says Lily quietly.

Of course he was, thinks Susie.

'Yeah. It's such a waste, isn't it? He had it all—' Miles stops. His face collapses. He lifts up his glasses and presses his thumb and forefinger into the corners of his eyes to quash the tears.

At midnight Miles suggests they go to bed. Lily wraps her arms around both of them until they form a tight little circle on the landing, hugging one another close.

Miles is the first to peel away. 'I made up my bed with clean sheets while you two were outside. You can sleep there, Lily, and Susie can have the spare room. The bed's made. I'll sleep on the sofa.'

'I don't mind sleeping on the sofa,' says Susie. 'Lily can sleep in the spare room. That way we won't be putting you out.'

'It's not a problem,' says Miles. 'And if Lily wakes in the night, you're nearer.'

Susie glances at Lily. 'Promise me you'll wake me if you need me.'

'I promise,' she says. She thanks Miles and kisses him on the cheek and gives Susie one last squeeze.

Lily undresses slowly in the unfamiliar room. The alcohol she's drunk, instead of slowing down her brain, has invigorated it. It's buzzing, whirring into overload, crowded with painful thoughts as if dozens of frantic mice are scurrying around beneath her skull. She slips under the duvet, tense and taught, and rolls on to her side. She forces her eyes shut and prays for sleep to overwhelm her but instead a kaleidoscope of Tarantino-like images flash through her mind. Adam's punctured eye, his lacerated body, his matted hair, the fraying coil of his guts spilling out of his abdomen. Images so vivid it's as if she's been transported back to the post mortem room. She can smell the antiseptic, can taste the acid remnants of her vomit while Marshall's pinpoint questioning reverberates in her ears. She opens her eyes and takes some deep breaths to calm her racing heart.

If only I had been at home when he got back, none of this would have happened, she thinks, hugging her knees to her chest. He wouldn't have gone jogging. He wouldn't have been murdered. He'd have stayed and talked to me.

Wouldn't he?

She cradles her head in her hands and presses her elbows together, to block out the question. If only he'd talked to me. If only he'd told me why he was so angry. Something must have happened, something he couldn't tell me about. But what?

Her mind is a tornado of gruesome emotions, fear, loneliness, helplessness and guilt, swirling around in wild confusion. And then it hits her. A sensation so powerful she feels she's being ripped apart, limb from limb, mind from brain by some monstrous sharp-clawed animal. The pain of earlier is a pinprick in comparison to the convulsions that consume her now. Despair, denial, anger, grief collide to detonate in one gigantic explosion, the searing, devastating, pain of a heart just broken. Her heart. The one she gave to Adam, happily and readily. The one that died with him today.

Her future lost, she squeezes herself into a tighter ball, clutching her knees to her chest in the hope that this new compact, rounder form will prove more effective at deflecting pain. She rocks backwards and forwards, crying into her pillow, trying to console herself that she, at least, is alive.

Broken-hearted.
But alive.

A memory sears her tortured mind. The night of Adam's proposal. Why now? she thinks, trying to dispel it. But it knocks on her conscience, refusing to be ignored.

'I'm taking you away for the weekend. Somewhere smart, so dress up,' he said. She didn't mind. She liked it when he surprised her, although this was the first time he'd specified a dress code. After trying on and discarding four or five outfits, she opted for an aquamarine wrap dress that Susie insisted made her look sophisticated. Adam picked her up in his brand-new BMW Roadster and drove her from the Clapham flat she shared with Susie to the Combe House Hotel in Devon, an imposing, Grade I Elizabethan Manor with a long drive surrounded by fields of Arabian horses. The manager greeted her with a dozen blood-red roses then led them to a cosy little room, where a bottle of champagne sat in readiness in a silver ice bucket, a plate of delicate canapés on a small round table.

Pan-seared scallops, pea puree and crispy pancetta, followed by best end of lamb with a sweetbread mousse and a Mediterranean vegetable tian, washed down with a bottle of Gevrey-Chambertin a wonderfully expensive Pinot Noir, Lily discovered from the sommelier. It was the most elaborate food she'd ever tasted and a menu she'd committed to memory.

Their room was large and predominantly cream – cream coverlet, cream chairs, cream drapes – apart from the two red scatter cushions on the king-size bed. An ice bucket with another bottle of champagne lay waiting on the glass-topped table. Adam took her hands and looked at her as if she was the most wonderful thing he'd ever seen.

'I want to spend the rest of my life with you,' he said. 'Marry me, Lily.'

'Yes,' she whispered, closing her eyes. 'Yes, I'll marry you.'

He let go of her right hand and dug around in his pocket. 'I can't wait to see this on your finger.'

Lily's eyes widened at the size of the solitaire diamond.

'I love you, Lily,' he said, slipping on the ring.

The cork exploded out of the champagne bottle and hit the ceiling. She giggled.

'A good omen,' said Adam, trying to contain the foaming liquid in a flute.

She hears it trickling into the glass. Her eyes snap open. Sunlight streams through a chink in the curtains. Disoriented, she sits up. She doesn't recognise the room.

'Adam?'

The present hits her like a slap across her cheeks. It isn't champagne she can hear but the sound of Miles running a shower in the bathroom next door.

17

DS Bella Day's short, layered, highlighted hair fits her head like a swimming cap. Her face is tired and worn. Two deep vertical lines bisect her cheeks, which combined with the deep, saggy bags under her eyes, give her face a lived-in look.

'If she wore her hair longer it would draw attention away from her bulbous nose,' Susie whispers at breakfast.

'Don't be mean,' says Lily.

'And as for her voice. I'm terrified I'm going to laugh every time she opens her mouth.'

'You'll get used to it. She's kind. She's dealt with everything. All the hassle from the media. DCI Marshall. I couldn't have coped without her.'

'Have you seen her tattoo?'

'Tattoo?'

'A small bee on the inside of her wrist. I noticed it when she took her watch off to do the washing up.'

After breakfast, the four of them sit down to watch Marshall's television appeal. It's a straightforward entreaty to anyone who might have seen Adam the day of his murder to get in touch with Sussex Police. A photograph of Adam appears on the screen. Lily stares at it, hypnotised. It's the one she gave DS Day last night. Miles had taken it on the white sandy beach in Saint Martin just after they were married. Adam, beaming proudly, looks handsome in his white dinner jacket and bowtie. It's a beautiful memento of the happiest day of her life. But, like a poster advertising a movie, she knows that from now on it'll be remembered as the image most closely associated with his death. She holds her hands in front of her face, wishing she'd chosen a less poignant one.

By Friday every British journalist has linked Adam's death to Carly Stoner's unsolved murder. *Serial Killer at Large* screams one headline. *The Jogger Murders* another. It's a logical assumption, thinks Lily; both victims attacked on the same path in a sleepy Sussex village while out jogging. If only DCI Marshall could see that.

'Don't let him get to you. He's going to end up with egg on his face,' says Susie. 'Just you wait.'

Bella's mobile rings continuously. The majority of the calls she takes are from the press, but Marshall telephones frequently, as do the Police Press and Public Relations Office. Bella deals with each call discreetly, retreating upstairs to the spare room. On one occasion Lily walks in on her when she's talking to her fiancé about honeymoon destinations. Both women are embarrassed. Lily apologies profusely and leaves the room. Bella cuts short the conversation and quickly returns downstairs.

On Friday morning, DS Day accompanies Lily and Susie to Orchard House. It's an inauspicious moment for Lily. She's been looking forward to going home but now, standing on the doorstep, she's not sure how she'll cope. She pauses, shell-shocked, unable to cross the threshold, unable to move, terrified as to what she'll find inside, as if she's been burgled not widowed.

'Follow me,' says Susie, picking up the grey envelope that's lying face down on the mat.

Lily takes a deep breath and steps into the hall. Apart from three days' worth of newspapers and a small pile of post next to the telephone on the table beneath the stairs, nothing about the room has changed.

Susie hands Lily the letter, one eyebrow raised. 'Hand-delivered but addressed to Lily Green. Weird. You haven't been Lily Green for five years.'

Lily stuffs the envelope into the back pocket of her jeans. She doesn't need to look at the handwriting. She knows who it's from.

'There's plenty more over there,' Susie says, pointing to the pile.

Lily tenses. The pile of sympathy cards and scribbled letters from well-meaning friends, relatives and acquaintances rams the truth home again. Yet more confirmation, as if she needs it, that Adam really is dead.

'We'll leave you to it if you want to read some of them,' says Bella.

'Oh I—'

Bella picks up the papers. 'Tea, Susie?'

'Actually, I think I'll try calling Fabian again,' says Susie, fiddling with her iPhone.

'Fabian?' Bella asks.

'Her boyfriend,' explains Lily. Her spirits slump. She likes Fabian. It's impossible not to. She just doesn't want to have to share Susie with anyone at the moment.

'Unusual name. Is he French?'

Susie shakes her head. 'As British as Prince Philip.'

'Oh!' Bella looks confused. 'I see,' she adds, laughing.

'Have you invited him down?' Lily asks.

'No. He's in Milan.'

Susie's off-hand reply is a dead giveaway. She's obviously missing him. Lily is embarrassed she hasn't asked after him but at the same time, she's relieved. 'Oh! I didn't know. When did he go?'

Susie screws up her nose. 'He was called out there on Tuesday. A business crisis. Ironic, isn't it?' She sounds annoyed.

'How did he take the news about Adam?' asks Lily.

'Actually, I haven't spoken to him about it yet.'

Lily is surprised. It's unusual for them not to speak. They're the kind of couple who keep in constant touch, calling or texting each other several times a day. Perhaps they've had an argument.

'Really? Why's that?' asks Bella, curious.

Susie fidgets. She looks agitated. 'He's not answering his mobile. Well, it's either that or he hasn't switched it on. And I don't particularly want to tell him in a message.'

'You should try phoning his office. They'll be able to get hold of him,' Bella suggests.

'Or Rose,' adds Lily reluctantly.

'Yeah. Maybe I should. Mobiles still work in the garden don't they?'

'Yes but feel free to use the landline.'

'Actually, I fancy some fresh air. Call me if you need me.' She smiles at Lily, lightly touching her back.

'I'll be in the kitchen reading the paper,' Bella calls out over her shoulder.

Lily grimaces. She'd seen Adam's photograph on the front page of *The Times* this morning, again. There'd been pages of editorial devoted to it yesterday, not that she'd read a single word. She didn't want to relive the ordeal. The media were bound to be interested in this story. Serial killers were always of great interest to journalists and the public, even though it made for gruesome reading. There's something fascinating about the macabre. People like to be scared. It's all part of the process. Some small detail, the most unlikely circumstance written about, may jog a reader's memory. There is nothing she can do about it, except hope that it does. I'll dig out another photograph, she thinks, picking the other dozen or so letters from the hall table, find one that I'm less emotionally attached to.

Clutching the post to her breast, she heads off to the sitting room and sinks into the larger of the two cream sofas. The thirty red roses, dry now and shrivelled, are still in their vase on the coffee table.

One for each year of your life.

She shivers and glances around the room for traces of disturbance. Every painting, every photograph, every piece of furniture, the smell of the place, is precisely as she remembers it. She is surrounded by memories. Adam is everywhere but nowhere. She wishes she'd stayed at Miles's.

Her life is in ruins. Being here, in the house they shared, is like having that point rammed home over and over again. She should have stayed away.

She wants to scream and run out of the room, the house, to somewhere far away but she knows there's no point. All that would achieve is more unwanted attention. You're just going to have to front it out, she tells herself. Get through each day, cope with your grief and deal with the uncertainty. She wriggles forward and pulls Finn's letter out of her pocket and adds it to the top of the pile of letters in her hand.

Lily Green, she reads.

Her forehead crinkles in annoyance. She isn't sure she wants to think about Finn right now. This letter has triggered another emotion altogether. Is it guilt she's feeling? Or embarrassment?

She places it at the back of the pile and flips through the other envelopes, one by one. There are two, maybe three white-windowed envelopes addressed to Mr and Mrs A Hutchinson, as if time has rewound and the last two days are nothing more than a figment of her imagination. According to Lloyds TSB, South East Water and BT, she is still one half of a married couple. The next three envelopes are from credit card companies and are all addressed to Adam, as is another one, from HSBC and marked *urgent*. Junk mail and the mortgage, no doubt. She puts them on the coffee table to deal with later and focuses on the next envelope. She knows the flowery handwriting well. Rose. But Lily is still smarting from their last conversation. She shoves it to the back of the pile and flicks briefly through the other handwritten envelopes, including one from her brother, until she comes face to face with Finn's again.

She eyes the envelope warily, as if it contains dreaded exam results. She groans and rips open the envelope.

My dear sweet Lily Green,

I read about your husband's murder in the paper and am sorry for you from the bottom of my heart. If the darkness gets too much, I am only a phone call away.

All my love

Finn xx

Written in his artistic hand in brown ink, it is short but heartfelt, like holding a mirror to the author's character. Two sentences stuffed full of concern. He must have figured out who I was from the papers, she reasons. So now he knows I've lied to him.

Susie's head peers round the door. 'Are you going to tell me who it's from?'

Lily frowns feeling awkward.

'At least tell me his name,' Susie says winking at her.

Her frown deepens. Is it that obvious the letter is from a man? She chews her cheek, stalling. She can't figure out why she doesn't want to reveal his identity, other than because her friendship with Finn has always been her secret. She's not entirely sure why, just that it has. She folds the letter.

'Finn Costello. He's a sculptor I met in Lewes at an exhibition I went to. I liked his work and we chatted for a bit. It's an advertisement for his next showing.' She speaks evenly although she can feel herself blushing.

Susie gives her a knowing look before she turns away. 'Really?'

She thrusts the folded letter in the back pocket of her jeans but offers no more.

At half-past-midday, DS Day produces a lunch of chicken sandwiches from a loaf of bread she's found in the freezer, and some cold chicken and salad in the fridge from Lily's trip to Tesco. It's a quiet affair. Lily isn't in the mood for idle chitchat and Susie seems preoccupied. After they've cleared the plates, Susie darts into the garden clutching her mobile without uttering a word. Lily presumes she's still trying to contact Fabian. Clearly his absence is worrying her more than she's letting on.

At least he's still alive, she thinks. He's bound to call her sooner or later.

She can't face the thought of sorting through Adam's papers, or worse, his clothes, so she decides to turn her attentions to searching for her mobile. At least if she found that she'd know if Adam tried phoning her the day he died. She hopes he did. She can't bear the thought that he called Miles and not her.

What if he didn't? her conscience goads. What will you do then?

If it's lost I'll never know, she replies.

But there's another reason she's eager to find it. She wants to send Finn a text. Thank him for his letter. Explain the Lily Green thing, to salve her conscience, if nothing else.

She scours the house, searching all the obvious places, her bedroom, the kitchen and the sitting room, but there is no sign of her mobile. To save herself the hassle of peering under beds and moving furniture, she takes the handset and dials the number, then wanders around the house listening for the sound of a ringing phone. She traipses from room to room redialling her number continuously. Nothing. The mobile is ringing. She can hear it down the landline, arriving infuriatingly, after three rings, at the answerphone. I must have lost it or left it somewhere, she thinks irritably, marching back into the hall. She racks her brains. When did I last use it? The phone only works in the garden. Maybe I dropped it out there. She crosses the hall and is about to open the front door when she remembers the text Finn sent last Tuesday, asking her to come over. I replied to that and then Honor appeared. After she left I drove to Finn's. That's definitely the last time I used it. She dashes outside. I'll check my car first, she thinks, making her way across the drive to the garage, and then the garden.

Susie is working herself up into a state. Why hasn't Fabian called? Where is he? And what the hell is he playing at? Unless …

She shivers. Don't even go there, she castigates herself. Adam's death and Fabian's disappearance are nothing more than a bizarre coincidence. She folds her arms and sits down on the bench under the apple tree. She loves this place. The blossom is almost gone but the baby green leaves are unfurling in the spring sunshine. She breathes in the smell, tips her head to the sun and enjoys the warm caress of the rays on her cheeks. For the trillionth time she wonders why Fabian has lied to her. On the off chance that Janice White had got her facts wrong, Susie rang the office in Milan. He wasn't in Italy, wasn't expected anytime soon. It isn't like Fabian, she thinks. He doesn't play games.

She casts her eyes back down and glowers at her mobile.

'Ring, goddamn you. Ring,' she says out loud.

But the phone remains obstinately quiet.

She drills her feet on the grass in frustration. The last time he called he was antsy because Adam, in a foul mood, had made an unexpected visit to the office and hit Delaney. Rose told Fabian something dodgy was going on at work. The rumours were about insider trading. Was Adam involved? Did it have anything to do with his death? No. Impossible. Whatever is going on at work has nothing to do with the murders. Does it? But what is going on at Golbergs? And where is Fabian? Why did he lie to her about going to Milan?

There's only one thing for it, she thinks, trying to ignore her sweaty palms and the panic rising in her chest. I have to speak to Rose.

She finds the contact and dials the number. *I'm sorry but the phone you've called is switched off.*

Her impatience growing by the second, she dials Rose's flat.

'I'm afraid I'm not here at the—'

114

Susie cuts the connection and dials Rose's office direct line, and goes straight to voicemail. This time she leaves a message.

Where the hell is everyone? she wonders angrily.

Defeated, she walks back up the garden to the house. Lily isn't about but the front door is open so she wanders through the hallway and out on to the drive. Muffled noises are coming from the garage. She hurries over, past a pile of reclaimed bricks outside the arched iron gateway that leads to the back garden.

The garage is full of the usual paraphernalia, a ladder, a watering can, coils of wire, garden tools, all neatly stacked against the sides. She inches past them towards Lily, whose top-half is submerged in her Mini. She taps her on her bottom. 'What are you doing?'

Lily jumps, banging her head on the car roof. 'Ouch!' She backs out, rubbing the crown of her head and turns round.

'Sorry,' says Susie, and starts biting her nails.

Lily frowns. 'What's wrong?'

'Fabian *still* hasn't returned my calls. I can't understand it. It isn't like him.'

'No, it isn't,' Lily replies quietly. 'He's probably been busy.'

'I left a message this morning telling him about Adam. He should have rung to reassure me, if nothing else. It isn't like him. We usually speak two or three times a day.'

'Maybe he hasn't picked up his messages yet.'

'But one of his closest friends has been murdered. They worked together. Somebody must have told him.'

'When did you last hear from him?'

She picks up on the irritation in Lily's voice but ploughs on. 'On Tuesday, around lunchtime.'

'There must be a very good reason. What deal is he working on?'

'I don't know …'

'Call Rose then,' Lily snaps and sticks her head back in her car.

Susie is about to tell her she's not an idiot and has already done that, when it occurs to her she's being a tad insensitive. She really shouldn't be complaining to Lily about Fabian, not now, when she's just lost her husband. 'What are you doing?' she asks, staring at her backside. It's tiny, she thinks enviously, unlike mine.

'Looking for my mobile.'

'Oh. When did you last have it?'

'Tuesday morning. I definitely had it then. I … I remember calling Adam. But I can't find it anywhere. I'm wondering if the police took it away for forensic examination.' She backs out of the car and straightens up.

'It's possible.'

'It's frustrating. There's someone I need to call.'

Susie smiles. 'Duh! Well use the landline then.'

'I can't. His number's on my mobile.'

'*His?*' she asks jumping on the pronoun like a dog on a rabbit. 'Who's *he?*'

'Er, Nat!'

'But you hate Nat these days! Why would you want to call him?'

'I thought …' Lily pauses.

'Thought what?'

'I thought he might know where Fabian is. I'd have asked you for his number but I didn't want to get your hopes up in case he doesn't.'

'That's a bloody good idea. Why didn't I think of it?' She thrusts her mobile at Lily. 'Here, use mine. You'll find his number's under Mephistopheles.'

'Mephistopheles?'

'That's right!'

Lily looks at her questioningly. 'I've a better idea. You call Nat. I'm going to go out and buy another phone.'

'Do you think that's a good idea?' Susie asks as she trails Lily, who is stomping angrily across the drive

116

'I can't see why not. I need one,' says Lily, running up the steps into the house. She picks up her handbag from under the hall table and darts outside again.

'What about the press? They know where you live. They're probably lying in wait. You might be mobbed,' says Susie, following Lily back to her car.

But Lily is not in the mood to listen. She climbs into her Mini. 'I'll see you later,' she says, slamming the door.

Susie bangs on the window. 'Hang on, Lily. I'll come with you.' She dashes round to the other side of the car. But she's too slow. Lily has fired the engine and is thrusting the gears into reverse. The back wheel spins, there's a spray of gravel and the car speeds off down the drive and onto the road.

It's approaching five by the time Lily returns to her Mini, swinging the plastic bag that contains her new mobile. Most of the shoppers have gone and the dimly lit, concrete underground car park is deserted. It's cold and the aroma of last night's urine hangs in the fusty air. But Lily doesn't care. She's on her own for the first time in ages and has completed a task all by herself. She feels liberated. The act of shopping itself has restored a semblance of normality to her life. I should try and get out more, she thinks, digging in her handbag for her keys. She presses the button on the remote unlocking device. The bleep echoes in the cavernous space and the brake lights flash red for a second, the colour bouncing off the walls. She grabs the handle and the door swings open with a loud squeak. Bending down she reaches across the driver's side and places her handbag and the carrier bag carefully on the front passenger seat. She backs out and is about to climb behind the wheel when she hears a rasping cough some twenty metres behind her. She shoots a wary look over her shoulder but all she can see is a black Renault Espace, the only other vehicle around. She lifts her left leg but almost topples off balance at the sound of another cough. She spins round, her eyes focusing on the

Renault, half-expecting to see the greasy haired reporter from the *Mirror*. She scans the area again, just in case. But she can't see anyone. Not a soul.

She exhales loudly, and levers herself into the car. As her buttocks brush the seat leather she hears the rapid thump of fast-approaching footsteps. She swivels her head swiftly to the right. A man in a dirty charcoal hoodie and too-big jeans is thundering towards her. A journalist? she wonders, reaching for the door handle, or some Easthaven low-life? But her eyes are fixed on the hooded figure and she swipes at thin air instead. Cursing herself, she tries again, successfully this time. But it's too late. Her pursuer has caught hold of the door and is pulling hard on it. Lily manages to stick the key in the ignition. In a flash, the man darts round the door and lunges at her. As she fires the engine, she feels his bony fingers on her arm. She cries out, pressing her foot on the accelerator, sweat trickling down her back, her pulse racing. The car revs noisily but doesn't move. She stamps her foot down hard. Nothing. She reaches for the gear stick and struggles with it, trying to force it into reverse. The grip on her arm tightens but she continues to jiggle the gears. Muttering incomprehensibly, the man rams his knee in her belly, winding her. As she gasps for breath, he stretches across and extracts the keys. His pale, acne-splattered face is skin-crawlingly close to hers. So close she can smell the sourness of his breath.

Lily opens her mouth to scream but the young man jerks backwards and covers her mouth with his filthy hand. Her bowels weaken. Terrified she's going to soil herself, she clenches her buttocks.

The man presses his lips to her ear. 'Scream and you're dead.'

His voice is low and hoarse as though he's been gargling gravel. Lily is aware of every muscle in her body tensing. She stays stock-still, pinned against the seat of her car, her guts churning uncontrollably. She feels a sharp stab of pain. Something hard is rammed into her chest. She squeals.

'Do that again and I'll shoot,' the voice rasps. 'Do I make myself clear?'

18

Lily nods furiously.

'Good gel,' he says.

Fighting the urge to vomit, adrenalin tearing through her body, she holds her breath. The man coughs again and removes his dirty, reeking fingers from her mouth. Pointing the gun at her head, he scrambles over her into the back of the car. He smells awful, like rotting meat. Lily gags again and covers her mouth.

'For fuck's sake,' he growls, nudging her head painfully with the metal barrel. He hands her the keys. 'Start the car.'

With shaking hands, Lily inserts the key and ignites the engine. She wonders if this is the man who killed Adam. Did he strangle Carly Stoner too? Is he about to do the same to her? Overwhelmed by the sudden need to urinate, Lily engages the deep internal muscles of her pelvic floor.

A single teardrop rolls over her lower lashes and tumbles down her cheek. She clenches her jaw, determined not to show her fear. 'What do you want from me?'

The man taps the back of her skull with the gun. 'Money.'

He wraps his free arm round her neck and squeezes hard. She feels the air drain out of her lungs, moisture between her legs. But suddenly it doesn't matter anymore. She is going to die. She clamps her eyes shut and prays it will be quick. But after a few seconds the man releases his hold. Aiming the gun at Lily's temple now, he presses his lips to her ear.

'Drug money.'

Lily clutches the steering wheel with both hands, unable to make sense of what he's said. Her hands are clammy, the inside of her thighs, damp. Thinking about it she realises she is slightly wet all over. The cold sweat of fear. What does he mean, drug money? Money for drugs? Is that what he's after? Is that why he's ambushed her? She glances in the rear-view mirror. He is scratching violently at his neck, as though he's trying to peel his skin off his bones. A couple of the pimples on his face have burst and are oozing puss.

'Coke,' he says, his upper lip drawn back in a snarl. 'That's what your old man was into. Only he never paid me, see. And now 'e's gone and got 'imself killed. And I ain't 'appy.'

Clearly the man is confusing her with someone else. Adam? Cocaine? No way. He is ... *was* ... an advocate of healthy living; a fitness fanatic. He drank a bit but not every day, he didn't smoke and he certainly didn't take recreational drugs.

'I ... I think you're confusing him with someone else,' she stutters through chattering teeth.

The man snatches a handful of her hair and tugs. Lily screams in pain as her head jerks backwards. 'I don't think so darlin'. Your old man's dead. Am I right?'

Lily tries to nod but she can't move her head. 'Yes.'

He lets go of her hair and cuffs the back of her skull with his hand. 'Adam 'utchinson. Ring any bells?'

Goose bumps prick her skin. Her blood is thundering down her arteries. Adam owes this low-life money for cocaine. And she had no idea. No idea at all. Not a clue. Her cheeks burn with humiliation.

'I'll get you the money,' she says evenly.

'Course you will. So drive the fuckin' car.'

Fighting back tears, Lily grips the steering wheel, her knuckles white beneath the skin, and tries to coordinate her leaden limbs. The car jerks several feet forward before she manages to bring it under control. She steels a nervous

121

glance at the dealer in her rear view mirror. He is lying on the back seat, the gun pointed at her head. He keeps rubbing his face and scratching at his abdomen, his body twitching as if it's got a mind of its own. He yawns, opening his mouth wide enough for her to see a layer of white fur on the surface of his tongue. L-O-V-E is tattooed on the base of the fingers of one of his hands, which are filthy and covered in scratches and there is dirt under his nails.

He catches her eye and glowers. 'Keep your eyes on the road, bitch.'

The urge to pee grows stronger. The air in the car is fetid and hot. She is nauseous, desperate for air but she doesn't dare open the window. She begins to wonder how she will react if he tries to rape her. Will she fight him off? Or will she submit? Will it hurt? A cold shiver of fear runs the full length of her spine. If only she'd listened to Susie and stayed at home.

'The posh bastard never called me back,' he says, as though answering her question.

Incensed, Lily turns round and glares at him. 'So you killed him.'

'Like fuck.'

He springs upright and jabs the snout of the gun into her neck. Petrified, Lily loses control of the Mini. She swerves and hits the curb before slamming on the brakes. The driver of the car behind hits his horn and overtakes them, screaming profanities through his open window as he passes. The dealer ducks out of sight.

'What you go an' do tha' for? You could 'ave got us killed.'

The irony of his words isn't lost on her. She shrugs not wanting to antagonise him further, rights the car and continues down Market Street.

A hundred metres further on, opposite a hole-in-the-wall, the dealer slaps the back of the seat with the flat of his hand. 'Stop the car!'

Quivering with fear, Lily pulls up on the single yellow line, puts the car in neutral and the handbrake on. Apart from a few parked cars, the street is deserted.

'Get out,' he orders, nudging her in the kidneys with the gun.

Lily kills the engine and opens the door. She is shaking from head to foot and climbs out clumsily. The man pushes the seat forward and follows, the gun concealed in the front pocket of his hooded sweatshirt.

'You'll be needing your debit card.'

Sweating, Lily bends down and reaches across the front seat for her handbag.

'Now cross the street.'

Lily does as instructed, the man walking to the right of her. He stops at the wall and leans against it, out of sight of the CCTV cameras, and tugs his hood down over his face. Fully aware of what's expected of her, Lily thrusts her hand in her cluttered bag and rummages around for her purse. She extracts the card, pushes it into the slot and taps in the pin number for their joint account, punching a wrong digit in the process.

The man jigs his leg impatiently. 'For fuck's sake.'

'Sorry. Sorry.' She takes a deep breath, willing her right forefinger to stop trembling, then slowly and carefully presses each of the numbers on the pad. The menu comes up.

'What's the limit on your card?' he hisses.

'A thousand pounds, I think.'

'Then wotchu waitin' for?'

She taps in the amount but the request is declined. She reads the balance. There's only one hundred and three pounds available. That can't be right. There was five thousand pounds last time she looked. Wasn't there?

'Get a move on, lady.'

'There's not enough money.'

'Don't make me laugh. I've seen your 'ouse.'

She takes out the card to her old current account she's never got around to closing. She's relieved when she remembers the pin. There's just over six hundred pounds in it.

'That'll cover it,' he says, peering over her shoulder at the screen.

The machine makes a whirring sound, followed by a clunk as it spews out the cash.

'Take the money, turn round acting real natural, and walk back to the car.'

Don't do it, urges a scared little voice inside of her. You'd be mad to get back in the car with this maniac. Once you give him the money, he'll kill you. Out of the corner of her eye she sees a couple of men exiting the pub, about ten metres from where they are standing.

'No,' says Lily, trying hard to ignore the frantic beating in her chest.

'You stupid bitch. I'm pointing a gun at you.'

'I know but you're not going to kill me in front of two witnesses.' It's a deadly gamble. Her heart is in her throat. 'The moment they've passed, I'll give you the money then I'll get into my car and drive away. Do we have a deal?'

The beat of her pulse pumps painfully at her temple. They are facing one another now, the gun in his large frontal pocket, flat against his belly. By the way his bloodshot eyes flicker uncontrollably, Lily can see he's anxious. She waits for his answer, fear crawling over her. The men reach them and the taller of the two stops.

'You all right?' he asks.

Lily manages to stretch her lips into a shaky smile. 'I'm fine. It's my brother. He's not himself today.'

This answer seemed to satisfy the man, who smiles briefly before moving swiftly away to catch up with his friend. A couple of cars pass by in the road.

'Give me the money and piss off,' mutters the dealer.

Faint with fear, Lily shoves the thick wedge of twenty-pound notes into his grimy, outstretched hand. She spins round and strides briskly towards her car, tensing her muscles in anticipation of the vicious sting of a bullet.

19

It is unbearably hot in the boardroom because the air-conditioning has broken down. As far as Rose is aware, Maintenance has been informed of the situation. On any other day she could rely on Janice White to sort it out. Janice knows everything anyone could ever need to know about the Goldbergs' fourth floor, including the whereabouts of every person, every hour of every day. She knows what deals they are working on and for how long, where they're working and whom they're working with. Nothing gets past Janice's hawk-like eyes; no misplaced letters, no holidays, no stationery, no fake expenses claims, no office romances. Not that Janice is one for gossip. The only time she ever lets slip information about an employee, is when they cross the line. There's no song and dance. Just a discreet word in Delaney's ear and the matter is dealt with behind closed doors. The staff respect her because of it. But since Delaney's dramatic departure, she's been a shadow of her former self. Delaney has succeeded in doing what dozens of former employees have failed to do before him. He's managed to pull the wool over Janice White's razor-sharp eyes. And she's mortified. She trusted Delaney, held him in high esteem. With Janice's mind no longer on the job, the office has descended into chaos.

Rose's sky-blue, cotton shirt, which was crisp and fresh when she slipped it on this morning, is now creased and sticky with sweat. The most senior member of the team following Delaney's departure, Adam's death and Fabian's absence, she is struggling to hold it all together. All she wants is to lie down in a dark place and yet she's stuck in the stuffy, airless boardroom, being interrogated by a charmless woman from the Enforcement Division of the FSA.

Deidre Marchant is a short woman of about forty-five with a roly-poly figure, dressed in a too-tight, pin-stripe suit. She has this infuriating habit of clicking her tongue while Rose is speaking. She wants to scream at the wretched woman to stop, but with an FSA Legal sitting in on the interview and the two tapes recording everything that's being said, she can't afford to put a foot wrong.

'The FSA has reliable evidence that an investor, acting on Delaney's recommendation, took out a spread bet on the share price of the target company before the takeover was announced,' says Deidre Marchant. 'A Goldbergs' employee overheard Delaney tipping-off the investor in a bar and rang the FSA to lodge a complaint.'

I know, I know, you stupid woman, she thinks, willing her to shut up.

'Insider trading is a financial crime with a potential sentence of up to seven years' imprisonment,' Deidre Marchant reminds her.

Yes, I know, thinks Rose angrily. Thanks to Alex Delaney's malpractices, she and Janice White and everyone else on the fourth floor are now part of a formal investigation.

'Have you managed to get in touch with Fabian Stephens?' Deidre asks, tapping her pudgy hands on the table.

'Not yet, I'm afraid.' Where on God's earth is he? she wonders. I've called him on his mobile and at his home, left countless messages but he hasn't returned a single one. It's as though he's disappeared into thin air.

And it's not just Deidre Marchant who's eager to find him. Rose winces, remembering the phone call she received earlier today from a DS Harry Mills of the Sussex Police.

'We want to speak with him about the murder of Adam Hutchinson,' he explained.

She'd put down the phone and retched into the wastepaper basket.

There is a click as Deidre Marchant turns off the tape. 'I think we'll call it a day. Thank you for your cooperation, Ms de Lisle, Ms White. We'll be in touch in due course.'

20

Shivering uncontrollably, Lily drops her bags, staggers across the hallway to the stairs and collapses on the bottom step. Her heart thumps in her chest, kicking painfully at her ribs.

'There you are,' says Susie, appearing from nowhere. 'The vicar called to see you.'

Lily jumps and cries out in shock.

'Blimey, what happened?' asks Susie.

Lily hugs her arms around her chest. 'I've just been held at gunpoint by a drug dealer.'

'Oh my God. Did he hurt you?' Susie asks, scanning her body for obvious signs of damage.

Lily shakes her head. 'Adam owed him money.'

'Adam? He didn't do drugs.' Susie throws Lily a quizzical look. 'Did he?'

'No,' she says, sighing. 'I don't know.'

'Holy moly. Did you get a good look at him?'

'Not really. He was wearing a hoodie.'

'But would you recognise him again?'

'Yeah,' she mumbles. 'I would. Why?'

'Adam owed him money and now he's dead. It kind of adds up.'

It's nearing seven-thirty when DCI Marshall arrives. DS Day answers the door and leads him into the kitchen, where Lily and Susie are sitting, and offers him the requisite cup of tea. He is wearing a crumpled beige linen jacket that is slightly too tight, Lily notices, and has an air of weary efficiency about him, as if she's one in a long line of distraught widows of murdered husbands he's had to deal with this week.

He listens avidly while Lily recounts her ordeal, then turns to Bella Day with a wry smile. 'Still planning on getting married, Detective Sergeant?'

Lily flinches, stung by the barb.

Bella, who's been absently fiddling with her small diamond engagement ring, silently admonishes him with a lowering of her eyebrows.

Marshall turns back to Lily. 'You weren't aware then, that your husband used cocaine?'

Lily recoils, shrinking into her chair.

'Chief Inspector. I really don't think—' begins Bella.

Marshall holds up a hand as he digs his notebook out of his jacket pocket with his other. He flicks over a few pages before he finds what he's looking for, brings his hand to his mouth and clears his throat. 'The pathologist found traces of cocaine in Adam's blood. I would say that corroborates your story, Lily.'

Lily gapes at the detective. She's too shocked by what he's said to be bothered by his sarcasm. Her life is becoming increasingly surreal. Held at gunpoint by a drug-crazed criminal one minute, sitting in the safety of her kitchen another. Has she imagined the last few hours? The past three days? She raises her feet on to the seat of her chair and hugs her knees into her chest. She feels vulnerable. And cold.

'Sadly, kids involved in drugs tend to lose sight of right and wrong,' Marshall says, blowing on his tea before taking a sip. 'There's a lot of money to be made, dealing cocaine. Cash is what the clever ones are after. The uneducated ones, however, peddle drugs to buy drugs. Judging by your description, I'd say your attacker was addicted to heroin and in desperate need of a fix. Addicts often resort to crime to get more of what they're hooked on. Given the press coverage, he'd have known where you lived. He's probably been watching the house, waiting to get you alone. I doubt he intended to kill you. The gun, if it was real, was for effect. He wanted to frighten you into paying the money Adam owed, and probably a bit more. I very much doubt he'll bother you again.'

Lily uncurls and sits up straight. The gun had been real all right. No question about that. 'Did he kill Adam?'

'I doubt it. But I still want to question him. You've given me a fairly detailed description of the man. He's probably on the drugs squad records already. We'll check the bank's CCTV of course, although from what you've told me it seems he was pretty clued up about them.'

'I thought Adam was angry because he'd argued with Nat,' Lily says almost to herself. She just can't get it into her head he was using coke.

The detective straightens up and slaps his palms on the kitchen table. 'Ah yes. Nathan Tyler.'

'Nathaniel,' says Susie.

Marshall ignores her. 'I spoke to him yesterday.'

Lily frowns. Why didn't he mention this before?

'They did argue, as it happens,' he says, thumbing through the pages of his notebook. 'Adam swung at Tyler almost breaking his nose. The afternoon of Adam's murder, Tyler was out celebrating with some mates from work. He was pretty drunk by all accounts.'

'Oh really, you do surprise me,' mutters Susie, under her breath.

'He works in insurance,' continues Marshall, reading from his notes. 'Apparently his team had signed a lucrative deal that day. He gave me the names of the people he was out drinking with and who've corroborated his story. However, they told me he left the party around six. Tyler says he then went home and watched TV. There are no witnesses to confirm that. Sometime later he received a phone call from Adam.'

Another call to another friend, thinks Lily miserably.

'Sadly, Tyler was too drunk to remember the conversation,' he adds. He runs his hand through his hair and fixes his eyes on Lily. 'Apart from the instance following his argument with Nathaniel Tyler, were there any other occasions when you noticed changes in his moods?'

Lily fiddles anxiously with the hem of her T-shirt. 'What sort of changes?'

'A heightened sense of euphoria followed by a period of irritability, paranoia, fatigue, possibly depression.'

She shakes her head. 'Why?'

'I think he may have been high when he hurt you,' continues DCI Marshall gently. 'It would explain why he acted out of character.'

'But I don't understand. He wasn't the type to seek cheap thrills,' says Lily blushing.

'That's more Nat's style,' says Susie.

'It's not always about thrills. Stress can lead to it.'

'Adam wasn't stressed,' says Lily

'Really? He owed money. That's stressful.'

She recalls the almost empty joint account. Had he used that money to buy cocaine?

'And as he obviously hadn't told you about—'

'What about the crank calls?' she interrupts, the blood rising in her cheeks. 'BT has given you the numbers, haven't they? Was that the dealer?'

'Given you were unaware of his expensive little habit, it's unlikely Adam gave him his home phone number. We're still retrieving the technical data from his mobile. Unfortunately, there's so much red tape nowadays, these things take far longer than we would like.'

Marshall's ever-so-slightly patronising tone grates on Lily's frayed nerves. She wants to stick her fingers in her ears and yell at him to stop talking.

'We found a shoeprint in the soft mud by the river where we found his body …' He pauses to refer to his notes, turning over a few pages. 'The make has been identified from the sole pattern, but not the size. A Converse All Star trainer. The tread is fairly worn at the front, which makes it unique because everyone wears their shoe down in a different way, depending on how they walk. It's as reliable as a fingerprint.'

'And it belongs to the killer?' asks Susie, enthusiastically.

'Adam was wearing a running shoe, so yes, almost certainly.'

'But loads of people wear Converse trainers,' says Lily, clasping the back of her head with her hands. This sudden barrage of evidence is giving her a headache.

'I know, but it is evidence, another piece of a large jigsaw that may well help us solve the crime,' says Marshall. 'The pathologist also discovered traces of animal blood on Adam's hand. And there are tiny spots of another human blood type on the shirt Adam was wearing.'

'Did the killer set a dog on Adam?' asks Lily, disturbed by the thought of Adam having to ward off a rabid canine as well as a knife-wielding madman.

'No. There are no bites on Adam's body. No saliva either. We're waiting for the DNA profile of the animal blood. Again, it may take some time.'

'What about the blood on his shirt?' Susie asks.

'We are extremely keen to find a match for that.'

Lily is exhausted. She doesn't want to listen to any more. She puts up her hand, as if she is a child in class, and stands up. 'Can I go and lie down?'

'Well, I did want to talk to you about the—' begins Marshall.

'Of course,' DS Day interrupts quickly.

Lily walks towards the door.

'Wait,' Marshall says, striding after her.

Bracing herself, Lily stops and turns round.

Marshall opens his jacket and produces an opened envelope from inside his breast pocket. He hands it to Lily. 'Forensics found this in the pocket of Adam's suit.'

Lily stares at it in stunned silence, at her name written in black ink in Adam's handwriting.

A letter from beyond the grave.

Susie's palms are sweating, her head spinning. Since Lily left the room, Marshall has honed in on her. His questions about Fabian are making her uncomfortable. She isn't sure what he's driving at and, with Lily out of the room, she feels horribly exposed.

'Where were you on the evening of Tuesday 6 May?' Marshall regards her intently.

Colour flares her cheeks. What is this? Surely he isn't accusing her. She thrusts back her shoulders, juts out her breasts and looks him directly in the eye. 'I was at home swotting up on *EastEnders.*'

He arches an eyebrow. 'On your own.'

'Yes. On my own.'

'And you had no idea where your boyfriend was?'

His eyes bore into her. She feels like a fly pinned on a board, still alive but squirming. 'No.'

'I gather he disappeared the morning of Adam's death.'

Susie usually exudes confidence as naturally as a heavyweight boxer oozes testosterone, but now she is untypically hesitant. 'He told me he was going to Milan.'

Marshall fixes her with a daggered stare. 'Have you tried calling him?'

Susie nods.

'So you're aware he lied to you?'

She screws up her nose. 'Yes.'

'Meanwhile news of Adam's death is making big, black headlines all round the country. A bit strange your boyfriend still hasn't been in touch?'

If I had a tail I would choose this moment to put it between my legs, thinks Susie miserably.

'One of my detectives called his office and spoke to Rose de Lisle. Like you, she's been trying, without success, to contact Fabian Stephens.'

She feels the blood drain from her face.

'Given the FSA investigation into Delaney—'

'Investigation?'

134

'—And Adam's murder, Stephens' whereabouts has become a matter of grave concern to the police. We've initiated a search, alerted the airports, train stations and so on. Fortunately he drives an ostentatious car. His Ferrari was photographed on an ANPR camera travelling through Brixton on the 6 May at around three in the afternoon.'

'Brixton!' repeats Susie.

'We've traced his route to the Marie Stopes centre.'

'Isn't that where women go to have an abortion?' gasps Susie, wide-eyed. What on earth was Fabian doing there? 'Oh my God. He was having a vasectomy,' she shrieks before Marshall has a chance to reply.

Bella, who is looking decidedly uneasy, smoothes the sleeve of her jacket methodically with the flat of her hand.

'Stephens was collecting a patient from the abortion clinic,' says Marshall, impatiently.

'What?' Knocked off kilter, Susie clutches two large clumps of her hair with both hands as if the force of Marshall's revelation might blow it away. 'I ... I don't understand.'

'The patient's name is Rachel Jones,' replies Marshall.

'Rachel Jones. Who's she?'

Marshall raises his eyebrows. 'A woman with an unwanted baby.'

Susie releases the two bunches of hair, eyes bulging in her sockets, stung by the casual nature of his remark. A sick attempt at a joke.

'My team are currently trying to trace her whereabouts,' he adds.

'Was it his?'

When Marshall doesn't reply, Susie leans forward, clutching her hair again. So that's why Fabian went into hiding. He was having a relationship with this Rachel Jones and she'd fallen pregnant with his child. That's why he lied to her to her about going to Milan. And just as things were going so well. Finally she has a boyfriend she really cares about. No, it's more than that. She's in love with him. She loves everything about him. She loves being with him. These past few months she's actually found herself daring to believe he's the one. But now this. It's as though the life she's longed for, that she dared to picture, has been stolen from right under her nose.

'I can see this has come as a bit of a shock but we are extremely eager to talk to him,' continues Marshall. 'A tall, slim, dark-haired, well-dressed man was filmed on CCTV talking angrily into his mobile on the platform of Berwick Station on Monday night around eight. As I understand it and from what I remember from the night of Carly Stoner's murder, Fabian Stephens fits that description.'

21

Lily lies on her bed, staring at the ceiling, the folded piece of paper pressed against her heart. She is worn out, her body heavy, spent right through to her bones. She turns towards the window. The sun's rays stream through the glass in dazzling spears of light. Blinded, she closes her eyes but is immediately confronted by the spotty addict holding a gun to her head. She snaps them open and hauls herself into a slumped seated position and looks at the note she's holding, at Adam's familiar handwriting. The paper is weighty in her hands. A burden. Something else she has to deal with. The last time she saw Adam he was violently angry. He hurt her and she was terrified. What if this letter contains more of the same? How will she cope?

She thinks about throwing it away or better still burning it without reading it. But she can't. Her curiosity is roused. She has to read it. With trembling fingers she unfolds the paper. Once. Twice.

It's a short note. Half a dozen lines, maybe more.

My darling Lily,

I've been a bloody idiot. You mean the world to me. You and you alone. But there are things I need to tell you. You weren't at home just now, so I'm writing this letter to stop me changing my mind. I've avoided this conversation long enough.

I'm sorry I hurt you. I don't know why I did and I really wish I hadn't. I was scared, Lily. But that's no excuse.

I love you, Lily, my golden-eyed girl. I always have and I always will.

Please try and forgive me.

Adam

She should be elated. But she isn't. The words slice through her like a razor. Without a mouth to explain them they are useless. Dead words from a dead man's heart.

She scrunches the paper into a ball, hurls herself on her front and buries her head in the pillow. She can't cry. She's drained of tears. But she hurts. Every inch of her. An all-encompassing pain, squeezing the life out of her. Barely able to breathe, she rolls onto her side and clutches the pillow to her chest. It isn't fair. If only she knew where Adam disappeared to after he hurt her, and what precisely happened between him and Nat. Something was wrong. But what? What could be so bad he started snorting coke? Is that what he wanted her to forgive? If only he was here to hold her, to tell her that he loved her, that everything was going to be fine. She feels cheated. Cheated out of a life she so desperately wanted to live.

'Of course I would have forgiven you. You were stressed,' she says out loud. 'I get that. I just wish you'd been able to confide in me sooner. Why couldn't you Adam? Was it because I was so wrapped up with getting pregnant? Is that why? Was that stressing you out?'

An idea nags her exhausted mind. Have I missed something? she wonders. She casts her mind back to Marshall's interrogation the day she identified the body. She'd been shocked when he told her Adam was still a suspect in the Carly Stoner murder. Was that what was bothering Adam? Is that why he couldn't talk to me? Why he was scared? Surely he knew I wouldn't have believed he was guilty.

A light goes on in her brain. A question she desperately wants to ignore but can't.

What if he did kill Carly Stoner? What if Marshall's hypothesis was correct and Adam had tried to kiss her then lost his temper because she wasn't interested, tried to rape her and ended up killing her in a freak, drug-fuelled accident. Coke could radically change a person's character and behaviour. If he had killed her, he'd have been stressed and scared. But that would make him a killer, she thinks miserably. Could I have forgiven him then?

A tear leaks out the corner of her eye and trickles down her face. She turns her head to the window looking to the sky for inspiration. The bitter paradox of the situation isn't lost on her. Outside the sun continues to shine.

22

It is late. The office is deserted. Even Janice White has left, willingly, as it turns out. The four-hour interview with Deidre Marchant has worn Delaney's loyal PA to a frazzle. Rose sighs and glances at the clock on the wall in the open-plan section of the M&A department, opposite her office. Seven-thirty. If she gets a move on she'll be home in time to read George a bedtime story. His nanny approves of that, not that Rose gives a jot what Lizzie Barker thinks. She's not much more than a child herself. How would she know what's good for him?

She yawns. What she really needs is a good night's sleep. She eyes the untidy and precarious towers of files on her large, rectangular desk. There's a ton of stuff to get through but since the conversation with DS Mills she's been unable to concentrate.

She reaches for the pink trainers she wears to and from work, and is about to slip out of her heels and put them on, when a door slams outside in the corridor interrupting the silence. Rose jumps.

'Rose?'

Quick as a flash, Rose ducks behind her desk. The last thing she needs right now is a confrontation with her furious boss.

'Rose. I know you're here,' Delaney bellows, charging into her office. 'A word please.'

With no place to hide, she rises unsteadily to her feet to face him. 'Alex.'

He is smartly dressed, as usual, in a Prince of Wales check suit, his dark hair slicked back. But the impact of Adam's fist is clearly visible. The cut on his top lip has formed a scab and the socket of his left eye is swollen and a livid blue-black.

He folds his arms. 'Tell me you had nothing to do with it.'

'I ... I had no idea.'

Delaney takes a step towards her and slams his hand down on the desk, dislodging a couple of files from one of the piles. They topple to the floor, shedding their contents. Anger glints in his irises. 'Don't fuck me around.'

Rose is rigid with terror. 'I ... I'm not.'

'Turns out that piece of shit you call your friend was a despicable hypocrite. He duped me into thinking he was a team player, when all the time he was manipulating me for his own ends. Tartuffe has nothing on that bastard Hutchinson.'

'I'm not sure I understand what you mean ...' She doesn't. Tartuffe? Who's he? The man is talking nonsense.

Delaney snarls. 'Keep up, Rose. It's not difficult to understand. He set me up.'

'But someone heard you talking about the shares in a bar. You can't blame Adam for that.'

He stares at her, his left eye twitching. 'That was you, wasn't it?'

Her heart skips a beat. Colour flares her cheeks. 'No. Of course—'

Delaney bares his teeth. 'You stupid bitch. I might have guessed. You're the sneak.'

He takes a massive swipe at the piles of paperwork. Rose dodges out of the way as papers, files and the framed photo of George fly across the floor. The glass shatters as it slams into the wall. She looks back at Delaney. His face is purple. A raised vein on his temple throbs angrily. The man is insane, she thinks.

Her pulse racing, she whirls round and bolts towards the door but her heel catches on the detritus on the floor and she slips. Delaney is on to her in a flash and snatches her wrist. She tries to wriggle free, hitting out at him with her free arm but he grabs that too and shoves her back towards the desk and bears down on her. Bent over backwards, she stares into his bloodshot eyes, at the unsightly triangles of foam that have formed in the corners of his mouth. He's on top of her now, his weight crushing the air out of her. He fastens a hand on her throat. Rose twists her head, trying to shake him off but it's no use. From the position she's in she can't wrest herself free.

She's gasping for breath.

She thinks he's going to kill her. She thinks of George.

Oh my God. What will happen to my little boy?

23

There's a gentle knock on her bedroom door. Lily raises her head and sees a pale-faced Susie, standing in the doorway, clutching her mobile.

'Can I come in?' she asks.

'Sure.' Lily hauls her aching body upright, and scrunches up her nose. 'Has he gone?'

'Yes, thank God,' says Susie, plonking herself on the bed beside her. 'That man is like a dog with a bone.'

'Been grilled have you?'

'Roasted more like.' She motions to the screwed up ball of paper. 'Adam's note?'

'Yeah.'

Lily leans over to retrieve it and hands it to Susie, who drops her mobile on the bed, smoothes out the creases then reads it. 'Wow. Heavy!'

'I should be pleased he wanted to apologise. But I'm finding it hard to accept his apology when I don't know what he's done.'

'It sounds like he was going to tell you about the coke.'

'Do you think?'

'What else could it be?' Susie wriggles closer and hooks her arm around Lily. 'Are you feeling any better?'

'Not really.'

'To be frank, I'm amazed you haven't collapsed in a heap.'

Lily sighs and rests her head on Susie's shoulder. 'Dear old Frank.'

Susie softly strokes her hair. 'It must have been terrifying, being held at gunpoint.'

'I thought he was going to kill me.'

Susie shudders. 'You were very brave. I'm proud of you.'

Lily pulls a face. She doesn't feel brave. 'I'm just glad you're here. I couldn't cope with this on my own.'

'Listen, Lily,' says Susie, letting go of her. 'There's something I should tell you. I would have told you earlier but you were upset about your mobile and I didn't want to add to your problems.' She blinks rapidly.

Lily doesn't like the sound of this. 'Go on.'

'The last time I spoke to Fabian was the day Adam died. He told me Adam returned to the office in a foul mood. He demanded a meeting with Delaney. Apparently he was furious and punched him. The rumour was that Delaney had got involved with an insider trading scam. And now, according to Marshall, the FSA has launched an investigation into the fraud. Do you think Adam was involved?'

'He'd never cheat ...' she stops. Why not? He took cocaine.

'It might explain why he was stressed and why he wrote you the note. Fabian and I overheard him and Rose arguing the night of your party. Rose was properly angry with him but when we asked her what was going on, she was very cagey about it and said it was a work matter. Fabian was upset they hadn't thought to include him, but maybe this is why.'

'We should call Rose.'

'My thoughts exactly, which is why I just did.' Susie raises her iPhone. 'But she's not at work and she's not answering her mobile.'

Lily wrings her hands. 'This is getting ridiculous.'

'What's getting ridiculous?'

Lily, still jumpy from her ordeal, starts and almost topples over backwards at the sound of Miles's voice.

Susie reaches out and steadies her. 'What did you do that for, Miles?'

144

'I'm sorry,' he says, sitting down on the other side of Lily.

'Lily's been held at gunpoint by a smack-head drug dealer who Adam owed money.' Susie's explanation explodes from her mouth.

Miles takes off his glasses and rubs his eyes.

'Were you aware he snorted coke?' asks Susie irritably.

'Forensics found traces of cocaine in his blood,' Lily explains.

'I had no idea.'

'The killer left a footprint at the scene,' continues Susie, filling Miles in. 'Forensics matched the print to a Converse trainer, slightly worn at the front. Marshall says the footprint is as unique as a fingerprint, although my guess is the killer chucked them away or burnt them. And Adam had some kind of animal's blood on his hands but not a dog's. Marshall's waiting to see what forensics turns up. Oh, and Delaney is being investigated for fraud.'

Lily scrunches up her eyes and is confronted by a pile of boxes neatly numbered and labelled: one – cocaine; two – holidays; three – phone calls; four – enemies. She quickly opens them again.

'What does Fabian make of all this?' Miles asks, replacing his glasses.

Susie frowns. 'I don't know. I haven't spoken to him yet.'

Bella orders in pizzas for dinner. Lily isn't the least bit hungry and neither is Susie, who picks at the olives and mushrooms but eats little else. Bella eats hers and Miles munches his way, slowly but manfully, through his, while the girls sip red wine. After supper Bella retreats to her room, and Miles helps Lily set up her phone. He sends her the numbers of their mutual friends and Susie does the same.

At twelve-thirty Miles looks at his watch. 'It's time for me to go. I've got endless meetings tomorrow. But promise me you'll call if either of you need anything.'

'We will,' says Susie.

Lily smiles. 'Thanks, Miles.'

They remain at the table until they've drained the last dregs of the second bottle of red, when Susie suggests they go to bed. Lily is shattered. Her emotions shot to pieces. But she is reluctant and dithers in the kitchen, busying herself with tasks that don't need doing, until Susie insists they share a room for the night.

It's nearing three in the morning when Lily's overloaded mind whirrs back into life. Breathing heavily, damp with sweat and, having lurched from one blood-soaked nightmare to another, she feels more exhausted than she did before she fell asleep. Running to escape a pockmarked addict brandishing a gun, she'd come up against a locked door, a brick wall and a car that wouldn't start.

Disorientated, she sits up and adjusts her eyes to the gloom. She can just about make out the green-checked curtains and the open fireplace with the painting of a dapple-grey horse hanging over it. The spare room, she remembers, tucked away at the back of the house. Susie's favourite room, the place she always sleeps when she comes to stay.

She glances at the sleeping body lying in the foetal position beside her, snoring softly, and experiences a stab of envy. She wishes she had Susie's capacity for sleep. She sighs and lies back down on her side and urges her taut, tense body to relax. But thirty minutes later she's still awake, her imagination in overdrive. The addict knows where I live. What if he's out there, watching, waiting? Not that he needs to wait. He has a gun. He can blast his way in anytime he chooses.

Don't think about him, she thinks, shivering. She lets her mind drift, back to the university skiing trip and New Year's Day. She woke up with the mother of all hangovers, spread-eagled on the bed in the apartment, saliva dribbling out the side of her mouth. Adam, face down on the floor, was snoring. It had been one hell of a night. A great party. Rose was pregnant, although none of them knew that yet, not even Rose who wouldn't find out for another six weeks. By mid-afternoon she and Adam had recovered enough to hit the slopes. It was one of those crisp winter days – sun, blue sky but skin-numbingly cold. They skied for an hour before taking the last chairlift up to their favourite run, and stopped in a mountain restaurant for a mug of hot chocolate, heaped with whipped cream.

'Delicious,' she said, taking a sip.

Adam laughed.

'What?'

'You've got cream on your nose.'

She wiped it off with the back of her hand and blushed.

'I love the way you do that,' he said.

'What?'

'Blush all the time over the silliest things.' He reached across for her hands. 'I love it that you make me laugh.'

Her blush deepened.

'I love you, Lily Green.'

It took her breath away that first time, hearing him say those three little words. To her. Adam loved *her*. It didn't seem possible. She wanted to scream with joy. Dance up and down. Go crazy. But she didn't. She just peered into his light, grey eyes and smiled. Later, she wondered why she hadn't told him she loved him too. She adored him, was infatuated with him, but wasn't that more like an ardent fan a pop star? Was that really love? She didn't know.

Valentine's Day duly arrived. Somebody threw a party, Nat maybe or Miles. She arrived late, looking for Susie who'd been in a terrible state all day. Justin Carter, Susie's boyfriend of the time, had chosen to celebrate the occasion by dumping her. *Be My Baby* was playing on the radio, she remembered. She searched everywhere for Susie but eventually found her throwing up in the toilet, Adam holding her hair.

That was the moment, she thinks. That was when I realised I was in love with him.

This is not helping, she tells herself, switching to her other side. Determined to erase all thoughts from her mind, she decides to count sheep. She reaches four hundred and thirty-nine before boredom leads her to list the farms, houses and cottages of Adlington. But counting thirty-five buildings takes no time at all. Registering the occupants proves harder, but by the time she's returned to the rectory and has listed the Reverend Cyril Beeton, his wife and their two Yorkshire terriers, she is wide-awake.

Irritated, Lily rolls over again. Even though it's a warm night, she tugs her half of the duvet up to her chin and tucks the bottom end under her feet to form a cocoon. If Susie can sleep then so can I, she reasons, squeezing her eyes shut. She's worried about Fabian. And so she should be. As one of Adam's closest friends, it's weird he hasn't been in touch. At the very least he should have rung me to pass on his sympathy. Maybe he's involved in the fraud and is keeping a low profile. No. That's crazy. Fabian is as rich as Croesus. Why risk his job? Unless ... unless he's suffered the same fate as Adam.

She shivers. Neat theory, Lily, but where's the body?

She sighs and rolls on to her other side but immediately starts thinking about Rose. Why hasn't she returned Susie's calls? And why hasn't she been in touch with me again. Okay, so I slammed the phone down on her but she must have realised that was down to shock. It's not like I shoved her head in a pile of warm manure and begged her to eat it. I'm the victim here. Not her.

It's not like Rose, her conscience nags. She's usually one hundred per cent reliable. A good friend. With Adam dead and Fabian missing and things kicking off with Delaney, she must be up to her eyeballs. Maybe you should cut her some slack. She did write to you, after all.

Lily sits bolt upright. Of course, Rose's letter. What with everything that's happened this afternoon and Adam's note, she's forgotten all about it.

Her curiosity roused, Lily slips quietly out of bed and tiptoes down the landing. She pauses halfway down the stairs and peers into the dark hallway. Sweat pricks her armpits and she shivers. I'm not up to this, she thinks, turning round. But the thought of what's in the letter is an itch she feels compelled to scratch. Her ears on red alert, she carries on, taking extra care to avoid the squeaking bottom step. Her breathing quickens as she gropes her way towards the hall table. She feels for the switch on the standard lamp and sighs with relief when she finds it. In the soft yellow light, she sees the post stacked in a neat pile. Rooting through she finds the cream-coloured envelope and holds it up to the light just to be sure. Satisfied her name and address has, in fact, been penned by Rose, she darts upstairs and scurries down the landing, back to the spare room and the comforting presence of the sleeping Susie.

She reaches out and touches the lamp base. The bulb glows dimly on its lowest level. It isn't much but it will do, she thinks, tearing open the envelope. She pulls out the single sheet of paper, lifts it closer to the light and begins to read.

Dear Lily,

There's something I need to talk to you about. Something you should know. I can't help thinking that I should have told you this before. And you have to believe me when I say I would have, Lily, I really would but it never seemed to be the right time. I was uncertain of the consequences, you see, for all of us. Only now with Adam dead, I realise that I was wrong.

You are and have always been a very dear friend. My greatest hope is that you will understand the reasons for my silence and that you will forgive me.

Please ring me the moment you read this.

Your loving friend

xx Rose

24

Susie is aware of someone trying to rouse her but it takes Lily a further five minutes of gentle cajoling before she's awake enough to focus on Rose's letter. Not a morning person at the best of times, and with the dawn unbroken, Susie thinks it's expecting a lot of her to click straight into top gear. She sits up, yawns and rubs her eyes. Huddled up in half the duvet, it strikes her that it's been a long time since Lily and her last sat in their pyjamas in the semi-dark, something they often did at university; party post mortems conducted amidst the jumble of her room. But those were fun times. There's nothing remotely amusing about the situation they are in now.

'What do you think she wants to tell me?' Lily asks.

Susie lowers the letter. 'It has to be about Delaney. Perhaps that's what Adam's letter was about too. Maybe he and Rose were on different sides over this one. There's a first time for everything.'

Lily crinkles her forehead in concentration, as though she is trying to crack a tough mathematical code. 'So you think Rose wanted to tell me Adam was involved in the fraud?'

Susie thinks for a moment before responding. 'It would explain the cocaine and the mysterious holiday.'

Lily shoots her a filthy look. 'You don't believe that do you? Adam is far too ambitious to risk his career.'

'I'm sorry. I didn't mean—'

'Besides, he doesn't … didn't need the …' Lily stops and frowns as though she's remembered something.

'What didn't he need?'

She waves her hand dismissively. 'If he was involved then Fabian would know by now.' She scratches her head and looks at Susie. 'Do you think Fabian's involved too?'

Susie puts down the letter and lowers her eyes. Since the conversation with Marshall, Fabian's deception has been eating away at her. It's as humiliating as it is heartbreaking. Lily is her friend. The person she turns to when her life hits the skids. If she can't talk to her then who can she talk to?

She sighs, lifting her head to look Lily in the eye. 'Fabian's having an affair.'

Lily's mouth drops open. 'Fabian? Impossible. He's nuts about you.'

Susie takes Lily's hand and squeezes it as she relates what Marshall told her earlier. 'And Rachel Jones has had an abortion.'

Lily is wide-eyed shocked. 'Oh my God, that's awful.'

'Yep.'

'Do you know this Rachel Jones?'

'Nope.'

'So you reckon that's why he's gone into hiding?'

Susie shrugs. 'It must be.'

'Why when what he's actually done by disappearing is draw attention to himself.'

'I know. It doesn't make sense.' That Fabian might be involved in Adam's murder is inconceivable. He is the gentlest of men. She skims through the letter again. 'I know Rose says to call her the moment you read the letter but I really don't think she was expecting you to read it at four in the morning.'

'Too late. I've already tried.

Susie arches an eyebrow. 'And?'

'Her mobile's switched off and there's no answer at her home.'

Susie sucks in her cheeks. There is no easy way to tell Lily what she has decided to do but her mind is made up. She steels herself. 'I'm finding it very difficult sitting around here speculating about what Fabian and Rose may or may not be up to. I'm going back to London to search Fabian's house.'

Lily's face pales. She grabs Susie by the arm. 'No you can't.'

'I have to do something. Not knowing is driving me crazy. I may find Rachel Jones's telephone number or some evidence to prove Fabian's having an affair. Or better still, something that proves his innocence.'

Lily's eyes widen further. 'Innocence?'

'He may have had an affair but I really don't think he killed Adam. If I go and have a thorough search of his place it'll speed up the process and Marshall won't waste any more time chasing after the wrong man.'

'Please don't go. Give the key to Marshall. He's the detective.'

'Lily, the man questioned me as if I was guilty. He certainly suspects Fabian.'

'It's what he does.'

'Yes but clearly Fabian's been up to something. I need to find out what.'

'It's unlikely he'll have left any evidence lying around. He knows you have a key.'

'Don't think I don't know that. I intend to ransack the place.'

'But I'm scared, Susie. I don't want to stay here on my own.'

The orange glow of the early-morning sky seeps through the narrow stripes of violet cloud and a fine mist hovers above the dew-drenched grass. Birds chatter noisily in the hedgerows and trees, but apart from that all is quiet. Susie is giving it her all; her palms flat against the boot of the Mini Lily is steering silently, engine off, down the drive.

'Marshall advised me not to leave the house,' Lily protested when Susie tried to convince her to come with her.

'He only said that to cover his back.'

'It's only a few hours since I was held at gunpoint. I'd be mad to chance my luck a second time.'

But Susie dug in her heels. She was going whether Lily came with her or not. 'And as I'm going to London I thought I might as well drop in on Rose.'

Desperate to talk to Rose, Lily caved in.

They leave a note for DS Day explaining their sudden need to get as far away from the drug dealer as possible. Susie thinks it best not to go into too much detail. It might lead to problems later. But fleeing the house at dawn with DS Day soundly asleep upstairs, Lily feels like a fugitive.

The car glides out of the drive into the road. Susie leaps into the passenger seat and gives Lily the thumbs up. Smiling grimly, her heart in overdrive, Lily turns the key in the ignition and the engine kicks into life.

'Quick! Lock the door,' she says.

'It's okay. No one's about,' Susie says, securing it anyway.

Lily, who is struggling to breathe, shakes her head but says nothing. She accelerates gently and they are off. But it isn't until they hit the A23 and are clear of the Downs that either of them began to relax.

'I feel like we're Thelma and Louise,' says Lily.

'Weren't they housewives on the run?'

'Okay, so a bit like them.'

Susie frowns. 'But they were criminals. They killed a man.'

'My point is they were having a tough time, they leapt in a car and hit the road. I didn't mean ... I wasn't ...' Lily tails off. She isn't sure what she's trying to say. She sneaks a peek at Susie. The whites of her eyes are speckled with a pattern of red, spidery lines, the only outward sign she's under any strain.

Susie turns to look at her. 'You trust me, don't you?'

Lily is taken aback. 'Where on earth did that come from?'

'This *Thelma and Louise* stuff!'

153

For the first time since the investigation began, the idea that Susie is somehow involved in Adam's death flashes into Lily's brain. Absolutely no way, she tells herself. Susie isn't capable of murder. No. No. No, she protests, stamping on the thought as if it's a troublesome ant. 'Don't be ridiculous, of course I do.'

'Do you mean that?'

'Yes. And I don't want to hear another word about it, okay?'

They travel on in silence until the A23 widens into the M23. Susie switches on the radio and fiddles with the tuner until she finds Radio One. One Direction is singing *Kiss You*.

'I love this song,' she says, cranking up the volume. She sings along to the chorus, bouncing up and down in her seat and drumming the dashboard in time to the beat.

Despite the situation, Lily smiles. It isn't Susie's style to brood. She lives in a black and white world. When she's happy she laughs, if she's sad she cries, sometimes both at the same time. And if you do or say something to make her angry, she won't waste time stewing about it but instead will tell you what you've done directly to your face. If you can take the crap as well as the compliments, then being friends with her is easy. You always know exactly where you stand. Lily appreciates her honesty. In fact she loves her for it.

The song ends and *Newsbeat* starts. Susie turns down the volume. 'I think men are overrated. Just when you think you've found one who's different, special, perfect even, you discover he's no better than all the rest. I really, truly, honestly believed Fabian was the one for me. I've trusted my instincts all my life but just when I needed them the most, they let me down big time.'

'Following his arrest yesterday afternoon, Alex Delaney, the Vice President of Goldbergs, was charged this morning with insider trading.'

Lily nudges Susie, who fiddles with the volume.

'Delaney, who was sporting a fat lip and a black eye, was released on bail in the early hours and is due to appear before magistrates next week.'

Susie whistles. 'No shit!'

Lily waves her hand to silence her. 'Listen.'

'The FSA is obliged to look at any unusual share trading activity before a major corporate deal and has been cracking down on insiders whose activities undermine confidence in financial markets. Delaney, the Vice President of Goldbergs' Mergers and Acquisition Department, passed market sensitive information on to an investor, who took out a spread bet on the share price of the target company before the takeover was officially announced. The FSA was significantly assisted in its efforts by an anonymous tip-off from a Goldbergs' employee, who overheard Delaney tipping-off the so-called *investor* in a bar. This arrest follows hot on the heels of the murder of a member of Delaney's team, the investment banker, Adam Hutchinson, who was killed on a bridle path while out jogging in the Sussex village he lived in, four days ago, not far from where the young nurse, Carly Stoner, was murdered eighteen days previously.' The announcer moves on to the next story.

'This *must* be what Rose was referring to in her letter. She must have been at odds with Adam about it, which can only mean Adam was involved,' says Lily, turning off the radio.

'It makes sense. Little Miss Squeaky Clean is hardly likely to have dirtied her nose.'

'Or maybe Adam was the Goldbergs' employee who overheard Delaney in the bar. That would've given him a pretty good motive to kill Adam,' says Lily, warming to the theme. 'Maybe Delaney had a fight with Adam and then killed him in anger.' It was simple but logical, the fragmented pieces slotting together seamlessly.

'Hang on a minute, Lily. He's been arrested for insider trading not murder.'

'But what about the anonymous calls? They could have been Delaney. He might have had an inkling of what was about to happen. He might have been trying to phone Adam. He'd have been angry he'd disappeared.'

Susie thinks about Marshall's tall, well-dressed man talking angrily into his mobile on Berwick station. The description fits Fabian but it also matches Delaney. 'I think we're in danger of jumping to all manner of wild conclusions.'

Lily's brain is a tangled knot. An air of mystery is hanging over the Goldbergs' Mergers and Acquisitions Department. Adam has been murdered, his boss arrested and Fabian is missing after visiting a friend who was having an abortion. That just left Rose? Where is she?

'I'm worried about Rose,' she says. 'She obviously wanted to tell me something. I think we should stop by her place first.'

'She's not in. You called. And her mobile is still switched off.'

'Maybe she's in but isn't answering her phone.'

It isn't quite seven by the time Lily parks her Mini outside Rose's flat in Kenyon Road. She rings the doorbell for a good five minutes while Susie dials the flat on her mobile. The theory being that, if she's inside but not answering, the irritating clash of ringing bells will flush her out.

The curtains on the first floor window of the neighbouring house are yanked apart. The sash window opens with a drawn out creak and an angry-looking woman, with bed hair, and a checked pyjama top, leans out.

'Fuck's sake, it's Saturday,' she says.

'We're looking for Rose,' says Susie.'

The woman frowns. 'She's not in.'

'Do you know where she is?'

'No but George is with her parents. They picked him up last night. Now if you don't mind.' Her head disappears and she brings the window down with a crash.

'That's odd,' says Susie.

'Perhaps there's a new man in her life she hasn't told us about,' suggests Lily. 'It's been ages since Brian.'

'Brian?'

'The accountant she saw for a while. You must remember? Forty, divorced, balding.'

'Nope.'

'It didn't last long. He wasn't right for her.'

'Well thank goodness she's had at least one shag these last nine years,' says Susie as they head back to the car. 'Still, I doubt she's got the time for relationships these days. She's such a workaholic. Fabian says she often works on Saturdays. Maybe we should try her at the office.'

But there's no answer at Delaney's Mergers and Acquisitions Department either.

Even though it's still early, the traffic is heavy and Lily drives the Mini at a crawl towards Notting Hill. She is tired and subdued and, as the traffic builds, increasingly claustrophobic. She's forgotten how infuriating it can be trying to navigate London by car. Her buttocks ache, her sleep-deprived eyes sting and her mind is filled with a sense of dread. She's not sure why that should be. Fabian is and always has been the perfect gentleman – charming, thoughtful and modest. She met him eight years ago on a Goldbergs' funded trip during Adam's first year at the bank. Although she was still at university, studying hard for her finals, it was an intensely passionate period in their relationship. Earning a salary meant that Adam could afford to whisk her off on romantic weekends to Paris, Florence and Amsterdam, but Milan was the first business trip he asked her to accompany him on.

When Fabian's Uncle Bruno heard his favourite nephew was coming to his city on business, he invited him and his Goldbergs colleagues to a party in his penthouse apartment. The place was crammed with Milanese socialites decked out in the latest designer fashion. Lily felt dowdy in her safe, black shift dress and spent the evening hugging the walls, trying to be as inconspicuous as possible, which was fine until the music started and a glamorous woman, with enviously long slender legs and waist-length hair, dragged Adam by the hand on to the dance floor. While she watched them gyrating in front of her, Fabian introduced himself. She was struck by his feminine looks, his fine bone structure and long eyelashes. Chivalrous to a fault, he introduced himself, holding her hand to his lips before leading her on to the dance floor where he whirled her around for almost an hour. She felt a million dollars after that. Perhaps they were wrong to mistrust him. Perhaps there was a perfectly logical explanation.

'Left here,' instructs Susie.

Lily indicates and steers the Mini off Holland Park Avenue into Ladbroke Grove. 'Are you sure this is such a good idea?' she asks.

'Right here, into Kensington Park Gardens. Why? Have you got a better one?'

'Susie, look!' Lily's heart drops to her stomach. Parked in pride of place outside the Victorian terraced house is Fabian's crimson Ferrari.

'Great. We'll be able to ask him what he's been up to.' Susie cranes her neck, looking up and down the crowded road. 'Drive around the block. There's bound to be a space somewhere.'

Lily follows Susie up the six stone steps, worn smooth by years of use, to the stylishly grey front door, flanked by two bay trees in square planters and skilfully clipped into balls. The downstairs curtains are drawn, she notices as Susie rings the bell. She peers up at the sash windows on the first floor, partially obscured by the balustrade of the small balcony. The curtains are open but there is no obvious sign of life that she can see.

'He's not here,' says Susie, ramming the key in the lock. 'Give me a couple of seconds to turn off the alarm before you come in.'

She disappears inside the house. The alarm bleeps for a moment, then dies. Relieved, Lily takes a few reviving breaths then walks into the narrow hallway, stepping over the river of post on the black and white tiled floor.

'Now what?' she asks, closing the door and bending down to gather up the envelopes and leaflets.

'I'm going to smell the sheets,' says Susie, one foot on the oatmeal-carpeted stairs at the far end of the hall.

'You what?'

'Ms Jones is bound to wear a different perfume to me. It's the quickest way to discover if he's having an affair.'

'Don't be daft. He won't have brought her here. You've got a key. If he was having an affair he wouldn't want you walking in on him.'

'He'll have worked out I'm staying with you.'

'But she's had an abortion! They're hardly likely to be having sex.'

But Susie isn't listening. 'I'm going to look through his diary, listen to his answerphone messages, read his emails, his post, see if he's booked into any hotels recently, check for dodgy correspondence from Delaney. Then I'm going to search the drawer in his study where he keeps his receipts. And if I still don't find anything, I'll ransack every wardrobe, cupboard and drawer in the house. I might even search the garden.'

She's been planning this, thinks Lily, shaking her head. 'But what if you're wrong and Fabian is innocent? He's going to be pretty pissed off when he finds out you didn't trust him.'

'That's the least of my worries. I know what I'm doing.' Her answer is emphatic. 'And while I'm doing it, why don't you make us some coffee and put your feet up. You must be exhausted.'

Lily sighs. It's pointless arguing with Susie when she's set her mind on something. Her opinion, however informed, is never wanted. And if she does push it, Susie might lose her temper, which is as terrifying as it is rare. In this sort of situation, it's far simpler to toe the line. After all, it's entirely possible Fabian deserves to be treated like this. His behaviour has been thoughtless and insensitive. No matter what is going on in his private life, he should have found the time to talk to Susie.

Unless he's hiding something far more sinister, she thinks with a shiver.

Shaking off her apprehension, she heads off down the hall. As she sets the mail in a pile on the slim console table, she notices the light on the answerphone flashing red. She deliberates listening to the messages. How would she feel if Fabian and Susie snooped through her things? Yeah but I've got nothing to hide, she reasons, as the light continues to blink.

She yawns. Desperate for a caffeine fix to perk her up, she decides to ignore it for the moment and continues down the hall towards the kitchen. It's so very Fabian, she thinks, flicking open one of the glossy, red cupboards in search of the smart, black box that contains the coffee for his glossy, red Nespresso machine. She finds it in a drawer beneath the matching kettle and selects a couple of the strongest capsules. She fills the machine with water, waits for it to heat then taps the button and watches the coffee trickle into the grey espresso cup. Above her, the sound of drawers and doors being pulled open and Susie's swearing, filters through the ceiling.

'Coffee's ready!' she calls up the stairs.

A door slams and Susie's flushed face appears over the banisters.

'I'll be down in a minute. Could you listen to his messages?'

Lily rests Susie's cup on the hall table and takes a sip of the hot, fresh coffee. It tastes as delicious as its seductive aroma. I've been drinking too much tea, she thinks as she hits the silver button marked *play*.

She listens to a message from a friend asking Fabian to play squash next Thursday, three or four increasingly urgent requests from Janice White asking him to call the office, one from DS Mills, who leaves a number to call as soon as possible, two from his anxious-sounding parents, ten or more messages from Susie, the last one verging on the hysterical, two from a very worried sounding Rose, the first telling him about Adam, the second begging him to call because the FSA want to talk to him and in amongst them, a brief message from a distraught woman with a foreign accent.

'Fabian, I really need to speak to you. I need help. You know I would not bother you but I have no one else to turn to. I will try your mobile.'

Lily replays the message a couple of times, trying to make sense of it. It must be Rachel Jones. The woman is clearly distressed about something. And Rachel Jones would certainly have been worried about an unwanted pregnancy. But the caller has an accent, which doesn't tally with the name. Rachel Jones is as British a name as you can get, unless she's Spanish, pronounces her name Raquel and is married to an Englishman, or a Welshman. Except that she doesn't sound Spanish or French for that matter. She listens to it again. There's something vaguely familiar about the voice, which is weird, because she's a hundred per cent certain she's never met anyone by the name of Rachel Jones.

'Anything?' asks Susie, bounding down the stairs two at a time.

'There is one that's a bit odd.'

Susie scrunches up the piece of paper she's holding and rams it into the pocket of her jeans. 'Let's hear it,' she says, picking up the coffee cup and taking a gulp.

Lily rewinds the short message.

161

'It should be Rachel Jones. She sounds upset and that would fit if she had a baby she wants rid of. But the accent isn't right.'

'Perhaps it's someone else involved in the Delaney scandal,' suggests Lily.

'When did she call?'

Lily replays the message. It was logged on Tuesday 6 May at twelve twenty-seven in the afternoon. At least seven hours before Adam was killed, she thinks but doesn't say.

'I spoke to Fabian around then when he rang to tell me he was going to Milan. It has to be Rachel Jones.'

'Or Mrs Raquel Jones.'

'Ew! An affair with a married woman!'

'Hang on, Susie. This message could be interpreted in hundreds of ways. Maybe she was a genuine friend in need.'

'She'd be very worried if her husband had just found out she was pregnant by another man.'

'If that's the case then Rachel Jones might be an alias.'

'Brilliant, Lily! Of course.'

'I'm guessing.'

'I know but it's genius,' Susie says, pirouetting happily.

It's a strange reaction, she thinks, almost as if Susie wants Fabian to be guilty. She's about to tell her as much but the sound of a key rattling in the lock has her swallowing her words. She points to the door with a trembling finger. 'Hide!'

'Don't be daft. It has to be Fabian. Which means it's showtime!' Susie says, planting her feet hip distance apart and folding her arms.

25

If Fabian is shocked to see Susie, he doesn't show it. Maybe he's already figured out she's here because the door is unlocked and the alarm turned off. But what strikes Lily most is that he doesn't look like a man whose life is in disarray. He's casually but impeccably dressed, in pristine jeans and a pressed turquoise shirt, his dark brown hair gelled in a stylish quiff. Unruffled by the sight of his girlfriend, standing legs astride in the hall, he moves to embrace her, a passable imitation of a smile on his lips.

'Darling!' he says, opening his arms.

'Don't you *darling* me,' Susie retorts. With a flick of her wrist she flings the cooled dregs of her coffee in his face.

Fabian flinches but doesn't protest and dabs at his cheek with the cuff of his shirt.

Susie glowers at him. 'Where the hell have you been?'

Fabian opens his mouth to speak but catches sight of Lily lurking awkwardly in the doorway of his kitchen. A flicker of incomprehension in his eyes is supplanted with pity. Gently removing Susie from his path, he strides purposefully towards her.

'Lily, I can't begin to tell you how sorry I am.'

She shifts backwards, uncomfortable and stares at the damp brown coffee stain on his sleeve.

'It's a bit late for that. Adam's been dead four days,' says Susie, stomping up the hall. She snatches his arm and yanks him round to face her.

'I know,' he says quietly before wheeling back to Lily. 'It's shocking. A dreadful tragedy. If there's anything I can do to help please don't hesitate to ask.'

The easy manner with which he offers his belated condolences is baffling. He appears to be a man completely at ease with himself.

'When did you plan to get in touch?' asks Susie, steering him around again. 'I've been going out of my head with worry.'

'I was going to call you today. The past few days have been very difficult. I've—'

'Oh, we know what you've been doing. We know all about Rachel Jones!'

For the first time since he entered the house, Fabian's air of relaxed calm deserts him. 'How do you—?'

'Who is she?'

'A friend in—'

'And you expect me to believe that?'

Fabian blinks rapidly. 'Susie, please. Let me explain.'

'Please, Susie. If not for you then me,' says Lily.

Susie rolls back her shoulders, her eyes locked on her boyfriend's. 'Okay then. Tell me all about your relationship with the tragic Rachel Jones. Every little detail including how you got her pregnant.'

Fabian bites his lower lip. 'I'm not involved with Rachel Jones.' His voice is clear and even, his eyes fixed on Susie's.

'But you collected her from Marie Stopes after her abortion, the day Adam was killed. That's a bit odd don't you think? He was your friend. Our friend. You should have been upset. You should have been comforting me, your girlfriend.'

His forehead creases. 'I didn't know.'

'What do you mean, you didn't know? Are you blind and deaf as well as insensitive?'

'I mean I didn't hear about his death until Wednesday. You were down in Sussex by then, supporting Lily. I read about his murder in the newspaper that day.'

He's telling the truth, thinks Lily. Adam's name wasn't released as the murder victim before the ten o'clock news on Tuesday.

Susie sticks her nose in the air. 'So you've listened to my messages but haven't bothered to reply because you've been too busy with Rachel Jones.'

The creases deepen. 'It's not what you think. She's an old friend. She called me out of the blue because she was extremely distressed. She's been having an affair with a married man and fell pregnant. Her lover was furious and threw her out of the flat he'd bought for her. She rang me because she didn't know what else to do.'

'But why you?' demands Susie.

Because she's working abroad and doesn't know anyone else, thinks Lily. 'Does she work for Goldbergs?'

'No. She's someone I know from Milan.'

'That explains the accent,' says Lily.

Fabian raises his eyebrows.

'We listened to your messages,' she explains apologetically. 'We were worried something had happened to you.'

Susie's eyes, which have darted from speaker to speaker, settle on Fabian's. 'What an incredibly tear-jerking tale. Let me see, you've had four days to make it up,' she says, driving her point home.

'Honey, you have to believe me. I'm not making this up.'

'But where did you go? Why didn't you bring Rachel back here?' Lily asks. 'Why all the secrecy and subterfuge?'

'She'd booked into a hotel. I didn't think anything of it.'

Susie gapes boggle-eyed. 'So you mean you've been staying with her in a hotel?'

Fabian squirms. Is he embarrassed? wonders Lily. Or is he lying to protect himself?

'I can see how it must look and I'm sorry, but Rachel was traumatised. She needed me.'

'Did you have something to do with the Delaney scandal?' Lily asks. 'Is that why you didn't get in touch?'

Fabian's eyes widen in surprise. 'No. Absolutely not.'

'But it still doesn't explain why you didn't get in touch after Adam's death. I've left you hundreds of messages here and on your mobile,' says Susie exasperated, as though Fabian is a wall she's banging her head against. 'It would have only taken a minute.'

'I can't explain beyond what I've told you.'

'Do you mean can't? Or won't?' challenges Susie.

The faintest of shadows passes across Fabian's face before he shakes his head. 'I love you, Susie. You must know that.'

The emotional warmth he manages to convey, even under pressure, is impressive.

'I want to believe you, I really do,' says Susie, gently now. 'So the baby wasn't yours?'

'No.'

'And you weren't involved with Delaney?'

'No. I wasn't.'

Susie stamps her foot. 'So why am I so utterly convinced you're lying?'

He shrugs disconsolately.

'This isn't getting us anywhere. Come on, Lily, we're leaving.' Susie barges past her boyfriend and marches towards the front door.

Fabian rushes after her, out onto the street. 'Susie! Wait!'

'The police want to speak to you,' says Lily, catching up with him.

He turns to look at her. 'Me? Why?'

'They didn't appreciate your disappearing act either. DS Mills has left his number on your answerphone.'

Fabian says nothing, just hangs his head.

Lily wonders if that's because he's regretting his behaviour of the past four days. She considers trying to reassure him that everything will turn out all right in the end. But how can she convince him of something she no longer believes to be true?

26

Susie is waiting by the car, spitting expletives. She clearly hasn't believed a word Fabian has said. Lily isn't surprised. His story is incredibly far-fetched. But the message on the answerphone seems to confirm some of what he's said.

Perhaps it isn't simply a question of Fabian lying to us, she thinks. More that he's keeping something back. But what that is and why he would, I've no idea.

'Could you drive?' she asks Susie, tossing her the keys. Her mind and body are flagging. She wants to go home, put her feet up and try to forget everything that has happened these past four days.

'Sure.'

Jessie J starts to sing. Susie sighs and pulls her phone out of her back pocket and checks the screen. She pulls a face and cancels the call. 'Fabian,' she explains as she unlocks the car. She squeezes in behind the steering wheel, plonks her phone in the small tray behind the gear stick, starts the engine and drives out into the road. The song begins again. She swears loudly but doesn't answer it and eventually the phone falls silent.

Most of the cars are gone, Lily notices, as they drive back down the road towards Fabian's house but a silver Porsche is reversing into the recently vacated space beside his Ferrari. As they pass, an elegant woman emerges, dressed in a white Macintosh, belted at the waist, a large pair of black sunglasses and black, patent stilettos, her long black hair cascading down her back in glossy waves. She sashays past, confident in her heels. There's something familiar about her, thinks Lily, shifting round in her seat. She watches, amazed, as the woman climbs the steps to Fabian's front door and knocks. Fabian appears in the doorway. A flicker of disappointment gives way to a smile. He kisses the woman on both cheeks then ushers her inside the house.

Rachel Jones? wonders Lily, staring open-mouthed.

'What are you gawping at?' Susie asks.

'A woman's just gone inside Fabian's house.'

Susie slams on the brakes. The seat belt cuts into the flesh on Lily's neck as the Mini skids to a stop. Susie crunches the gears into reverse, puts her left arm round the back of Lily's seat and careers, far-too-fast backwards in a wiggling line. Lily clings on and closes her eyes but fortunately the road is free of traffic and they arrive in one piece. Susie undoes her belt and reaches for the door handle.

Lily grabs her arm. 'Wait! I thought I recognised her. I mean I did recognise her. I just can't think where from.' She stares at the Porsche and racks her aching brain. Where has she seen her before? Where has she seen the car? It comes to her in a flash. The car. The Porsche. That's the link.

'Susie, I do recognise her. I've met her. She came looking for Adam the day he died.' Lily closes her eyes reliving the scene. The words she spoke in her soft, accented voice before she went away. The voice she listened to earlier on Fabian's answerphone. The woman they assumed was Rachel Jones.

'Really? Who is she?'

'Honor Vincente.'

'Who?'

'I don't know but I'm pretty sure she's Italian. I only met her that once. She drove to Sussex to see Adam. She didn't say why. Only that she was an old friend. She left the message on Fabian's answerphone. The one we thought was Rachel Jones.'

Susie whistles. 'Holy Cow! So Fabian was telling the truth. She is an old friend from Milan.'

Well he wasn't being completely honest, Lily thinks. He let us believe she was Rachel Jones. 'Do you want to go in?'

Susie chews her cheek, drumming her fingers on the steering wheel. 'No. I don't think I do. You?'

Lily wants to say yes. She wants to ask Honor why she came looking for Adam. Did she want to talk to him about Fabian? But if Susie sees Fabian's damsel in distress is a sleek, slender, beautiful Italian, there's no telling what might happen.

'No. I don't think I do.'

'Good.' Susie shifts in her seat and tries to squeeze her hand in the front pocket of her jeans. They're skin-tight and she has to wriggle around to fit it inside. With much groaning, she manages to pull out a scrunched up scrap of paper, which she unravels.

'What's that?' Lily asks.

'An address.'

Lily doesn't like the sound of that one little bit.

'Aren't you going to ask me whose?'

'No!' she says, crossing her arms.

Susie stretches her mouth into a sad yet sympathetic smile. 'I'm really worried about Rose.'

'And?'

Susie pats Lily's leg, her expression grave. 'Time for Plan B!'

The address that Susie hastily scrawled on the dog-eared scrap of paper is in Wimbledon, which, she explains, is not too great a distance from Notting Hill.

'A twenty-minute journey tops, providing the traffic isn't heavy. It's pretty much on the way home.'

Lily is furious. The encounter with Fabian has sapped the last grains of energy from her. 'Drive to the nearest tube station. You can take the underground, because I'm going home. It was a bad idea coming here in the first place.'

'You didn't have to,' Susie points out quietly.

Lily glares at her.

'Listen. How about we grab some sandwiches then drive to Wimbledon. You can stay in the car. I won't be long.'

Lily purses her lips. Dropping Susie off is an idle threat. She needs her. But she is desperate to go home. This Sarah Lund routine of hers is wearing pretty thin. If anything they are far more confused than when they started out but she knows it's pointless to protest. Susie has made up her mind. She folds her arms. 'Fine. We'll go to Wimbledon. But after that we go home. Promise?'

'Brownie's honour.'

Lily groans. She doesn't bother asking who they are going to see, because she doesn't want to know. Her stomach grumbles, a reaction to Susie's mention of food. They've had nothing to eat all day.

The egg sandwich they buy from Marks and Spencer on the Fulham Road does the trick. It's the most substantial meal she's managed in days. She puts the empty cartons in the plastic carrier bag on the floor and glances at Susie. Her face is a study of concentration as she swerves across the lanes on Putney Bridge, narrowly avoiding a Tesco delivery van.

Lily clutches the side of the seat. 'You may as well tell me what Plan B is now.'

'I will if you promise not to shout.'

Oh God, she thinks. 'Okay.'

'We're going to have a little chat with Alex Delaney.'

'What? Are you mad? He's just been charged with insider trading. The last thing he could possibly want right now is a visit from the widow and girlfriend of two of his employees.'

Susie frowns. 'You promised you wouldn't shout!'

'I'm sorry. I wasn't aware … No, Susie. I absolutely put my foot down about this.'

'I thought you wanted answers? We know he's at home, so we won't be wasting our time. And he'll certainly know what's been going on at Goldbergs. He might even know what happened to Adam.'

'What makes you think he'll tell us if he does?'

'We won't know until we've tried.'

On one level, Lily can only admire Susie. She's an up and at 'em kind of girl, which is why, unlike Rose, she dropped everything and jumped on a train to Sussex the moment she heard about Adam. Her actions spring straight from her heart, always. It is both her best and her worst quality. She hits problems straight on without a care for the consequences, which are sometimes disastrous. And this, Lily suspects, is going to be one of those occasions.

It is almost two by the time they turn into Bathgate Road. Alex Delaney's house is easy to find. The cluster of journalists and press photographers, camped beneath the privet hedge at the end of the gravel driveway, are a dead giveaway. The way Susie's lips part and curl as she drives past the little gathering, implies this is a problem she hasn't anticipated. She makes no comment, however and parks the Mini about a hundred yards down the hill.

Lily is dying to say *I told you so*, but there's no need. The journalists' presence presents a barrier. An insurmountable barrier. All she has to do is patiently wait for Susie to reach the same conclusion.

'Okay. Here's what we do,' Susie says eventually. There is something about the way she stabs the air with her forefinger, her forehead furrowed in concentration, which suggests their road trip isn't over yet. 'We pretend to be his cleaners. The press won't bother with us after that. Then we go round to the back door. That way we'll be out of sight of their lenses.'

Lily's shoulders sag. 'Oh my God, you're serious.'

Susie throws her a despairing look.

'But we don't look anything like cleaners,' says Lily.

'Dat iz because ve are Polish.'

It is a passable imitation of the accent. 'We are?'

'Yes. Ve are. And I am ze only von of us dat speaks English, so I vill do all ze talking.'

'So that year at LAMDA wasn't totally wasted then,' mutters Lily.

But Susie isn't listening. She's rummaging around in the glove compartment. 'Ta-dah,' she says triumphantly, pulling out the blue duster that Lily uses to clean the inside of the windscreen. She folds it in half and ties it over her head like a scarf.

'Who in their right mind would wear a duster on their head?' Lily asks.

'A cleaner.'

There's no answer to that. She folds her arms. 'I'm not coming with you, remember?'

'Fine. I'll go on my own.' Donning her sunglasses, Susie gets out of the car. She waves at Lily then saunters down the road towards the house, confident as anything.

Incredibly, the press swallow Susie's story whole. They wolf-whistle at her and laugh and one of them asks how many other illegal immigrants work for *that fraudster* Delaney. Susie smiles sweetly and shakes her head as if she hasn't understood a word they're saying then continues boldly down the drive. She has no real plan other than a determination to speak to Delaney. With Britain's media poised for action, she decides against marching up to the front door and ringing the bell. It would blow her cover and her photograph would be splattered across the front pages of all the national newspapers.

It would be ... It would be great coverage, she thinks smiling to herself.

To the right of the double garage she spies a wrought-iron gate, hidden amongst the rhododendron and camellia bushes. Without faltering Susie marches up to it, praying it's unlocked. She presses down on the handle and the door swings open. Her heart beating erratically, she walks through to the back garden.

Phew, thinks Susie. Made it. She eyes the swagged and tailed, wall-to-ceiling windows at the back of the vast neo-Georgian mansion and whistles. So this is what he's done with all his Goldbergs' bonuses. This place must be worth at least three million.

Her eyes scan the manicured lawn, the stone Venus fountain in the centre, the well-tended herbaceous borders bulging with shrubs, and the modern, grey wicker furniture on the limestone paved patio. It certainly is an impressive place. Delaney has obviously done well for himself. So why the fraud? Greed, she thinks, ignoring the barks from the dogs inside. Buoyed with adrenalin, she scuttles across the grass to the back door. She raises her knuckled fist and knocks and, a mere two seconds later, it sweeps open. Delaney, ashen-faced and bristling like the two athletic-looking mouse-grey dogs whose collars he's holding, glares at her. Despite a sudden surge of fear, she finds herself staring at the scab on his top lip. Adam took quite a pop at him, she thinks.

'Who is it now?' a woman's voice calls out from inside. She sounds irritated but nervous. Still Delaney says nothing.

'Don't worry, I'm not a journalist,' Susie says cheerfully.

Delaney clenches his jaw prompting a worm-like vein on his temple to swell.

'Susie Ashton,' she says, smiling. 'We've met a couple of times. You probably don't remember. I'm Fabian Stephens' girlfriend.'

Delaney glowers at her, his cheek muscles working furiously. She can hear the enamel of his molars grating as he grinds them together. The dogs start to whine. His head twitches and he clenches his fists into tight white balls to restrain them.

'Lovely dogs. Weirmaraners aren't they?'

Still Delaney doesn't speak.

'Obviously a lot has been going on at Goldbergs, what with Adam's death and your ...' she stops to clear her throat. 'I thought you might be able to throw some light on—'

'If that bastard wasn't already dead, I'd take great delight in removing the sanctimonious smirk from his self-satisfied face with a very sharp knife.'

Susie has no time to dwell on the connotations of this remark because Delaney's wife appears behind him, her face puffy from crying, blinking rapidly. 'What's going on?' she asks, then, 'Who are you?'

Simple questions but they tip her fuming husband over the edge. He explodes with rage. Susie watches transfixed as his shoulders rise up past his ears, his cheeks turn puce and swell, until his eyes are little more than two thin lines. The wiggly, blue vein on his forehead begins to pulse. He thrusts out his chest.

'ROCKY, TYSON, KILL!' He exhales the words in a monstrous roar and releases his hold of the dogs. Then, without a backward glance, he retreats inside and slams the door.

The Weimaraners growl and bare their sharp, pointed canines in anticipation of this unexpected meal. Elastic drools of saliva hang from their mouths. I don't stand a chance against these angry bundles of muscle, she thinks. Blood beating at her eardrums she turns and sprints. She sees the table and flings herself face down on the glass top, kicking over two of the chairs with her feet. The dogs spring in the air. One of them snaps at her ankle that's dangling over the edge. Her face contorts with pain as she draws her legs to safety. She crawls to the centre of the table and lifts up the bottom of her jeans. There's a ring of tooth marks above her anklebone, some bruising, but the dog hasn't punctured her skin.

Claws clatter on the glass. She looks around and sees that one of the dogs has managed to climb on top. It wobbles precariously on the slippery surface before it gains its balance and creeps closer, nose to the ground, snarling. Terrified, her confidence evaporating, she stares into its grey-blue eyes.

He's going to rip me to shreds, she thinks, sliding backwards on her buttocks. She pivots round at the far end, but comes face to face with the other animal, its front legs resting on the table, barking manically. She is well and truly cornered. In the distance she hears the wah-wah of a police siren, but she doesn't dare take her eyes off the dogs. There's a very real chance she's about to lose a limb. The drone grows louder. Rocky and Tyson stop growling and prick up their ears. Distracted, they start to whine again then bound off the table in the direction of the noise. Susie sighs with relief. She takes a few deep breaths to recover her composure as the journalists yell to one another in the drive. The police car speeds down the hill towards the house, the siren deafening now. She sees a flare of blue light as the car screeches into the drive. The siren emits one last strangulated bleat before it dies. Another car follows and skids to a stop. The dogs are going mad. Car doors slam. Cameras flash. A voice shouts *get the fucking dogs under control.* Footsteps approach the house and somebody bangs a fisted hand on the front door.

'Police. Open up!'

Susie slides off the table and runs to the gate, out of sight of the driveway but within earshot. The police bang on the door again. A fleeting silence is broken by a cough. After what seems an age, the front door opens.

'Alex Delaney?'

Susie starts. She recognises the voice, although its timbre is even sterner than usual.

'Yes?' Delaney says with undisguised irritation.

'We have some questions we want to ask you in connection with the murder of Adam Hutchinson.'

27

Delaney's wife lets out an anguished howl, a horrible wailing sound like a widow from the bible. Susie's heart skips a beat.

'Oh for God's sake,' Delaney replies impatiently.

'You were seen fighting with Adam Hutchinson in your office around midday on Tuesday 6 May, shortly before his death.'

'Oh really?' He sounds bored.

'Mr Delaney, you've clearly been in a fight.'

Susie is surprised to hear Delaney laugh. 'If you must know, I walked into a filing cabinet.'

Marshall clears his throat. 'A witness has come forward who says they saw a tall, dark-haired, well-dressed man talking angrily into his mobile on the platform of Berwick station at around eight on Monday night.'

She pictures Delaney's face, the worm-like vein at his temple pulsing with anger.

'Now you're being ridiculous.'

'We're asking you to accompany us to the station.'

'Absolutely out of the question.'

'Mr Delaney, if you refuse to cooperate we'll have no option but to arrest you.'

'But that's preposterous. You don't have any evidence.'

'Were you or were you not in a fight with Adam Hutchinson the day of his murder?' persists Marshall.

'We were in this together. But he changed his mind at the last minute and the next thing I know, one of his colleagues, a 'close friend' of his, I might add, went sneaking to the FSA. I hit him but I didn't kill him.' Delaney speaks quickly, nervously, as though he's finally grasped the trouble he's in.

'And yesterday, Friday 10 May, you assaulted another member of your team.'

'I've already been charged for that.'

'You won't mind accompanying us to the station for questioning then.'

'I DO MIND!'

'In that case you leave me no alternative. Alex Delaney, I'm arresting you on suspicion of the murder of Adam Hutchinson. You do not have to say anything but it may harm your defence if you do not mention, when questioned, something which you later rely on in court. Anything you do say may be given in evidence.'

His wife lets rip an ear-piercing scream. Susie flinches.

'I HAVE THE RIGHT TO SEE MY SOLICITOR,' bawls Delaney.

'Of course. You can call him when we get to the station.'

A scuffle ensues as Delaney resists arrest. Marshall raises his voice. Delaney swears and says something Susie can't hear. There's a metallic snap as handcuffs are clicked on his wrists. Blue lights flash. Journalists hurl questions at Delaney. Their cameras exploding with flashlight. His wife screams again, loud and shrill. A plain-clothed policeman comes into view, dragging Delaney down the drive against his will. A car door slams. Voices are raised again, in excitement and anger. One of the cars kicks into life and drives away, without the siren this time.

Susie leans against the wall, shocked. So Adam was involved but changed his mind. And which of Adam's 'close friends' told the FSA? Rose or Fabian? Would Rose sneak on her best friend's husband? Would Fabian? Is that why Fabian vanished? Was he hiding from Adam?

'Susie Ashton?' Marshall calls out.

Her bones jolt with surprise. Footsteps crunch across the gravel. Before she has time to compose herself, Marshall has shot through the gate. He draws back in surprise when he catches sight of her, pressed against the wall.

'So Delaney wasn't lying.' He runs his hands through his hair rapidly, clearly perturbed by the sight of her, transfixed by the blue duster she's wearing on her head.

'He set his dogs on me. I think he intended them to kill me. You arrived just in time.'

'What the hell are you doing here?' he asks.

'I was—' begins Susie.

He waves the air. 'No. Save it. I don't want to know.'

'Did he do it? Did he kill Adam?'

Marshall sighs and runs his hand through his hair again. 'You shouldn't have come here. Delaney is a very bitter man. Anything could have happened.' He glances around suddenly tense as if he's lost something then turns back to Susie. 'For one awful moment I thought you'd dragged Lily up here too.'

Following the dramatic arrival of the police cars Lily sits waiting in the Mini, leaning forward with her hands over her ears and her eyes closed. She hates to think what's happening to Susie.

She peers in her wing mirror and is surprised to see an exasperated-looking Marshall hurrying towards the car, Susie, flustered and breathless, in pursuit. With no place to hide Lily sits upright and opens the passenger door.

'We heard about his arrest on the news this morning,' says Susie, catching up with Marshall as they reach the car. 'We wanted answers. We thought he might be able to tell us what's been going on.' She pulls the duster off her hair. 'It's my fault. I brought her here.'

Marshall rolls his eyes. 'With all due respect I suggest you leave the detecting to the detectives.' His voice is sharp. He squats down in the road beside the Mini. His hair has fallen over one eye but he doesn't bother to sweep it into place. 'I realise you've been under a great deal of strain but you should have stayed at home.'

'We were trying to find Rose. We're worried about her,' explains Lily, staring at the loose strands of his hair.

'Then let me put your mind at rest. She's been helping the City of London Police with their enquiries regarding the Goldbergs' scandal.'

So that's why she wasn't answering her phone, thinks Lily.

'When she found out what was going on she got in touch with the FSA.'

'No way!' shrieks Susie.

'Delaney stormed into her office last night and assaulted her. Fortunately the Police found her in time and she wasn't hurt. Delaney claims he and Adam were working the scam together.'

Susie whistles in astonishment and shakes her head.

Lily trembles. She can't believe Adam was involved in a crime. There must be another explanation. Surely Delaney is lying. 'Do you think Delaney killed him?'

'The facts infer his guilt but we have no evidence yet.' Marshall groans and stands up, his knees creaking. And now at last he coaxes his hair back in place. 'I suggest you get back to Sussex. I'll call Bella Day; let her know I've seen you. Oh, and I'd like to take a note of your mobile number, Lily. Just in case this happens again.'

'What about the drug addict? Have you found him yet?'

'No. Not yet. But the drug squad are on the case. You gave us a good description. He doesn't sound the most adept criminal. I'm sure they'll find him.'

Marshall opens his notepad and writes down the number that Lily, after looking it up on her new phone, gives him. Her nerves are jangling like loose change. But Marshall doesn't notice. He thanks her and even manages to smile in response to something witty Susie says as she climbs into the car.

'By the way, we've traced the anonymous calls,' he says, still standing by the open passenger door.

Lily braces herself.

He puffs out his chest. 'Two phone numbers as it happens. A foreign mobile and your Chelsea flat.'

Lily's heart collides into her ribs. She isn't sure she's heard him right. 'Our flat?'

'That's right. In Chelsea.'

'But we haven't got a flat in Chelsea.'

A glimmer of surprise flickers in the detective's eyes. He sucks his teeth. 'The deeds are in Adam's name.'

'I don't understand. Adam was crank calling me from – from his flat?'

Marshall pauses before replying, as if he's searching for the appropriate answer. He screws up one eye, clearly uncomfortable with the situation. 'Lily, I'm sorry. I don't know. Look, you need to get home. You've had a lot to deal with these past few days. Maybe Delaney can shed more light on things. I'll call you the moment I have any news.'

Marshall closes the door gently but Lily recoils as if he's slammed it in her face. She hears a thud overhead as he pats the roof and then he's off, striding purposefully down the street towards his car, mission accomplished.

'Are you okay?' Susie asks.

Lily's cheeks are burning, her stomach churning with anxiety but she nods and closes her eyes. She wonders if her mind is playing tricks on her. Why would Adam buy a flat and not tell her? Was it because he intended to spend more time in London and was worried she'd be upset? How ironic. She was going to ask him about renting a flat there so she could return to work, but she didn't have the chance. It was staggering to think he could make such a big decision without consulting her. Why? Why would Adam do that? Still, now she knew where Adam had gone the days he went missing. He'd been in his flat, crank calling her. He wanted to scare me, she thinks, but why?

But worse than Adam's lies is Marshall's pity. She is humiliated by it. He hadn't been able to disguise his surprise at her ignorance. Then there were the crank calls, the foreign mobile number, the fraud, the cocaine, the holiday, his fight with Alex Delaney that she knew nothing about either. Marshall would have formed a fairly clear picture of their relationship. He would see their marriage for what it was. A sham, held together by Adam's carefully woven web of lies.

28

'Don't worry, darling. You've got an awful lot on your plate at the moment. Dad and I will look after little Georgie for as long as you need us to. Now why don't you try and get some rest.'

Rose thanks her mother and cuts the connection. She is sitting at the round, smoked-glass table in the small kitchen at the back of her flat. It's eleven o'clock in the morning and she's sipping a glass of chilled white wine. She is completely shattered. Too tired to return Lily and Susie's calls. Too tired to sleep. She hopes the wine might remedy that. Last night's tussle with Alex Delaney has left her physically and emotionally drained. She honestly thought she was going to die. Delaney was choking the life out of her. Thank goodness she had both the strength left and the wherewithal to bring her knee up hard and fast between his legs. He backed off immediately, and doubled over on the floor, howling like a baby. Seizing her chance she kicked off her shoes and sprinted out the door and ran slap bang into a man she'd never seen before. DI Barrett, she discovered later, once he produced his ID and flashed it at Delaney, of the City of London Police. She could still recall the look of horror on Alex's face.

A good night's sleep was what she needed after that, but DI Barrett had other ideas. She spent the entire night answering his questions at Wood Street police station. She protested of course.

'What about my son?'

But DI Barrett insisted so she phoned her mother who came to the rescue. She's been doing that a lot recently, thinks Rose. Coming to my rescue. She takes another sip of wine. Why would anyone want a baby? she wonders, when a cute little puppy would be so much easier. At least puppies grow into faithful companions who accept every decision you make with a wag of their tail, not demanding sharp-minded little boys who take up so much of your time, and question and oppose everything you do. God help me when George hits adolescence.

It would help if I had a bigger place, she thinks. But that's not going to happen anytime soon, unless Goldbergs decide to reward me for what I did. It's been ages since my last hefty bonus. Thanks to Delaney it'll be a dry old pot again this year. In fact I'll be lucky if I still have a job.

'After the bravery you've just shown, sweetheart, you'll be promoted,' her mother said when she voiced her concerns.

It was brave of me, she thinks. It takes guts to be a whistleblower. Not that I had any choice. I have my principles. Alex and Adam broke the law. It was not about revenge. It was my duty as a law-abiding citizen to inform the FSA.

The phone rings. Work no doubt, she thinks and answers it. But it isn't Janice White. It's Miles.

'Oh good, you're there. I've been trying to get hold of you,' he says, sounding pleased.

'I'm having a day off.'

'That's not like you.'

She thinks about elaborating. 'No. I suppose not.'

'Listen, I've decided to have a lunch tomorrow for Lily. It would be great if you could come down. She's having a rough old time. She needs as much support as she can get right now. It's up to us to rally round.'

29

Susie is driving them over to Lewes for lunch at Miles's. He'd rung last night to suggest it. Susie explained what had happened in London and about the flat in Chelsea that Marshall told them Adam owned.

'It was a terrible shock for Lily.'

'The change of scene might do you both good,' he said.

Lily stares listlessly out of the car window. The blue sky of the past few days has been replaced by a low ceiling of grey-white clouds. Rain is forecast later but the first spots of rain are already visible on the windscreen. The countryside, so colourful and vibrant in the sunshine, is faded and listless in the gloom. Even Mother Nature is depressed. She is thinking about Adam. The new version, not the man she met and fell in love with. This is a different Adam. A brilliant liar. A skilled cheat. An arch deceiver. It's like being told the god she's worshipped all these years is a fake.

Returning from London last night, she swiped up the pile of post on the table and charged upstairs. In the privacy of her bedroom, she ripped opened all the envelopes addressed to Adam. It made for chilling reading. No wonder he hadn't paid Liam Smith. Adam owed a lot of money. She'd seen he'd taken out another mortgage to buy the Chelsea flat from all the payment reminder notices but he had a huge overdraft as well and three credit cards, all spent to their limit. It explained why he'd raided their joint account. But if he was in so much debt, why on earth did he buy her diamond earrings for her birthday?

You know the answer to that, Lily, she tells herself. Guilt.

What a God-awful mess. She doubts there is anything Miles or Susie can say or do to wash away the stain of Adam's lies. They are scorched on her skin like a brand.

Miles's front door opens and Nat's freckled face appears. Lily tenses and balls her hands into fists. She didn't think things could get any worse. It takes all her willpower not to turn around and run straight back down the road to her parked car.

'I'm so terribly sorry,' he says, moving towards her.

His eyes are bloodshot and rheumy. There's a slight scar on the bridge of his nose, evidence of his fight with Adam. Lily recoils and stumbles backwards off the pavement into the road. An oncoming car swerves to avoid her and the driver hoots and glares at her. Susie reaches for her arm and pulls her on to the pavement as Nat jumps in the road and flicks a V-sign at the departing vehicle.

He turns back to Lily. 'Are you okay?'

His breath reeks of alcohol. She doesn't want to talk to him. Has he forgotten their last conversation, that awful leery, late night phone call which set in motion the terrible events of the last eleven days? She backs away, into the house, wondering why he's here. Miles knows how much she hates him.

'I'm very sorry,' he says, trailing her. 'Is there anything I can do? Anything at all.'

She wants to scream at him to go away but when she opens her mouth she finds she has neither the energy nor the inclination, so she ignores him instead.

The television is on in the living room and the smell of lasagne drifts into the room from the kitchen around the corner. On the coffee table is a half-drunk glass of red wine beside an empty bottle.

'Sit down,' says Nat, swaying slightly. 'The others are arguing in the kitchen. I'll get you a drink.'

'Others?' she says.

'I don't believe you,' Miles shouts, as if on cue.

'Please don't shout at me. It's the truth, I tell you.'

'Rose,' says Lily. 'Why's she here?'

But Nat doesn't hear her. 'They've been arguing for ages. I left them to it to watch the Grand Prix.'

'But you're her friend,' Miles shouts.

'Yes I am.' Rose's tearful reply is barely audible.

No you're not, thinks Lily, as every one of her muscles tenses. She has a few choice words to share with Rose. She makes a beeline for the kitchen. 'I assume the *her* you are talking about is me,' she says, fronting up to them, her blood simmering.

Rose and Miles stop arguing and look at her. There's an awkward silence.

'You've got some front, Rose, I'll give you that,' says Susie, joining them.

Lily opens her mouth to speak but her words desert her. She stares at Rose tongue-tied.

'If I'd known what she'd done I wouldn't have asked her,' says Miles.

Susie frowns. 'How could you, Rose?'

Rose's face is pinched and pale, her eyes unnaturally wide. She juts out her chin. 'I had no choice.'

'We all have choices. It's just a question of making the right ones. Adam was your friend,' says Susie.

Rose stamps her foot. 'Hang on a minute. I wasn't the one who broke the law.'

'Stop it, Rose,' says Miles, wiping his forehead with the back of his hand. 'At the very least you owe Lily an apology.'

'I have my principles.'

'Principles! It was sneaky and underhand and you know it,' says Susie. 'And it may well be the reason Adam's dead. Delaney's been arrested on suspicion of Adam's murder.'

Rose does a double take. 'Delaney?'

Lily stares at her in disgust.

'I'm sorry,' Rose mumbles, shaking her head and frowning as if she can't quite believe she's having to apologise for something that's clearly not her fault.

'Sit down, Lily. I'll get you a glass of wine,' says Miles, softening. He takes her by the arm, guides her to a chair and presses her into it.

She leans forward and clutches her head. 'What's Nat doing here?'

'He turned up an hour ago in a terrible state. I couldn't turn him away.'

'I don't suppose any of you have seen my trainers?' says Nat, wandering into the room with an empty glass. 'I lost them a few weeks ago. They were my favourite pair. It's damned annoying.'

'Grow up,' says Susie under her breath.

Miles walks over to the wine rack. He reaches for two bottles of Rioja and plonks them on the table. He opens one with a large metal corkscrew. The cork makes a gentle popping sound as he prises it out. Nat thrusts his glass at Miles, who fills it and the other four glasses on the table.

'We're going to get you through this,' Miles says, handing Lily some wine.

Lily takes a large slug. She knows he means well but, with Nat and Rose around, his words are meaningless. Nat's already drunk and as for Rose, she's crossed a line. She already feels far worse than she did this morning. She puts the glass to her lips, tips back her head and drains it.

'Did you know about the flat?' she asks Nat as he sits down at the head of the table.

'What flat?'

'He didn't know. None of us did,' cuts in Miles, crouching down in front of the oven, his hands encased in oven gloves.

'I've just filmed a tissue commercial,' says Susie, in a desperate change of subject. 'My agent told me I was chosen for my pert little nose.'

188

Nat snorts with laughter. 'And should the company decide to advertise bog roll, then I'm sure your ample arse will prove just as virtuous. Tell me, Susie. Does selling Kleenex amount to a demotion in your line of work or should we be viewing this as the pinnacle of your career?'

Susie sticks out her tongue.

'Must you?' groans Nat. 'I'm hoping to eat in a moment.'

Lily's already taut shoulders stiffen still further.

'Arguing is pointless. I think it's important we stick together,' says Miles, carrying the lasagne over to the table. He sits down next to Lily, removes the gloves and loops them over the back of his chair. He takes a large spoon to the pasta and starts to serve.

'Here, here,' says Susie, sitting down opposite. She picks up the bread knife and starts sawing away at the French stick.

'Aren't you going to sit down, Rose?' asks Nat.

Frowning, Rose pulls out the chair next to Susie, who's covering a slice of bread with a thick layer of butter. Nat picks up the bottle and fills her glass then tops his up.

'I honestly didn't know Delaney had been arrested,' says Rose. 'I wish you'd believe me when I say I was only doing my job. I have George to—'

Nat's eyes drill into her. 'It's not your pathetic little career we're worrying about. Get off your fucking high horse. Adam is dead, you stupid bitch.'

Rose gasps and covers her mouth with her hand. She looks as though she's going to cry. Miles, who would normally leap to her defence, says nothing.

'Who's to say it won't be you next,' continues Nat nastily.

Susie shoots Lily a look, her heaped forkful of food suspended in mid-air.

'Me next what?'

'Murdered! Or worse, discovered dying in a pool of your own blood but–just–a–little–too–late.'

189

'If you continue to talk to me like this I shall go.'

Lily can't think of anything she'd like more, right now, unless Nat was to leave with her. She gulps down more wine to steady her nerves.

'Nat, take it easy. We're trying to solve a crime, not commit another,' says Miles.

Nat holds up his hands. 'I'm sorry, Rose. I'm not myself.'

Rose blanches visibly. She fiddles with her napkin as her eyeballs flick anxiously in her sockets. 'Good, because I mean it. If you're going to shout at me, I'm going home.'

'I won't shout, I promise,' insists Nat.

Miles sighs. With relief, Lily supposes.

'Meanwhile Fabian vanishes, only to reappear with a cock-and-bull story about being too busy with a friend's unwanted pregnancy to put in an appearance. It's all a bit vague don't you think?' continues Nat, turning his attention to Susie.

'What?' says Susie, spraying a few morsels of lasagne. 'Are you accusing Fabian now?'

Nat pours yet more wine into his glass. Lily stares at him with contempt. How dare he swing the conversation round to Fabian? What about him? According to Marshall he was drunk the night of Adam's death. So drunk he couldn't remember the conversation he'd had with Adam. And when Nat's drunk he loses his temper in a flash. What if *he'd* been angry enough to kill him?

'What about you?' she asks quietly. Four pairs of eyes zoom in on her like searchlights in a fog. 'You had a motive,' she continues bravely. 'I bet you were angry about Adam coming over and having it out with you about those drunken late night phone calls you'd been making to his wife.'

Nat's eyes narrow into two sharp blades.

'Or perhaps you forgot!' she says, her voice heavy with sarcasm.

'I take it you think I haven't been telling the truth.'

190

'You're a drunk, Nat. Drunks are aggressive and drunks lie.'

Nat snorts. 'Oh la-di-da-di-da.'

'You seem pretty drunk today,' says Susie.

'Shut the fuck up, you stupid bitch.'

'That's enough, Nat,' says Miles. 'You're not doing yourself any favours.'

Glowering, Susie picks up her fork and continues to eat. Nat drains his glass and stares into nothingness. Lily, fuming with rage, turns away and allows her eyes to wander round the room. It's small but tidy, everything in its place. The stainless steel colander on the wall, tea, coffee and sugar in glass jars in a neat row on the speckled graphite surface, blue and white striped mugs hanging from a tree.

'And then of course there's you, Lily.' Nat's voice echoes through the morgue-like stillness of the room.

Miles slams his hand on the table. The cutlery rattles with the force. 'Shut up, Nat. You've gone too far.'

'But don't you see? She has the biggest motive of us all.' Nat kicks back his chair with such force it falls over and hits the floor with a loud crash. Oblivious, he picks up his glass and the full bottle of wine, and staggers towards the door. 'Adam was a rich and successful man. Maybe this supposedly innocent little creature bumped off her husband for his money and her freedom. Why don't you all think about it, while I go for a slash.'

Susie leaps to her feet. 'Great idea. Go and piss off. How dare you even imply Lily could have killed him? She's totally distraught. How you've got the audacity to sit there with that smug look on your ugly face and accuse her. I'm amazed you sleep at night.'

Nat stops in his tracks, swivels around and waves the bottle at Miles. 'Why don't you rein in these girls before they become hysterical.'

'Nat just—' begins Miles.

'Oh that's typical of you, you arrogant little shit,' says Susie.

'Don't, Susie!' implores Miles.

'You tell the little drama queen, Miles. And while you're at it, remind her what a sad little nobody she is. A fat one at that. This is real life, dearie, not a soap opera. No wonder Adam found you irritating.' Nat replenishes his glass, spilling wine before dropping the empty bottle on to the wooden floor where it tips over and rolls across the room.

The last vestiges of Lily's patience desert her. Seeing red, she charges at Nat, mewling like an irate cat.

'Lily!' shouts Susie.

Blood hammering at her eardrums, Lily launches herself at Nat, pummelling him with her fists, kicking wildly at his shins. Nat laughs as Miles wrenches her off him. She tries to wriggle free from his grasp, but she can't, his grip is too strong.

'I'm going for a piss,' says Nat in a bored voice.

Miles lets go of Lily and Susie takes her hand. 'He's not worth it,' she says. 'Not when he's like this.'

But Lily doesn't hear her. Nat's poisonous words have infiltrated her mind. Maybe it's the alcohol she's drunk on an empty stomach. Maybe it's a build up of stress. Lily neither knows nor cares. She is consumed with hatred for Nat. He shouldn't be allowed to bully his way through life. They're all too scared to front up to him. It wasn't Delaney who killed Adam and it wasn't Fabian. It was Nat. She is sure of it. And retribution is what she's after. Yanking her hand free of Susie's, she grabs the bread knife and runs out of the room.

30

Lily charges up the stairs, her heart beating rapidly. She'll catch him unawares while he has his hands full, she thinks, flinging open the unlocked door of the bathroom. She raises the knife above Nat's doubled form and gasps, horrified by what she sees.

'Lily, no,' yells Miles. He grips her wrist, removes the knife and turns to look at Nat. 'What the—?'

'Blimey!' says Susie, joining them.

'What the hell are you lot gawping at?' Nat asks, annoyed that he's been interrupted, oblivious of the knife.

'Lily was about to kill you,' says Susie.

Lily wonders fleetingly if it's true. If she is mad enough to stab Nat? Or would the remnants of her sanity hold her back?

Nat glances at Miles who's clutching the knife. 'Don't be ridiculous. Why would she do that? We're friends, aren't we, Lily?'

It's as if the vicious argument had never happened. If he doesn't think I'd murder him then neither do I, thinks Lily.

It's claustrophobic in the tiny room, all of them standing on top of one another, inches from where Nat is kneeling, a rolled up banknote in between the thumb and index finger of his right hand. On the lavatory seat, next to the wine glass, is a small rectangular mirror with a length of white powder running across it, and traces of two other lines.

Nat grins. 'Any of you want some? I've got plenty.'

'How long have you been taking it?' asks Miles.

'About six months. Adam got me into it.'

'Adam?' says Lily.

'Don't sound so surprised. Someone at Goldbergs offered it to him. He was feeling down, a bit of a failure. He couldn't get you pregnant. Work was going badly. He thought he'd give it a go, see if it improved his mood.' He places the twenty-pound note to his nose and sniffs up the powder.

Nobody says a word.

'It takes the edge off,' he says, leaping to his feet. He thrusts the mirror and note in his pocket, and brushes past them out of the room. 'I wouldn't have got through these past few days without it.'

Lily follows him downstairs and into the living area. He must have been high when he called me, she thinks. Was that why Adam was angry with him? Did he think Nat was going to tell me about his secret habit?

Nat walks over to the window that looks out on to the High Street and flings it open then spins round on the ball of his foot. He sees Lily and links his arm through hers and twirls her round the room like a mad sprite.

'Stop it, Nat,' she says angrily as the others join them.

'Why? You're a pretty good dancer.'

'Let go of me.' Scowling, Lily wriggles free but Nat continues, one arm around an imaginary back, the other extended, like an inmate of a lunatic asylum, ballroom dancing alone.

'Christ!' mutters Susie.

There's a loud knocking on the front door. Miles takes a deep breath and disappears to answer it. Nat continues to dance as Miles's exasperated voice filters through from the hall. 'Mate, I'm not sure this is a great idea.'

'Please. I really need to talk to you,' Fabian says, backing into the room.

Susie presses her lips together and marches over to him, eyes flashing. 'What the fuck do you want?'

Nat stops dancing and frowns in Fabian's general direction.

Miles sighs. 'Like I said—'

'There's something I have to ... it's about—'

Susie shoves him in the chest with the palms of her hands. 'Piss off. You're not wanted here.'

'No listen. It's about Honor.'

'Honor?' asks Rose.

'Honor Vincente,' explains Fabian, turning his attention to Lily. 'She's an Italian—'

'Yes I know. I've met her. She came to visit me the morning Adam died.'

Fabian's eyebrows shoot up in surprise. 'She did?'

'She's Rachel Jones isn't she? The girl you collected from the abortion clinic,' continues Lily.

Fabian glances from Lily to Susie and back again. 'That's right.'

'Susie and I saw her arrive at your house yesterday.'

Susie nods in confirmation. She's wearing a triumphant expression as though she's pleased to have caught her boyfriend out.

'Oh. I see,' he says.

'Why you couldn't tell me the truth about her in the first place is beyond me,' says Susie.

'Would somebody mind telling me what the hell is going on,' says Nat, collapsing into a chair.

'Honor is a very dear friend of mine. We've known each other since we were children,' says Fabian, wringing his hands. 'My aunt, Uncle Bruno's wife, was friends with her parents. I used to spend a lot of time in Milan. Honor and I always got on well and I feel a certain loyalty to her because of that.'

'And your point is what exactly?' hisses Susie.

Fabian marches across the room to where Lily is standing. Unlike his fresh appearance of yesterday, his face is ragged. His cheeks are sunken and cloudy black patches darken the skin beneath his eyes. He picks up Lily's hands and looks directly at her. 'I've thought long and hard about this. Forgive me, Lily but I want to tell you the truth.'

She stares at him, her stomach churning.

'It isn't me who's having an affair with Honor. It was Adam.'

31

Lily coughs. She clutches her throat and coughs some more, desperate to dislodge the cloying morsel of reality that's lodged there, choking her. She hurts. Every inch of her. This must be how it feels to be told the lump you hoped was a swollen gland is a malignant tumour, she thinks. No. It's worse than that. More like torture; a needle behind a toenail; an iron to the sole of the foot; electrodes on the genitals. Each day a little worse than before.

She staggers to the French windows. 'I need some air.'

'I'll come with you,' says Susie who, along with everyone else in the room, is staring bleakly at Lily.

'No. Please don't. I want to be alone.'

'But—'

'Please, Susie.'

Aware of the eyes of her friends on her back, Lily opens the glass door at the far end of the living area and steps outside into Miles's small walled garden. She closes the door and walks around the corner. When she's sure she's out of sight, she bends over and gulps up lungfuls of air. Her mind is reeling. Now she understands why Adam bought a flat. He needed a love nest for his Italian mistress. The exquisite Honor Vincente, one of the beautiful people of Milan. Life doesn't get more humiliating than that. Tall, chic and effortlessly elegant, with soft, slender hands and manicured nails. She remembers her mouth, unsmiling and lipstick red. An image of Adam and Honor making love on a king-size bed crashes into her mind. Her guts twist. She gags and clutches her throat again, and sinks to her knees on the patio and throws up what little lasagne she's eaten. She retches and retches, ejecting nothing more than wine-tinged bile on to the paving stones. Her throat burns. Her eyes sting. Adam led a parallel life and she didn't have the faintest idea. How pathetically trusting she'd been. How blind. How stupidly naïve.

After a few moments crouching dog-like, she dares to move. She staggers weakly to the end of the garden and sinks on to a wooden bench. When did it begin? she wonders, leaning forwards and clutching the back of her head with her hands. When did they meet? Was it that night at Fabian's uncle's party? Was the affair already well underway when we were married? No it couldn't have been. He would never have bothered marrying me if it was. He would have chosen Honor. Wouldn't he?

She casts her mind back. Had there been a shift in their relationship? A moment when Adam's attitude towards her had changed? She racks her brains for a sign she might have missed, a clue, a hint even that he was in love with someone else. But there's nothing. He gave her diamond earrings for her birthday, thirty red roses, told her he loved her in front of all their friends. And their sex life. There'd been nothing wrong with that. Nothing at all. He couldn't get enough of her, couldn't keep his hands off her. She shudders. The same hands that had explored Honor's body.

Had Adam told her that he loved her too? Had he given Honor diamonds and roses? Honor! What kind of a name was that for a mistress? She didn't know the meaning of the word. She knew he was married. She must have known he was happy. She must have known everything about them. Everything.

Lily gasps and clutches the wooden slats of the bench to steady herself. Honor must have known we were trying for a baby. Is that why she got herself pregnant? Because I couldn't? Was she trying to rub my inadequacies in Adam's face to tempt him away? Adam was going to be a father. It's what he'd wanted these last two years. What he was desperate for. No wonder he wasn't bothered about getting his sperm tested. He knew he wasn't firing blanks. Would he have left me for her?

It's a question too far. She can barely breathe. She tips her head back and gulps for air. Inside her chest her heart shrinks to a pebble, tiny, cold and hard. She's been such a fool. She could never have been enough for Adam, childless. She hurls herself forward and buries her head in her hands and sobs huge tears of self-pity.

She feels a thud on the bench beside her, an arm around her back. Flinching, she opens her eyes.

'It's okay,' says Miles.

She flicks her tears angrily away with the flat of her hand and shrugs her shoulder to dislodge his hand. 'Did you know?' Miles inclines his head on one side and puts his arm around her again and tries to draw her to him but Lily resists. 'Well did you?'

Miles presses his lips together but says nothing.

'I really hope you didn't because if you did, you should have told me.'

'I had no idea.'

She rises unsteadily to her feet. Miles stands up too. 'Promise me.'

'Lily, believe me. I didn't know.'

'Promise!' she screams, drumming her fists on his chest.

Miles catches her wrists, and looks her directly in the eye. 'I promise. I didn't know. I'm as shocked as you are. I can't believe he could behave so despicably.'

She retches again and tilts her head to spit out the bile that has risen in her throat. It trickles down her chin. She wants to wipe if off but she can't. Her legs give way and she drops down, dangling now from Miles's grasp. He lowers her to the ground and sits beside her on the cool paving stones, stroking her back with one hand, holding on to her wrist with the other.

'I thought he told you everything,' she whispers.

Miles let's go, wipes her chin with his sleeve and sighs. 'I thought he told *you* everything. Seems we were both wrong about that.'

'Do you think he was with her those last ten days?' she asks, her voice barely audible.

'I don't know. It's possible.'

'Oh my God. Oh my God,' she says, her breath coming in ragged bursts.

Miles finds her hand and squeezes it tightly. 'I'll take care of you. I promise.'

Lily looks into his tired, brown, bespectacled eyes but the image she sees impressed on his irises is Adam. And he is laughing at her. She jumps up, her cheeks burning hot. Resentment seeps through every pore in her body. She's clammy with it. If she didn't feel so violated, she would laugh. Nobody cares. Nobody ever did. She glares at Adam's number one disciple. 'So–why–do–I–feel–as–though–I'm– swimming–in–shit?'

Miles opens his arms and envelopes her, pushing her to his chest. He presses his lips against the top of her head and kisses her hair.

Lily hears a loud sob, then another and another. They are coming from her, from her heart, or what's left of it. It's been broken into so many pieces, ground down by the relentless march of Adam's secret skeletons, into a useless dust.

Rose, Fabian and Susie leap to their feet when Miles leads Lily back into the house.

'How are you feeling?' Susie asks, her voice a weird, high-pitched squeak.

'Oh my God. I can't do this anymore. I can't, I really can't,' Lily shouts.

Startled, Susie takes a step back.

Miles clasps Lily firmly by the arm and guides her to the sofa. He presses her on to the cushions, and sits down beside her. 'Susie, why don't you make Lily a cup of tea?'

Lily groans. 'I don't want tea. I'm sick of the stuff.' She stares at her friends blankly, over swollen cheeks. They're gawping at her, all of them, as if she's some kind of freak. Susie's jaw is hanging open, Fabian is twitching nervously, Rose is as white as a sheet. She glances around the room for Nat. But she can't see him. She wants to talk to him. He told her Adam would leave her. Did he know about Honor? Did he know about the flat? 'Where's Nat?' she asks.

'He's gone to have a lie down,' says Fabian gently, sitting down in a chair.

You, she thinks angrily. You knew all about this. You knew Adam was having an affair. She glares at him. 'How sweet of you to keep his sordid little secret.'

'I'm sorry. I realise now I should have told you. It's just that—'

'It's—just—what?' asks Susie, leaping to Lily's defence.

Fabian inhales deeply and leans forward on his chair. 'I should explain.'

Susie throws open her arms. 'What's to explain, for heaven's sake? The bitch was pregnant with Adam's child and you were helping her.'

Lily shivers and crosses her legs. Everyone knows her business. She is cold to the bone as though she's sitting naked in an Arctic wind.

Fabian's face reddens. He shifts his position. 'I know you're hurting, Lily. What I told you is a terrible thing for a wife to hear.'

'At the very least, you should have tried to stop them,' says Susie, her face clouded with anger.

'Believe me I did. I was furious with her. I reminded her he was married. I begged her to think of Lily. I tried everything in my power to persuade her to leave him alone but it was too late. She'd fallen in love with him. It was beyond her control.'

Lily understands what he is saying, deplorable though his words are. 'Did he love her back?' she asks in a small voice.

Fabian springs to his feet, rushes over and kneels in front of Lily. 'No he didn't. He loved you.'

'Oh right. Terrific. Thanks for your opinion,' says Susie, rolling her eyes.

'How long had it been going on?' Lily asks.

'About eighteen months.'

She smarts at another direct hit.

'The last thing I want to do is cause you any more hurt but there's something you should know.'

'Go on,' says Lily weakly.

'Adam left Honor.'

Lily's head feels light. She thinks she might faint and bends over to stop herself. 'Is that meant to make me feel better?'

'When Honor told him she was pregnant, Adam accused her of entrapment. The only person he ever loved was Lily, he said. Honor asked him if he loved his wife why was he sleeping with another woman? Adam laughed and told her she'd never meant anything to him. She'd been nothing more than a cheap thrill. And he couldn't care less about her baby. He wanted nothing to do with either of them. She was a whore.' Fabian pauses to wipe away the beads of sweat that have formed on his brow with his sleeve. 'That's why she had the abortion. That's why she was upset.'

Lily sits bolt upright, horrified. Is that why he'd disappeared? Is that why he'd been so angry? Is that what he'd meant when he yelled at her about being so fucking perfect? Is that what he'd wanted to tell her, what he was referring to in his note? Had it all been about his guilt?

'The bastard,' mutters Susie.

Lily is trembling. She tries to tell herself that she is fine, that she can cope. But she once loved this man.

'He ordered her out of the flat and then left,' says Fabian, rising slowly to his feet. 'When he came back he was high on cocaine and stood over her and jeered while she packed her bags. She was sobbing. She was heartbroken, she was pregnant with the child of the man she loved but who no longer had any use for her, and she had nowhere to go. This happened on Saturday, ten days before Adam died. She took herself off to a doctor then booked into the nearest hotel. The day he died she went back to the flat to try to appeal to him but of course he wasn't there. She rang both his mobile and Orchard House from there and then she rang me. It was lunchtime. She was in a bad way. She hadn't eaten or slept. She was incapable of making the simplest decision.'

Fabian stops and turns to Susie, his forehead furrowed to a central point. 'I couldn't tell you because you would have had to either tell Lily or lie to her and I didn't want to put you in that position. And I couldn't tell you, Lily, not once I'd heard the news of Adam's death. You'd been through too much already. And anyway, I had to look after Honor because she was alone in a foreign country. She'd already booked into the Marie Stopes. I tried to convince her to keep the baby, but I couldn't. She'd made up her mind. She wanted to get rid of it. The child would have been a constant reminder of the man who'd caused her so much pain.'

Can you measure pain? wonders Lily. Because if you can, surely the pain I've suffered is greater than hers.

'I don't understand why you didn't take her home,' says Miles.

'She wouldn't leave the hotel and I didn't want to force her.'

'Do you think she did it? Do you think she killed Adam? She sure as hell had a motive,' Susie asks, wide-eyed.

'Don't be ridiculous,' says Fabian. 'She was discharged from the clinic at five that evening. I drove her back to her hotel. Adam and Adam's child both died that day.'

Rose gasps and grabs the back of her neck.

'You should have called me,' says Susie quietly.

'I know that now.'

So that's why she came to his house that day, thinks Lily. She wanted to see whom she'd lost out too. How very disappointed she must have been.

'Did you come down to Sussex that evening too? Did you call Adam from the station?' Susie asks.

'Yes I did. I was furious with Adam. Honor was in a terrible state. I cooled down a bit after I'd phoned him and left a message telling him what I thought of him. So I crossed the railway line and caught the next train back to London.'

'How can we be sure you're not covering for Honor?' asks Miles.

'Because she was in the clinic.'

'But it was Rachel Jones who was booked into the clinic,' says Susie.

'She booked in under an alias. I can assure you, it was Honor.'

'And yet you came down to Sussex and left her alone, even though she was in a terrible state,' says Miles.

'I was angry with him. Adam behaved abysmally. Not just to Honor but Lily too.'

Miles rises from the sofa. 'I think you should tell the police.'

There's a commotion in the hallway. Nat appears, colliding with the doorframe as he sways precariously into the room. He makes a grab for Susie's arm but misses and falls to the floor. His body tenses then starts to shake violently.

Susie crouches over him. 'Nat? Are you okay?'

Drool dribbles out the corner of his mouth.

'He's having a seizure,' she says. 'Call an ambulance.'

Miles kneels down on the other side of Nat as Rose, ashen-faced and trembling, grabs her handbag and pulls out her mobile. 'Ambulance please ... Lewes High Street ... he's drunk and he's taken drugs ... cocaine.'

Lily watches impassively as the scene unfolds in front of her. She thinks Susie is just the sort of reliable, clear-minded person needed in a crisis, and Rose, absolutely no sentimentality, just cool, calm efficiency. But unlike the rest of them, Lily isn't the least alarmed by the sight of Nat convulsing on the floor. In her opinion, Nat has got what he deserved.

32

By the time the ambulance arrives, Nat's seizure has passed and he is lying on the floor in the recovery position Susie has placed him in. The paramedics bundle him on to a trolley, strap him down, then wheel him out to their waiting vehicle. Susie follows and stands on the pavement under the dim light of the amber streetlights.

'I want you to make sure Lily gets some sleep tonight,' says Miles, joining her.

'What do you want me to do? Hit her over the head with a baseball bat?'

'Don't you start,' he says, rummaging around in his jacket pocket. 'These might help.'

Susie takes the small bottle of pills, scrutinising the label. 'Zopiclone?'

'Sleeping pills,' explains Miles. 'I've been having trouble sleeping since Adam died.'

'Good idea,' she says pocketing them.

Fabian joins them on the roadside. She feels his eyes on her but keeps hers fixed on the ambulance.

One of the paramedics comes over. 'Is anyone coming with him?'

'Yes. I will,' replies Miles.

The paramedic gesticulates to the open door of the ambulance. 'Hop in then.'

Miles touches Fabian on the arm. 'Get yourself down the police station, mate.'

Fabian sighs. 'I was on my way. I just wanted to talk to you first. I thought Adam might have told you. I thought you would know what to do. I didn't expect this.'

Miles throws him a reassuring look then leans down and kisses Susie on the cheek. 'Look after Lily,' he says.

'Of course I will but what about Rose?'

'She'll have to stay at Lily's tonight.'

She pulls a face. 'Do you think that's wise?'

'You can't send her home. I'll pick her up as soon as I can tomorrow,' he says, climbing into the ambulance. He pulls the door closed and the ambulance drives off.

Terrific, thinks Susie, as it speeds up the hill, blue lights flashing. As if Lily is going to agree to that.

'Susie,' says Fabian, holding out his hand.

'Goodbye,' she says turning her back. Pressing her lips together, she folds her arms and walks back into the house without a backward glance.

Lily can barely walk for the weight that's bearing down on her. When Susie offers to drive home, she hands her the keys, and slides onto the front passenger seat of her Mini without uttering a word. Rose pushes forward the driver's seat and climbs into the back but Lily is past caring. Fabian's tale has sucked the last drops of optimism out of her. As a young bride she dreamed of happy endings. Of course she realised even then that life isn't like that, not even in the happiest of marriages. It's impossible to foresee the trials and tribulations of the future, just as it is to predict the diamond times. But she was certain she had a husband who would catch her should she fall. A safe pair of arms is as attractive as an honest heart. But it turns out Adam had neither. He'd lied and cheated her out of a life. Everything she believed to be good and true had been a fake. Adam hadn't caught her as she fell. How could he when he was the reason she'd fallen in the first place? He'd enticed her to the cliff edge of her sanity and pushed her over. And here she was, lying at the bottom helpless, broken and alone. Her dreams of happiness turned living nightmare.

They arrive back home in silence. Lily unlocks the front door and heads straight upstairs. She kicks off her shoes, flops onto the bed and stares at the ceiling.

A few moments later there's a knock on the door. 'You okay?' asks Susie gently, peering around.

Lily clenches her teeth. Can't Susie see she wants to be alone?

Susie holds out a small brown bottle. 'Miles gave me these. They're sleeping pills. Do you want to take a couple?'

She shakes her head and closes her eyes.

'I'll leave them on the table in case you change your mind.'

Lily knows she's being unfair, giving Susie the cold shoulder. But her world is rocking precariously on its axis. Nothing in her life makes sense any more. Any moment now a gigantic chasm might open up and swallow her whole. She can feel herself hanging on, desperate not to fall.

'I'll be in the kitchen if you need me,' Susie says, quietly closing the door.

Lily lies there staring into space, her eyes unseeing, like a foetus in a jar suspended in jelly. But unlike Adam and Honor's baby, she isn't dead. Stunned, damaged, scarred for life but very much alive. A widow in mourning, that's what she's supposed to be. Only Adam's death has cast a filthy shadow over her life. The trust that she placed in him, shot to pieces. She doesn't know him anymore. She certainly doesn't love him. No worse than that, she resents him.

She clamps her eyes shut, longing for sleep to overwhelm her. But instead she finds herself battling Sumo-sized images of Adam and Honor, love-drenched naked and locked together on a bed. She rolls over but her legs get caught up in the tangled duvet and she has to wrestle free. She is totally beyond sleep. She thinks she will never sleep again.

He used to tell me everything. If he was stressed at work, why couldn't he talk to me? I would have understood. He wouldn't have needed the cocaine. I might even have understood about Honor. I'd have been upset. Of course I would. He'd betrayed my trust. But we would have talked about it. He would have explained why it had happened. I'd have forgiven him. Wouldn't I?

What's the point? He didn't tell me, so how could I know?

Exasperated, she hurls the pillows to the floor and slides out of bed. How different is Adam and Honor's relationship from the one I share with Finn? she wonders as she pads across the thick white carpet to the wardrobe. Are they in any way comparable? Ours is a platonic relationship but I kept it a secret. Does that make me as bad as him?

She opens the door and delves around behind the shoes at the back, for the box she hid in here, all those months ago. She finds it and carefully places it on the bed. She lifts the lid, takes out the bubble-wrapped sculpture and unravels it. Her impulse buy. She hasn't set eyes on it since she bought it, can barely remember it even. She runs her hand over the smooth, cold stone, studying the semi-naked man, lying on his back, his arms behind his head. After a while, she hugs it to her chest.

Could I? Should I? she wonders as the rain, which has been threatening all day, pelts the window panes.

Without bothering to agonise further on the rights and wrongs of her actions, Lily places the sculpture on the floor. Her mind is made up. She has to see him, if only for an hour. There's no way she can sleep. She has to escape.

She puts on her denim jacket and creeps out on to the landing and listens. Music floats up the stairwell from the kitchen where Rose and Susie are talking. About her, no doubt. Holding her breath, she descends the stairs on tiptoe, skipping the creaking bottom step. She steals across the hall, opening and closing the front door silently. Rain splatters the gravel as if someone is chucking it in bucket loads from the clouds. She reaches the garage, unlocks the car and slides in behind the steering wheel. She combs back her wet hair with trembling fingers then tries to steady her hand enough to place the key in the ignition. Concentrating her mind, she has another go. This time she's successful. She fires the engine and turns up the air-con.

How wonderful it would be to run away from all this, she thinks as she drives her Mini slowly down the drive, casting a weary eye through the fuggy windscreen for the dealer or any journalists. She rubs the condensation with the sleeve of her jacket creating a circular aperture big enough to see through. There's no sign of life. She's cold and yet beads of sweat prickle her forehead. And she's tense, her shoulders up around her ears, her clawed hands locked around the steering wheel, her arms rigid. The wipers squeak as they sweep across the glass. Relax, she tells herself. Relax and drive.

Susie is in Lily's kitchen with Rose. She's raided Adam's wine cellar and unearthed a pretty decent looking bottle of Burgundy, her reward for having to spend an evening cooped up with a screwball. She's also found two of Adam's obscenely large wine glasses and has half-filled them. She hopes that Rose, with a bit of alcohol inside her, will loosen up. She's hardly uttered a word since they've been back and keeps twitching nervously and throwing Susie sideways looks as if she's worried she's about to get another bollocking. But Susie can't see the point in dragging it up all over again. Rose has been an idiot. They've all told her how they feel. And now she's got to live with it. She wouldn't like to be in Rose's shoes when she goes back to work. She doubts her colleagues will be all that sympathetic.

She takes a sip of wine. It's full-bodied, sweet and aromatic, almost a deep purple in colour. Delicious. Her mood improves immediately. She slots her iPhone in the dock on the worktop and scrolls through her albums until she finds Adele. Perfect, she thinks, sitting down on the opposite side of the table to Rose, who's staring glumly at her glass.

'How's George?' she asks, holding the stem and swirling the contents around.

'He's with my parents so I'm sure he's having a lovely time.'

'You know what? You're way too hard on yourself.' She's about to add George is lucky to have a mother like you, but she's not sure even she can make the lie sound convincing.

Rose, ramrod straight, shakes her head and continues to stare at her wine.

'It can't be easy, looking after a child and holding down a career. Hats off to you, Rose. I know I couldn't have managed it.'

'I'll talk to Lily tomorrow,' says Rose quietly. 'Explain everything.'

Susie frowns. 'I don't think that's a good idea.'

'But it's got nothing to do with you,' she says crossly.

'Look, you've got to try to understand, Lily loved Adam no matter that he's turned out to be a Class A bastard. You're going to have to agree to disagree on this I'm afraid.'

Rose's face falls in on itself, her nostrils pinched. 'But you don't know what it's like for me.'

'I've a pretty good idea. I've worked with plenty of unscrupulous directors in my time.'

'What's that got to do with anything?' asks Rose irritated.

'It's called empathy. It's what friends do. You should try it some time.'

Rose frowns. 'It's the principle of the thing,' she mutters, almost to herself. 'And it's about responsibility.'

She's off her rocker, thinks Susie. Totally bonkers. She reaches over and pats her hand. 'Not everyone's perfect. The sooner you get the hang of that the better.' She picks up the wine and fills up her glass then points the bottle at Rose. 'Drink up. It'll put some colour back in those cheeks of yours.'

Lily isn't a good night driver and the hammering rain only makes it worse but eventually she arrives at Finn's. Slamming the car door shut behind her, she makes a dash for the porch. She knocks on the door but there's no answer so she runs round to the back and knocks again. The distant sound of music drifts across the lawn from the studio. She turns towards the soft light, shining in speckled beams across the silvery grass that shimmers in the rain. One of the windows has been boarded up, she notices as she sprints towards it. She slips on the wet ground and almost falls but rights herself. By the time she reaches the open door, she's soaking wet and panting. She hangs on to the frame to catch her breath.

The CD player is cranked up and Mumford & Sons are singing loudly about the *Little Lion Man*. The dying embers of a fire burn in the grate. Finn stands at his workbench, his back to her, totally absorbed in his work. The room is warm and snug after the rain. Motionless, she watches Finn smooth out the chisel marks on the stone with a hook-ended riffler, oblivious to her presence. The figure of the girl he's working on is clothed but striking a wanton pose, her back arched, her head and arms thrown back. She glances at the piece Finn calls *The Secret* in its usual place on the rickety, oak mantelpiece above the fireplace. There are similarities between the two – large eyes, slender body. The same girl, perhaps? She looks back at Finn who has stopped smoothing and is stroking the stone, intimately, lovingly, as though he's involved with his creation somehow.

He smiles, puts it down and moves towards his tools. Catching sight of her lurking in the shadows, he starts in surprise. 'Lily!'

She bites her lip. 'I'm sorry. You're working.'

Finn smiles and scrapes back a handful of his hair. 'Never mind that, it's good to see you. How are ya?'

'I'm okay,' she begins hesitantly, looking down at her hands. 'I just … I had to come.'

Finn rushes over and embraces her. 'You're soaking wet.'

She clings to his shirt unsure of how to explain herself.

'Let me get you a towel.'

'No. Wait. Hold me.'

He squeezes her tight. 'I've been thinking about you,' he whispers.

'I got your letter. I was going to text you but I lost my phone. I'm sorry, Finn.'

'Do *not* apologise. You have nothing to be sorry for. I'm very glad you're here.'

Lily sniffs. She pulls away and wipes her nose with a soaking wet sleeve. 'Adam had a mistress. A secret flat. He took cocaine. He broke the law ...' she pauses.

Finn just looks at her, head on one side, listening.

'His mistress ... She was pregnant. And it hurts. It really, really hurts, right here.' She thumps her chest with her fist. 'She's beautiful, of course.'

'But not as beautiful as you, I'll bet my life on that.'

'She's tall and foreign and elegant. Nat was right. I was punching above my weight with Adam.'

Finn leans down and wipes the lone tear that has escaped her control. 'That's absolute shite, Lily. You're beautiful in every way it's possible to be.' He places his hand over his heart. 'Real beauty comes from here and it's far more precious than a pretty face or a lovely pair of legs. You're radiant. You glow from inside. You only have to walk into a room and my spirits lift. You can't buy that. It's innate.'

'You don't know what you're talking about. You don't know me.'

Finn reaches out and holds her face in his hands. 'I do know you. I've known you for a year, give or take a few days. We're friends and not a day goes by when I don't think how lucky I am we met.'

Lily feels as though she's tried and failed to pass through a doorway only to collide with the frame. Her body doesn't seem to belong to her. It's a separate thing, awkward and cumbersome. She pushes his hands away and walks over to the broken window.

'How's Archie?' she mumbles.

He places one hand on her shoulder and gently steers her round to face him. 'He flew away.'

She peers into the fathomless pit of his coal-black eyes. 'Oh no. That's terrible. I loved that little dove. Did something frighten him?'

Finn fiddles with the bangles on his wrist. 'Yes I think it did.'

'Will he come back?'

'I don't know.'

'It's a ghostly parallel. I lose my husband and you lose a dove.'

'It's not quite the same in terms of tragedies,' he says, scratching his upper arm, as though the conversation is making him uncomfortable.

'I'm sorry. Am I being morbid?'

'A little.'

He takes Lily's hand again and opens his mouth a fraction, as though he's about to say something but touches his top lip with his tongue instead. He moves closer and cups her face again. Lily's heart is beating rapidly but not with shock this time. She inclines her head, pressing it into his hand. His gorgeous mouth, slightly parted, is a millimetre from hers. Finn draws closer and their lips meet but only for a second. The tips of his fingers caress her neck as his mouth skims across her cheek then back to her lips. Her body tingles at the touch of his tongue, soft and sweet. One kiss. The most natural thing in the world.

'I can't do this,' she cries, crashing back down to earth. She wrenches herself free and starts pacing haphazardly around the room, pulling at her jacket. What was she thinking?

'Lily, it's okay.'

'No it isn't. Well, maybe it is for you. But Adam hasn't been dead a week. You can't possibly have any idea how I feel. I was disorientated for a moment. You were being so kind. I didn't know what I was doing.'

'I didn't mean to frighten you.'

She frowns. 'I'm not frightened.'

Finn reaches out to her and gently draws her to him. He runs his fingers through her hair and kisses her neck. Lily arches her back and moans as every part of her body starts to tremble. No. No, she thinks. She has to stop this, now. It feels so good but – no. This shouldn't be happening. She straightens up and puts her hands on his chest.

'I was watching you. You were totally absorbed in your work.'

'Yes I was but now you're here and—'

'You looked involved with the figure, somehow. Emotionally, I mean.'

'Well I guess that's because I am. Come on. I'll introduce you.' Bewildered, Lily allows Finn to lead her to the table. 'She's a friend and very dear to me. She's not like all the rest. I've watched her for ages, studied her in detail – her bones, her muscles, her mannerisms, her unique characteristics. No one knows her like I do. I've held her, touched her, felt and worked every inch of her body with my hands. It's an intimate relationship, as binding and powerful as if I'd made love to her.'

Did he mean to say that? Lily wonders. Is he making fun of me? She feels even more awkward than before, her body and mind in turmoil. She looks at the figure offering herself and feels inexplicably jealous.

'She's very beautiful, don't you think?' he asks.

A cold shiver creeps down Lily's spine. She feels like a gooseberry. 'She looks as though she knows what she wants.'

'Don't you recognise her?'

'Your girlfriend?' she asks, dreading the answer.

Finn smiles. 'Don't be daft. It's you, Lily.'

Her eyes bulge in amazement. 'But you work from models and I've never modelled for you.'

'No but your image is engraved in my mind – the way you bite your lower lip when you're anxious, the light in your golden eyes when you're happy, the self-conscious way you sometimes smile, the straight line of your lips when you're being brave, resolutely concealing your unhappiness from me.'

It's as though he's read her from cover to cover, like a book. Feeling giddy, she moves forward to steady herself. But instead of the tabletop, her hand rests on one of his instruments. A knife. The sharp blade slices into her finger. She gasps and puts her finger in her mouth to suck the blood.

'Let me wash it for you.' He steers Lily by the arm towards the small sink in the corner and holds her hand under the cold stream of water. She hopes he can't feel her shaking as he dabs the wound with a towel. 'I've got a plaster somewhere.'

'I'm fine. It's superficial. Not deep at all.'

He rifles through a drawer. 'Here we go!'

He wraps the plaster around her finger while words tumble out of her mouth. 'I'm not brave. I haven't got a secret. And I'm not beautiful either. I don't know why I'm here. I thought I had to be with you. I was wrong. And now I've made you angry. I should go.'

'Angry? I'm not angry. How could I be when you are all I want?' He opens his arms.

Lily hesitates. 'I thought you were making fun of me.'

He moves towards her and closes his arms around her. 'I felt it the moment I first saw you. I knew then that you were the one. And I've hated sitting back, knowing that you're hurting.'

She feels his lips on her neck, his hair on her cheek as tenderly, slowly he starts to removes her damp clothes. 'I want you,' he whispers.

216

Their lips brush, light as feathers. He presses his mouth to her ear. She feels his tongue, insistent but soft, and sighs, aching with desire. She pulls frantically at his clothes and moans. 'Oh God. Oh yes. I want you too.'

He leads her to the rug in front of the fire. 'Over here, away from the broken glass.'

33

Susie wakes from a night of uninterrupted sleep, a new woman. Fabian's Big Confession has stilled the turmoil in her mind. She wonders why she ever doubted him.

If you cut him in half he'd have loyalty running straight through him, she thinks. Of course he'd rush to the aid of a friend in crisis. That's the kind of man he is. It's one of the many qualities I love about him. And on this occasion in helping one friend he'd tried his damnedest to protect another. Three, if I include myself in the equation. That's why he lied to me. But that's where he went wrong. The idiot should have told *me* the truth. He should have trusted me. And if he had, we could have broken the news to Lily gently. It was tough on her, finding out this way. I wonder how she is this morning? I hope she had the sense to take a sleeping pill. She needs to sleep. Her tiny frame can't take much more.

Susie sighs and slips out of bed and tiptoes down the landing, to Lily's bedroom at the front of the house. The door is ajar so she pokes her head through the gap. The bed looks as though it's come second in a wrestling match. The duvet is lumped in a crumpled mound in the centre and the fitted sheet has come adrift, exposing a corner of the quilted mattress cover. On the floor beside the discarded pillows and an open shoebox and some bubble wrap, she sees an object lying on its side. Intrigued, she wanders over and sees it's a sculpture. She bends down and picks it up. It's fairly heavy and surprisingly cold to the touch. She scrutinises it for a while, running her hand over the smooth stone, trying to make sense of its significance. A present from Adam perhaps? A memory of happier days? But why keep it in a box?

She puts the figure back where she found it and quietly, so as not to wake Rose, makes her way back down the landing and the stairs. The bottom step creaks loudly. She stands in the hall and listens but the house is silent. She heads towards the kitchen. Lily isn't there. She crosses the hall and goes into the sitting room. No sign of Lily here either. She tries the dining room, the study. All empty. With a growing sense of panic, she opens the front door and scuttles painfully across the gravel in her bare feet. The garage is empty, the Mini gone.

Lily opens her eyes. She can't believe she's slept let alone overslept. Sunlight streams through the leafy branches of a lime tree and the open windows. She raises her head a fraction and peers at the naked body of Finn tangled up with hers, the crumpled sheet over the lower half of their legs, covered in dappled shadows. A somnolent smile plays on his lips. She wonders if he's dreaming about her. Memories of last night come flooding back, the two of them making love, first in the studio and, later, in his bed, as if their happiness depended on it. She closes her eyes and breathes in the peppery scent of him. Was it naïve of her not to have detected the signs? Or was she so deeply in love with Adam the idea had never sprung to mind. Happily married people don't have affairs.

Well that's not true, she thinks bitterly. If Fabian is to be believed then Adam did. Perhaps it was the rush he was after. The buzz he got from being unfaithful. Or was it simply because he could, because like Mallory's Everest, Honor was there.

I could drive myself mad wondering, she thinks. I thought I knew Adam. I mean, really knew him: every mannerism, every ritual, his likes, dislikes, dreams and fears, his superstitions. His favourite food, pasta, his favourite music, rock, and his favourite colour, green. I thought I knew him better than I know myself. But I didn't know he was cheating on me. Didn't even guess. And now he's dead. And here I am lying in the arms of another man barely a week later. Am I ready for this?

She snuggles closer and runs her fingers over the tanned, hairless skin of Finn's chest, as smooth and unsullied as one of his sculptures, but warm. I might as well enjoy it, she thinks. Who knows how long it will last.

'Mmm. That feels good,' he says, his voice gravelly with sleep. He opens his eyes, slides on top of her and kisses the top of her breast. 'Oh God, the smell of you.'

'I can't,' she whispers, as his tongue toys with her nipple. 'No,' she says, eeling out from under him. 'I've got to go. If I'm not back soon I'll have some difficult explaining to do.'

Finn rolls on to his back. He yawns loudly and stretches his arms above his head. 'I was looking forward to a whole day in bed with you,' he says, turning on to his side and resting on his elbow. 'My God, Lily, look at you. You're—'

'Finn, don't.' She places a finger to his lips and frowns. 'Susie and Rose have probably got the police out searching for me.' She checks her watch and levers herself up like a sheet of metal folded in two. 'It's eight-thirty already. What was I thinking?'

Finn reaches out and strokes her back. 'Will you be all right?'

'Probably not.'

'Then let me come with you.'

'You know you can't do that.'

The sun that was shining so brilliantly when she woke has disappeared behind leaden clouds. Lily drives home in silence wondering what it is that she's just done. The cold hand of reality grips. Dread and despondency return with a vengeance. She parks the car in the garage and sits in silence for a moment before crossing the drive. With a bit of luck,

220

Susie and Rose will still be asleep, she thinks as she unlocks the door.

Susie intercepts her in the hallway, hands on hips. 'Where have you been?'

'I just popped out.' She is about to add *to get some* milk but she is empty-handed. She's never been any good at lying, so to speak now would be to betray herself. She sidles around Susie and heads for the stairs.

'I've been up for hours, you know,' says Susie.

Her heart beating a guilty rhythm, she continues to climb. She can feel Susie's eyes on her back but she doesn't turn around.

'Lily! Where have you been?'

She stops, one hand clinging to the banister and looks over shoulder. Susie's face is mottled, her fists clenched stiffly by her sides like an irate mother faced with a naughty teenager.

'I needed some air. A change of scene.'

'With him?'

'Him?'

'Yes him!'

'Who?'

'You know perfectly well who I mean. The sculptor who wrote that letter you keep in the drawer of your bedside table.'

Anger prickles her skin. 'You had no right going through my things.'

'I found a stone figure on the floor of your bedroom. You'd disappeared. I was worried about you.'

This is torture. Finn is *her* secret. He always has been. Susie has no right to interrogate her. She purses her lips.

'Fine. Don't tell me. You don't have to anyway. Your body language says it all.'

The phone rings. Sensing an opportunity to end the conversation, Lily charges back down the stairs, barging past Susie to answer it.

'Hello,' she says breathlessly.

'Lily?'

'Hello, Miles.'

'You okay?'

'Yes fine.'

'Good. Nat's recovered.'

She's forgotten about Nat. He's alive. Well bully for him. There's silence on the other end of the line as Miles waits for a response. When none is forthcoming he continues.

'He'll be discharged later today. I think he's a bit embarrassed about his performance yesterday, even though he can't remember much.'

Susie, watching her like a hawk, folds her arms and starts tapping her foot.

'I'm not surprised,' Lily says.

'Are you okay? Did you sleep?'

'Yes I did,' she says truthfully.

'I thought you sounded better. How's Rose?'

She groans. She's forgotten about her. 'Still asleep, I think.'

'I'll drop by and collect her just as soon as I can.'

Lily replaces the receiver and turns around slowly to face Susie. 'Miles,' she says.

'I gathered.'

Like a boxer taking to the floor again, Lily braces herself for round two.

'You're supposed to be my best friend. And as far as I can remember best friends share secrets and support one another,' says Susie.

'So support me why don't you. I've had a pretty shitty time.'

'Do you think I don't know that? Do you think I don't know how much you're hurting? But if I'm going to continue to support you, I need to understand what the hell is going on? Are you seeing the sculptor?'

'Finn. His name is Finn.' The moment she speaks his name her spirits lift. She feels lighter. The ease with which she has transferred her affections to another man astonishes her. Her husband hasn't set one bony metatarsal in his grave but she has Finn. She is going to be all right.

'So you *are* seeing him.'

The urge to share her secret with her best friend is overpowering. 'Yes. Yes I am.'

'You lying cow!' screams Susie.

'I was upset. Honor. The baby. Nat. Rose. Delaney. You know, they got to me. I had to see him,' says Lily all in a rush, knocked off balance by Susie's response.

Susie thrusts a thumb to her chest. 'I was here. You could have talked to me.'

'But Finn is a friend too. Just a friend.'

'And that makes it all right I suppose.'

Clearly it was not *all right* with her. 'No, that's not what I'm saying. I meant I slept with him last night for the first time. I'm devastated by Adam's death and—'

'You're a fast mover, Lily. You claim to have been besotted with Adam, yet all the time you've been seeing another man. Okay, so maybe you weren't screwing him when Adam was alive but now he's oh-so-conveniently-dead, you leap into bed with him without a thought for the consequences.'

'If you mean how it would affect us then I'm sorry Susie but I'm finding Adam's secrets a bit difficult to digest at the moment.'

Susie stares at her contemptuously. 'I'm well aware of that. And I'm as shocked as you are, which is why I am amazed you're so certain Finn had nothing to do with his death.'

'What? Are you mad? Finn never met Adam. Besides, the police have arrested Delaney.'

'And you're sure he's guilty are you?'

'Marshall told me that seventy per cent of all murders are committed by—'

'Just listen to yourself, Lily. You're pathetic.'

'Oh that's rich coming from you. Your boyfriend disappeared—'

'So tell the police then,' she interrupts defiantly, hands on hips.

'Tell them what?'

'About your relationship with Finn. If you're so sure he's innocent, you won't have any problem telling the police. Unless, of course, they know already.'

Lily can't believe what she is hearing. She stares at her friend incredulous. 'Are you jealous? Is that what this is about?'

Susie throws back her head and laughs. 'Be reasonable!'

'No I won't be reasonable. I'm fed up with being reasonable. Being reasonable got me into this mess. No. Reasonable is the wrong word. I've been walking around for eighteen months with blinkers on. And I'm not prepared to do that any longer. I deserve a life as much as the next person.' Lily's voice has risen to a furious crescendo, her face an angry red. 'Stand by Fabian by all means.'

'I wasn't aware that I *was* standing by Fabian.'

But Lily isn't listening. 'Ruin your life but please leave me alone to get on with mine.'

She crosses the hall and opens the front door. 'When Fabian is arrested for the murder of my husband, don't come running to me,' she says, slamming the door behind her.

34

Storm clouds are gathering above the farmhouse, scudding across the sky, large and menacing as horror-film villains in billowing black cloaks. Lily tears round the house to the garden. She hears Finn before she sees him, metal scraping stone as he rakes out the soiled wood shavings in the dovecote. He smiles when he sees her, his broad grin stretching up to his eyes, drops his rake and gathers her up in his arms.

'I didn't expect to see you again so soon,' he says, spinning around.

'I didn't expect to be here.'

Finn sets her down and holds her gently by the arms, aware that something is wrong. 'What happened?'

'I had a fight with my best friend. She wasn't pleased when she found out where I'd been.'

'Ah!'

She tilts her face to his. 'Make love to me again.'

The smell of their lovemaking lingers in the sultry air above the bed. Lily lies naked in Finn's arms. His liquorice eyes fixed on her, she recounts the events of the past five days.

'My poor, dear Lily Green,' he says, when she has finished.

She waits for him to say something more, tracing the crease that bisects his cheek with her index finger. She wonders what it is she hopes he might say. He knew nothing about her life with Adam. Now here she is revealing everything to him in all its sordid glory.

'It's funny you still call me that,' she says eventually.

'You'll always be Lily Green to me.'

She attempts a smile but fails, her mouth quivering at the corners. 'I can't help wondering why Adam didn't leave me for her. He was desperate to start a family.'

Finn stares pensively into the distance, holding his top lip between his teeth a second before letting it go. 'The man without eyes is no judge of beauty.'

Lily isn't sure she understands what he means. 'Maybe I got what I deserved.'

He turns back and throws her a cock-eyed look. 'How do you work that one out?'

'For deceiving him about being friends with you.'

Finn crinkles his forehead. Thinking she's upset him, Lily slides on top of him and kisses him, searching out his tongue with hers. He returns her kisses but without the passion of earlier, then gently prises her off him, back on to the bed.

He props himself up on one elbow and runs his fingers through her hair. 'I need to tell you something.'

She tenses. It's a phrase she's heard a lot recently but not, as yet, from Finn. Something about his downbeat tone startles her. She reaches for the sheet and covers herself, suddenly self-conscious. 'Go on.'

Finn flings himself on his back, his hands behind his head, and stares at the ceiling. 'I sort of knew Adam.'

She stares at him incredulous. 'No you didn't.'

'The flat he bought for … the one in Chelsea …' He pauses, twists on to his elbow and looks her in the eye again. 'My sister rented one of the rooms and I was helping her move out the day Adam took possession. Honor was with him. I could see they were close because they couldn't keep their hands off each other, not that I thought anything of it at the time. I had no idea who they were. I thought they were just another happy couple moving in together. We spoke briefly on the stairs. He introduced himself as Adam. It wasn't until he died I made the connection. I recognised his face from the picture in the newspaper.'

She cannot believe what she's hearing. 'But you didn't tell me.'

'It didn't seem the right time.'

Is there a right time? she wonders. 'So you knew he'd been unfaithful when we made love.' Duplicity, an ever-persistent bully, has punched her below the belt once too often.

'Yes, Lily. I did.'

'After everything I've just told you, you think that's fair?'

'It's not a question of being fair or unfair. I'm telling you now because of how we feel about each other. I don't want us to have secrets. You've been honest with me and I am being honest with you too.'

'But you haven't been honest, have you?'

'Please, don't be angry.' He sits up and wrenches the sheet from Lily's hand and laces his fingers through hers.

She pulls her hand away. 'But you knew Adam had a mistress. You'd worked it out and yet you didn't tell me. I had to find out about it from Fabian,' she says, unable to let the comment go.

'Lily, I'm sorry. I know you've suffered and I hate that. But it didn't feel right that I should be the one to tell you.'

'Why not? Too scared, is that it?' Her voice is fierce.

'No. That's not it at all.'

'I trusted you, Finn.'

'It's because I love you. I couldn't bear to hurt you. I hoped you wouldn't find out.'

She bristles. 'I have to go,' she says, sliding off the bed with the sheet clasped to her chin.

'Stay. Please.'

Lily drops the sheet to the floor and quickly pulls on her T-shirt. She tugs on her knickers and wriggles into her jeans, staring at a point beyond him.

He leaps out of bed and drapes his arms around her shoulders. 'I'm begging you.'

But Lily can't get out of there fast enough. She shrugs him off, zips up her jeans, picks up her shoes and hurries out of the room without a backward glance.

The first time Rose woke up it was to the sound of Susie and Lily arguing downstairs. Unable to face the world and its worries, she wrapped her head in her pillow and fell back into a deep sleep.

Waking a second time, an hour later, all is quiet. Sleep has revived her. Feeling better than she has in ages, she sits up and glances around the large room, at the blue and yellow floral curtains and the large mahogany chest of drawers, at her folded white shirt with the pinks spots and her jeans on the lemon slipper chair, her pale pink trainers stacked beneath. He had it all, she thinks. Good looks, money, a fabulous home, a pretty wife, but it wasn't enough for him. She recalls the last conversation they had and sneers. Selfish bastard got what he deserved.

I like it here, she thinks. I like the peace and quiet of the countryside, the birdsong, the lambs, the fresh air, the endless space. It's healthy. I should have come down sooner. She springs out of bed and pulls the curtains apart with one swift movement. It's dark outside, black clouds threatening rain. She peers up at the sky hoping to spot a chink of blue. When she can't, she sighs and pads across the soft, beige carpet to the en suite bathroom. She lingers in the shower, luxuriating in the hot water and jasmine gel, before getting dressed and trudging downstairs. She calls out but no one answers. The house is deserted. She wanders into the kitchen and sees a note addressed to her on the table.

Hi Rose,
Sorry to desert you but I need some space.
Lily has gone walkabout.
Will call later.
Susie.

'Some friend?' she says out loud, screwing the paper up into a neat little ball.

Lily drives about half a mile down the country lane before pulling up in a lay-by. She wishes she'd had a shower. The smell of Finn cleaves to her skin like a reproach. She winds down her window and fans the air with her hands then checks her mobile that's plugged into the cigarette lighter, charging. Two missed calls from Rose and one from Marshall. Brilliant. That's all she needs. She dials home.

'Oh, Lily. I'm glad you've called,' says Rose, her gratitude evident in her tone of voice. 'Susie's gone.'

She grits her teeth. 'Good.'

'Oh. Right.' She sounds surprised. 'Are you okay?'

'I'm fine. I'm on my way home.'

'Oh, that's good. I was worried.'

'Well don't. It doesn't suit you.'

She cuts the connection not wanting to get into a conversation. She's annoyed she's still there. She thought Miles was picking her up. He must have been held up at the hospital. Poor Miles. Running around keeping everyone sweet. They'd all be lost without Miles.

She puffs out her cheeks and, with a certain amount of trepidation, dials Marshall's number.

35

Marshall's car sweeps into the drive as Lily is parking the Mini in the garage. She climbs out quickly and hurries across the gravel to unlock the front door, wondering how to broach the subject of Finn. Marshall follows her, without uttering a word, into the kitchen. His chin is covered in a day's worth of spiky growth, sandy in places, grey in others, she notices. His linen jacket is crumpled and his shirt, less-than-white. Either he's slept in his clothes and hasn't bothered to shave, or he's worked through the night. The dark hollows beneath his eyes hint at the latter. He's a tough bastard, she thinks as she switches on the kettle, but I suppose he has to be. It's a tough job. I wonder what kind of backup he's got. What his domestic life is like. Maybe he's married and lives in a comfortable home with lots of mini-Marshalls running around it; a retreat he escapes to each evening, the welcoming smell of home-cooked food greeting him as he walks through the door. That would keep him sane. Or maybe he's been unlucky in love. Maybe he's living the life of a confirmed bachelor, married only to his job, flopping tired and hungry onto a threadbare sofa in a messy flat at the end of each working day, a white-paper parcel of fish and chips for supper again.

Marshall pulls out a chair simultaneously suppressing a yawn and drops the buff file he's carrying on the table.

'Late night, Chief Inspector?' she asks.

'Yeah, you could say that. My soon to be ex-wife was up to her tricks again, banging on the door of my flat in the middle of the night demanding to talk.'

So married but unhappy, she thinks. 'I'm sorry to hear that. Have you been married long?'

230

'Ten years. That's a pretty hefty sentence by anyone's standards. So yes, I'd call it long. It certainly feels like it. My wife can't stand my job, the unpredictable hours. She hates having to cancel things. I guess that's why she has affairs. She won't admit to them but the evidence is there – the cheery disposition, the dramatic weight loss, the drawer of sexy underwear. Fortunately we don't have kids, her choice not mine, so no lives will be ruined.'

It's more information than she's bargained for. She wishes she hadn't asked. 'I'm sorry.'

'No need. Marriage is overrated. The sooner the divorce comes through the better. I gather from the elusive Mr Stephens you had some bad news yesterday.'

What a way to prove a point, she thinks, frowning. The kettle boils. She swallows her irritation and smiles at the detective. 'Can I get you something to drink? Tea? Coffee?'

'Tea would be great, thank you. Listen, seeing how we're spending so much time together, how about you call me Danny?'

Danny? His sudden friendliness surprises her. 'Okay.'

'You'll be pleased to hear that at last I have some good news.'

'Oh?' she asks, fishing for the teabag with a spoon.

'DI Hammond had another little chat with Carly Stoner's boyfriend, Liam Smith, this morning. It turns out he was Adam's pusher.'

'Really?' It seems unlikely, she thinks as she hands him the mug. By all accounts – the press, Adam's – Carly Stoner was a fitness fanatic. The dealer, Liam Smith, was an unhealthy no-hoper.

'Thank you.' He rummages through the file with his free hand and produces a police photo, which he places on the table. 'Is this the man who held you at gunpoint?'

She casts her eyes over the familiar acne-covered face. Her skin crawls at the memory. 'Yes it is. Did he kill Adam?'

Marshall clicks his tongue. 'No, he didn't.'

Lily frowns, confused. 'What makes you so sure?' she asks, walking around to the other side of the table and sitting down. 'He owns a gun and has a motive.'

'Liam was involved with a drug ring run by a depraved individual who goes by the name of The Baron. Not very original, I know. Anyway, Liam was late with his payments. He owed The Baron thousands of pounds. The Baron wasn't amused and sent one of his henchmen to instil a little sense into him. If Liam didn't cough up in three days, someone close to him would be hurt. Liam couldn't so they went for Carly. I thought all along there were two killers at work. Carly's murder bore the hallmarks of a professional killer. Adam's didn't.' He takes a sip of tea.

'Could Liam be lying?'

'No. He's agreed to act as an informant in exchange for police protection. It's great news for the drug squad. They're about to bust one of the biggest rings in the country. And it'll be one in the eye for the media.' Marshall leans back in his chair. 'By the way, Stephens was more than happy to give us a written statement about what he's been doing these past few days. We'll check his movements to and from the hotel and speak to Honor Vincente as well. Meanwhile, Forensics has confirmed the blood on Adam's shirt is Alex Delaney's. Unfortunately it's not enough to convict him.'

Lily winces. She'd forgotten about him. 'Why not?'

'His wife rather conveniently provided an alibi. According to her he never left London. Mind you, wives of bullies are not the most reliable sources. They're often too scared to tell the truth.'

'Poor woman,' mutters Lily.

'We all have choices.'

It was uncharacteristic of him to offer an opinion. Is that how he thinks of me? she wonders.

He leans forward, and rests his elbows on the table. 'Susie Ashton not with you?'

'Er ... no. She left this morning.'

Marshall raises a quizzical eyebrow. He has another sip of tea then puts the mug down and removes his notebook from the outer pocket of his jacket. 'Now about this bizarre piece of forensic information I mentioned on the phone. It's a bit of a long shot but I wanted to run it by you on the off-chance.'

'Okay,' she says, as yet another opening to tell him about Finn closes.

'It concerns the animal blood on Adam's hands. The team finally tracked down the relevant specialist. It matches the blood of a family of birds called Columbidae.'

'Bird blood?'

'Extraordinary, isn't it? Zenaida macroura, in fact. It took them a while because Zenaida macroura is not an indigenous species.'

'Latin never was my strongest subject,' she says, suppressing a yawn.

'A Mourning Dove. They're common in America, apparently. Very occasionally, they migrate south from Canada in winter. There's been the odd sighting in Western Europe but never one in Britain.'

It's as if she's charged into an unstable brick wall at full speed. She listens, stunned.

'I've been mulling over this conundrum for the past few days, trying to make sense of the unlikely coupling of a murder victim and a Mourning Dove. I rang the RSPB in case a sighting has been reported in Sussex, but it hasn't. The Mourning Dove, like most other doves I'm told, lives off a diet of grain so it's likely to have ended up on farmland. It's a long shot but does it mean anything to you?'

Lily is struggling. Her heart is in her throat. She coughs suddenly and violently and grabs her neck.

Marshall springs up and hurries over to her. 'Are you okay?'

'Archie! It's Archie.'

'I'm certain it's a Mourning Dove,' he says, not comprehending.

'Yes. Archie. The dove. Archie.'

'I'm not following you. Try and get your breath back. Take a few deep breaths, in through your nose. That's right. Good and slow then out through your mouth.'

Lily does as she is told, heaving up air, the solid form of Danny Marshall hovering over her while she inflates and deflates her lungs. How great does a shock have to be to kill? she wonders miserably. Can an accumulation of shocks kill a person? And if so how many shocks does it take? Is she lucky to be alive?

'Well done, Lily. Keep breathing. Take your time. I'm just going to get you a glass of water.'

Her mind is racing, hurtling around the hairpin bends of her brain. Why did Adam have Archie's blood on him? Did he know where Finn lived? How was the dove involved? Didn't Finn tell her Archie had flown away? Did Adam find him bleeding to death somewhere near our home? No. Surely Finn would have told me. Wouldn't he? A couple of days ago she'd have answered yes. But after this morning, she wasn't so sure.

'The Mourning Dove that settled at Finn's place,' she says quietly, taking the glass of water offered.

'Finn?'

It's the moment she's been dreading. 'Finn Costello. A sculptor. He keeps doves.'

'A friend of yours?'

She takes a sip of water then places the glass on the table. 'Yes.'

'Was Finn Costello a friend of Adam's also?'

'No, he wasn't.'

'Could you tell me a little bit about your relationship with Mr Costello?'

Lily's shoulders droop. She is weary, wrung-out like an overused rag. 'A friend. A sculptor. I met him in Lewes at an exhibition about a year ago. I used to visit him in his farmhouse just south of Lewes.'

'And did Adam know of these visits?'

'No. I didn't tell him.'

'Why? Were you having an affair?'

'No. Not then but—'

Marshall's stare is penetrating. 'But you are now?'

'Yes. No. I was but—' Lily breaks off unsure of what she is trying to say.

Marshall leans down and thumps the table. 'But what?'

Lily jumps. 'The affair, if you can call it that, began last night and ended today. I loved my husband. But I was lonely. Since Adam was killed it's as if I didn't know him.' She stops. What could she possibly say that would explain her actions? 'I was in shock. Finn was a friend.'

Marshall draws himself up to his full height. 'So you're telling me that the affair lasted less than twenty-four hours. Why was that? What happened?'

There is a discernible tinge of anger to his voice. He seems to tower over her. She lowers her eyes. 'I'm sorry, I can't do this.'

'Lily, you do realise that in concealing your relationship with Finn Costello you've been perverting the course of justice. If it was deliberate then it is a crime. So I suggest you answer my question however reluctant you might be.'

When Lily speaks again it is in a small voice. 'Finn met Adam a year ago at the London Flat. His sister had been renting a room and he was helping her move out the day Adam and Honor moved in. I didn't know until this morning.'

Marshall strokes the stubble on his chin. As she watches him, the skin beneath his eyes seems to sag and darken. 'Is it possible Adam was aware of your relationship?'

'No. Definitely not.'

'So you never kept in touch, by email, for example?'

Lily shakes her head.

'Or sent one another text messages?'

She gasps. 'My mobile. I lost it.'

'When?'

'The last time I remember using it was the day Adam died.'

'And had you texted Finn that day?'

She groans inwardly. 'Yes. I texted him to tell him I was coming over.'

'So you were with Finn Costello the day of Adam's murder and not in Lewes shopping as previously stated?'

She feels like a steak on a grill, raw on one side, roasting to the point of burning on the other, aware that she's about to be flipped over. 'Yes.'

The air whistles as he blows it through his teeth. 'So you lied to the police and wasted a great deal of our time.'

'I can't begin to tell you how sorry I am,' she says idiotically, her humiliation complete.

'Why did you lie about Finn? What were you hoping to achieve?'

'Our friendship was a secret. I suppose I lied out of habit. As far as I was concerned, Finn didn't know Adam.'

'But Adam was dead. It didn't matter who knew about Finn, did it?'

'It mattered to me. I didn't want Nat to know for one thing. Carly's boyfriend supplied him too, by the way, not that it's relevant now I suppose.'

'How many times ...' he stops and inhales deeply through his nose, as he clings desperately to his patience. Lily slinks lower in her chair. 'Adam would have been angry if he read the messages on your phone. Violent most probably, given the stress he was under and the cocaine he'd taken. Was Finn Costello's number entered under his full name?'

'Yes,' she replies, thinking Susie's idea of making up nicknames was not so crazy after all.

'You've been unbelievably stupid and naïve. I should caution you on the spot.

Lily cowers under the intensity of his gaze.

236

'It's no longer inconceivable that you killed your husband. You sure as hell have a big enough motive,' he says snatching Liam's photo and stuffing it back in the file.

'But I didn't ... I couldn't—'

'You lied before. You could be lying now.'

'I wasn't being wilful. Truly I wasn't.'

'Listen to yourself. This is a murder investigation, not a frigging Mills and Boon.'

She bows her head. 'I'm sorry. I'm very, very sorry.'

'Write down Mr Costello's telephone numbers while I call the station,' he says, tearing a page out of his notebook and thrusting it at her. 'The mobile only works in the garden, am I right?'

'Yes but feel free to use the—' But Marshall has already prised the glass doors open and has one foot outside.

Lily slumps forward, her elbows resting on the table and holds her head in her hands. Had something gone on between Finn and Adam on the night of the murder? And if it had, why had Finn kept it from her? She can think of two reasons. One: Finn didn't want to hurt her. Two: he was her husband's murderer. She shivers. The second reason is too awful to contemplate.

Think, Lily, think, she urges herself.

If Adam read the text messages, given the mood he was in, the stress he was under, then he might have put two and two together and made at least five. Finn is a local sculptor, well-known with a good reputation. It wouldn't have been hard for Adam to find out where he lived. He expected to find me at home. He wanted to speak to me about something – cocaine, Delaney, Honor, the flat – I don't know. He'd have been frustrated I was out. He might have driven round to Finn's farmhouse and attacked him. And maybe Finn, in defending himself, stabbed Adam with one of his knives. She glances at the plaster on her finger and shivers, recalling how easily the blade had sliced through her skin.

But Finn is such a gentle man. I can't believe he's capable of harming anything or anyone. Adam's death was brutal and savage. Do I really believe Finn continued to slash at Adam's body well after he'd died then hauled him into his Land Rover, before driving to the bridle path to dump his body?

And what about Archie? His blood? What happened to him?

She bangs her forehead on the table. Susie advised her to tell Marshall about Finn but she ignored her. And now she is paying the price. She feels dirty, contaminated by Finn; his lies, his flattery, his body. What an idiot she's been jumping into bed with him. Talk about on the rebound. It wasn't as if he lured her either. Lonely and desperate, she leaped into his open arms quite willingly. Worse still, Susie offered her support but she turned her down.

If only she was here, she thinks, as she writes down Finn's address.

Marshall strides into the room, sliding the door closed behind him with undisguised aggression.

Trembling, Lily hands him the piece of paper. 'I've written down his address and his mobile number.'

Marshall snatches it. 'Some advice, Lily, before I go. Be careful. Don't turn detective again, and be selective about who you speak to.'

36

Lily stands in the hallway, disembowelled by Marshall's words. Her body feels hollow yet as heavy as lead and worse, she still reeks of Finn. Overpowering, irritating, offensive, it animates her and she charges upstairs desperate to get rid of it.

Rose pops out of the front spare bedroom, on to the landing. She's wearing running shoes, Lycra leggings and a crop-top that reveals her taut stomach. 'Is everything all right?' she asks. 'I heard voices. Thought it best to stay out the way.'

'DCI Marshall,' says Lily, staring at the red ribbon Rose has tied around her ponytail. 'And you thought right.' Her skin itches, distracting her. She scratches her wrists.

'Are you coming out in hives?' Rose asks. 'Stress can do that you know.'

'I need a shower.'

Rose shifts her weight. 'Can we talk?' she asks, as if she hasn't heard her.

Lily frowns. 'Later.'

Rose reaches out to touch her arm but Lily recoils and Rose withdraws her hand. 'It's important.'

'I'm tired. I really want a shower.'

'When I get back then?'

'Why? Where are you going?'

'For a run.'

'Are you completely mad?'

'I'll stick to the roads as I always do.'

Lily shrugs. She's too tired to argue. She dodges past Rose and backs into her room quickly, so that Rose doesn't get a whiff of Finn's odour.

'I'll be back in an hour,' says Rose.

'See you later then.'

Relieved Rose does not possess Susie's nose for deception, Lily closes the door behind her. She rips her Finn-infected clothes from her body and hurries into the limestone-tiled cubicle in the bathroom. Standing beneath the powerful jet of water she scrubs the perfumed bar of soap frantically over her skin.

Fifteen minutes later the water runs tepid. Lily places what's left of the soap in the metal tray and sniffs her arm. It's red and stinging but smells strongly of grapefruit. She steps out of the shower, wraps a fluffy, white towel around her and collapses on to the bed. Her body is clean to the point of sterilised but no amount of washing can erase the dark and dismal thoughts that plague her mind.

An aching silence hangs over Orchard House. She groans and squeezes her eyes shut and coaxes her bewildered brain back to the evening of Adam's death, the only time she spoke to Finn about her husband. He handed her a glass of wine. They sat in the sun. She felt relaxed and was on the verge of pouring out her heart. Finn had hugged her. Nothing unusual about that. But he'd been bare-chested and had suggested she stay and meet his sister. She remembers she felt awkward, which is why she left. Adam must have arrived home when she was out. Did he find her mobile, read the messages, then drive over to Finn's place to have it out with him?

Lily drags herself to her feet and delves through the wardrobe for some clean clothes. She finds a pair of white jeans and a beige cotton jumper and puts them on, then picks up the Finn-infested ones in the tips of her fingers. Holding them at arm's length, she negotiates the stairs and the hall and deposits them in the washing machine in the utility room off the kitchen. She pours twice as much washing liquid into the tray as necessary and turns the programme to sixty degrees/heavy stains. As she is setting the dial, she hears a loud knocking on the front door and jolts half out of her skin. Cautiously, she walks into the hall.

'Who is it?' she calls out.

'It's me. Miles.'

At last, she thinks.

'And I've a surprise for you.'

Lily is not in the mood for surprises. She's had enough to last a lifetime. She opens the door, fearing the worst. But a pleasant sight meets her eyes. Standing beside Miles is Susie. She smiles and is about to fling her arms around her when a strange thought enters her head.

What if I can't trust these two?

'Have you eaten anything today?' Susie's tone is motherly, protective. 'Do you feel up to some soup? I picked some up from the village store on the way over. It's chicken. Kosher medicine.'

The smile on Lily's lips fades and she stares at them, rooted to the spot as the wheels of her imagination turn.

'I'll take that as a yes then,' says Susie, stepping inside. 'Excuse me while I go and warm it up.'

Miles peers at her over the top of his glasses. 'You okay?'

You're losing it, she thinks, shaking herself. Susie and Miles are your best friends. 'Yes, I'm fine. And thanks for bringing Susie back.'

'It was easy. She walked to Berwick station, caught the train to Easthaven, called me and asked me to drive her back. Now where's Rose? I'm in a bit of a hurry.'

'Er … Actually, she's not here. She's gone for a jog.'

'Really? Is that wise?'

Lily feels a prick of guilt. She'd been so desperate to jump into the shower and get rid of all traces of Finn, she's barely given Rose a thought since then. 'She said she'd stick to the roads.'

Miles shakes his head in disbelief. 'Stupid girl.'

'Quite,' she says, relieved. She half-expected him to be cross she hadn't talked her out of going.

'Did she talk to you about Adam? Goldbergs?'

She sighs. 'Not yet, no. She wanted to but I couldn't face it.'

Miles puffs out his cheeks and looks at his watch. 'I've got to dash. Fabian called from the police station to ask if he could drop by, and Nat's on his way back from the hospital. They're probably both camped on the pavement waiting for me.'

'You can't go. What about Rose? Supper?'

'I'll pick up Rose tomorrow. I promise.'

Lily pulls a face.

Miles reaches out and softly pinches her cheek. 'It'll be okay. Susie will look after you. Call me if you need anything.'

She manages a weak smile. Poor Miles, she thinks. He must be finding it difficult too. Adam was like a brother to him. 'Thanks, Miles.'

'What for?'

'You know,' she shrugs sheepishly, 'everything.'

She walks to the front door with him, hugs him goodbye then hurries into the kitchen. Susie is at the hob, stirring the soup in the saucepan. She takes a deep breath. 'I'm sorry I was such a bitch.'

Susie shrugs without taking her eye off the soup. 'S'okay. I probably deserved it.'

'It seems you might have been right about Finn. It turns out he lied to me. He knew Adam. Even saw him the day he died.'

Susie's jaw drops open. She turns and looks at Lily, wide-eyed. 'Blimey!'

'You were right. I should have told the police about him.'

'It was just a feeling. I had no idea.' She opens the cupboard where Lily stores the crockery. 'Is Rose still here? '

'She's gone for a jog.'

Susie rolls her eyes. 'A jog? She's off her rocker, that girl. We had the weirdest conversation last night. She kept banging on about responsibility and principles and how tough life is with George. I'm telling you, she needs a shag. It might knock some sense into her.' She takes some bowls out of the cupboard then ladles up the soup.

'I'm not sure I agree with you,' says Lily, carrying the steaming hot bowls to the table. 'My mind's a mess.'

'Ah!' says Susie, sitting down. 'Good point, Lil.' She sighs. 'So Adam knew Finn?'

'Not exactly,' she says before explaining what Finn and Marshall had told her today. 'It was Finn's dove's blood on Adam's hand. Why? I don't know. It's a terrible mess and I feel incredibly stupid. I really trusted Finn.'

Susie puts down her spoon. 'How long did you say you'd known him?'

'About a year.'

'Long enough to know him quite well then.'

'I was bored, Susie. Finn was always so welcoming. I used to go to his place and watch him work. Feed his doves.'

'So you never hung out together in Lewes?'

'No. Why?'

'You'd have had some explaining to do if Miles had seen you.'

'You haven't told him then.'

'Of course not. I didn't want to break his heart.'

Lily pulls a face. 'What's that supposed to mean?'

'He thinks the world of you. He always has,' says Susie. She marches to the cupboard and collects two wineglasses. 'I think we could both do with a drink, don't you?' She walks over to the fridge and takes out a half-drunk bottle of white.

'I won't. But thanks,' says Lily.

Susie pours herself a large glass, has a sip then sits down at the table. 'He needs a girlfriend. What happened to Jules? I haven't seen her for a while.'

'They broke up.'

'Aw! Shame. I liked her. Jules Diamond. Great name, don't you think? Shows real imagination from her parents.'

'She was christened Julia. I doubt they realised. People don't.'

'She should have been an actress, with a name like that, not a dentist. What happened?'

Lily shrugs. 'Dunno.'

'Probably got bored of him.'

'Don't be mean. Miles isn't boring.'

'He soooo is.' Susie has a sip of her wine. 'Did I ever tell you we kissed?'

'No way.'

'I cornered him after a slow dance at one of Nat's parties in our third year and snogged his face off. Poor guy didn't know what had hit him. I was pleasantly surprised. He's an incredible kisser, soft yet seductive. He should get together with Rose. Who knows, a bit of sex with sensible Miles might put Little Miss Uptight right. Jesus. I mean I know Rose has her strict regime but I can't believe even she could go jogging at a time like this. She's mad as a box of frogs.'

Lily glances at the kitchen clock. It's twenty-five past six. 'Oh my goodness. She's been gone almost an hour.'

An hour later and Rose still hasn't returned. Susie and Lily sit on opposite sides of the kitchen table, the handset and their two signal-less mobiles between them. They've tried calling Rose's mobile but of course there's no answer.

'I think we should call Marshall,' says Susie.

'Would you mind talking to him? I'm still a bit bruised from this afternoon.'

Susie screws up her nose. 'Okay. As it's you.'

Lily finds his number on her mobile and stands nervously behind Susie as she makes the call from the landline in the hall.

'Rose de Lisle,' says Susie. 'She's staying with Lily … Oh, I see. Well she only arrived last night … About two hours ago … Okay, I'll hand you over.'

'He wants to know what Rose is wearing,' she mouths, handing Lily the receiver.

Lily describes Rose's running gear to Marshall in as much detail as she can remember, including the red ribbon she'd tied in her hair.

'She's the one friend of Adam's I haven't managed to track down for a chat. Any idea why that might be?'

Lily is about to confess she'd been upstairs when he was here earlier but thinks better of it. She hasn't quite recovered from his last dressing down. 'She's been busy dealing with the Goldbergs' mess.'

'So she's not hiding anything?'

Lily pauses. She'd been about to say no, but the way things have panned out recently, she can't be sure of anything anymore. Rose said she needed to talk to her. Perhaps she was. 'Not that I know of,' she says cautiously.

'We'll organise a search party. I'll need an item of her clothing so the dogs can pick up her scent. I'll send someone round immediately.'

She hadn't expected him to take her fears seriously. 'Okay.'

'There's no sign of Finn Costello yet,' he adds. 'He's not answering his mobile. Harry Mills is parked outside his house, waiting for him. Speak later.'

Lily puts down the phone feeling nauseous.

'We'd better call Miles,' says Susie.

'I'll call him on his mobile,' says Lily. That way, she reasons, I'll avoid having to talk to either Fabian or Nat. She snatches her mobile and dashes out of the back door into the garden. Her phone beeps emphatically. She has five new messages, all from Finn begging her to call him. Behind her a twig snaps. Her heart leaps into her mouth. She spins round and peers into the dark, wet night, walking backwards to the house before wheeling around and breaking into a sprint. She hurls herself into the kitchen, sliding the door behind her, her fingers trembling as she struggles with the lock. She leans against the glass, breathing heavily.

'What's the matter?' asks Susie, rushing back into the room, carrying a pair of shoes.

'Noises. I heard noises in the garden,' Lily replies, breathlessly.

'Is somebody out there?'

'I don't know. I heard a twig snap.'

'Did you speak to Miles?' Susie asks trying her best to sound casual.

Lily shakes her head and grimaces as she tries to ignore the goose bumps that are spreading rapidly across the entire surface of her skin. 'What are you doing with Rose's shoes?'

She holds them up. 'Look at the make.'

Lily shrugs. 'Converse All Star.'

Susie rolls back her shoulders. 'Have you forgotten the footprint? Adam's killer was wearing Converse trainers.'

'You think Rose killed Adam?' Lily asks incredulous.

Susie lowers her arm and shakes her head. 'No. I don't know. Maybe. She's been behaving very weirdly.'

'I think we're letting our imaginations get the better of us,' Lily says, shivering slightly.

They stare at one another for a moment, unsure what to say or do. The phone rings, shattering the silence. The girls jump. Susie answers it.

It's Miles.

'Did Rose get back okay?' he asks.

37

Rose is gasping for breath. Her eyes are bulging, straining in her sockets like two lumps of jelly about to pop out of her head. She starts to writhe and twist, jerking her body like a fish on a line, gulping for air. But that only makes matters worse.

She feels a tug.

The ligature around her neck tightens.

The pain is excruciating, cutting into her flesh. She claws at the wire with her fingers as she fights for air.

She's aware of a large weight on her back. Heavy. Solid. A body forcing her to the ground. Her legs buckle. She topples over, trying to break her fall with her arms. But the force from behind is too strong. Her elbows give way. There's a sharp crack as the side of her head hits the tarmac. Snow-white dots dance in front of her eyes. Her left cheek flat against the damp road, she closes her eyes and drifts into unconsciousness. But then she's moving, sliding backwards through dense vegetation, her head at an unnatural angle. Nettles sting the grazed skin of her face. Briars tear the bare flesh of her arms and belly. Bluebells brush her hair. Mud slithers up her nose, viscous and cloying. Light becomes shade. The air cools. She watches a worm wriggle into the earth, burrowing for its life. She wants to follow it, tunnel to safety. Too late, it's gone.

She stops. Rain slashes at her body. Her heartbeat frantic in her ears, she tries to scream. The wire is yanked tight.

A hand is pulling at her leggings. She clings to the waistband, determined to resist but with one rough movement, the Lycra is torn from her body. Her legs are prised apart. The steel blade is cold against the inside of her thigh, in stark contrast to the warm wetness of her urine trickling down her goosy skin. The knife is thrust inside her. A searing unendurable pain splitting her in two.

Rose screams a silent scream. George, she thinks. George.

And the inky starless sky comes crashing down.

38

Miles arrives as promised, early in the morning. He brings breakfast and Fabian, who is empty-handed, and Nat who brings lilies. An over-the-top bunch of white lilies he thrusts at Lily with an awkward jerk of his arm.

'These are for you,' he says.

'Lilies for Lily,' says Susie. 'Cute.'

Funeral flowers, Lily thinks, accepting them silently. Nat's eyes are pink and sticky from lack of sleep and a smattering of pimples has broken out on his cheeks and chin. He is rocking on his feet in a self-conscious manner, as though he is aware of his own unattractiveness. Lily has never seen him like this. He is always so cocksure.

'I went too far on Sunday,' says Nat. 'And after everything you've been through, there's no excuse. I was bang out of order.'

Lily steels herself and heads to the sink. She's not the least bit interested in Nat's apologies. She doesn't want him here. No doubt Miles felt sorry for him again. Fabian too, who's probably the last person on earth Susie wants to see right now. She drops the flowers on the draining board and goes into the utility room to retrieve a vase. Outside the whine of a police siren fades as it speeds into the distance.

'I saw myself in the mirror yesterday and it wasn't a pretty sight,' continues Nat. 'I don't want to go down the same route as my father, a sad old drunk at forty-five, with liver disease and dead five years later. I'm giving up the drink. The drugs. The lot.' His head droops, weighed down by guilt.

'Your father was an alcoholic?' asks Susie, who is standing opposite Nat, her back to Fabian.

'Blimey, Nat, I'd no idea,' says Miles, unpeeling rashers of bacon before dropping them in a large frying pan.

You're way too kind for your own good, Lily thinks, watching Miles. She turns back and sees Fabian catch Susie's eye for a second. But Susie looks away quickly.

'That must have been tough,' says Fabian.

'His death tore the family apart,' says Nat.

No mention of Rose, thinks Lily, angrily ripping the brown paper and raffia off the flowers. She fills the white china vase from the tap then stabs the water with the lilies, not bothering to arrange them.

'My mother had a breakdown. I was the eldest. I should have taken charge but I couldn't bear to be around her. I couldn't bear to watch her crying all the time. I moved out the day I graduated from university and haven't been home since. I'm pretty ashamed of myself. When I'm sober, that is. It all goes away when I'm drunk.'

Lily glances over her shoulder just as Susie reaches out to touch Nat on the arm. She cringes and turns away.

'Why didn't you say anything?' asks Susie. 'We could have helped.'

'Denial, I suppose.'

'Well we're here for you now,' she says.

Still a sucker for a sob story, thinks Lily as she fiddles with the flowers. Out of the corner of her eye she sees Fabian gaze fondly at Susie. Behind them, Miles is working hard, frying bacon with one hand, stirring eggs with the other. The situation is surreal. She feels detached, as though she is floating above them, outside the scene yet looking in. Rose is still missing. An army of police are trying to track her down. She was furious with her for double-crossing Adam, but she doesn't wish her any harm. Was she the only one in the room who cared?

Last night a couple of uniformed police called round to collect an item of Rose's clothing. Susie handed them the skinny jeans Rose had been wearing earlier and the trainers.

'Why?' Lily asked her later.

Susie shrugged. 'You just never know.'

The rest of the night they huddled under duvets on the sofas in the sitting room, listening to the rain lashing at the windows, waiting for Rose. Dawn broke and there was still no sign of her. At seven, when the phone rang, they leapt to their feet.

But it wasn't Rose. It was Harry Mills.

'We had to abandon the search last night because of the terrible conditions.'

'But Rose insisted she would stick to the roads,' she said.

'The tracker dogs are already hunting the roadside from your house down to the river. After that we'll search the woods, in and around the lake and the surrounding countryside. The forecast for today is sun. It'll make our job a whole lot easier.'

As if on cue a sunbeam eased through the leaves of the horse chestnut tree outside the window in dappled rays across Lily's face. But DS Mills's news was too bleak to be altered by a favourable change in the weather

'What about Finn?' she asked, catching sight of Adam's roses, dark and shrunken in the crystal vase.

'He eventually showed up at ten. He's been with us at the station since. As DCI Marshall is the SIO on this case, the interview has had to be halted for a few hours while he coordinates the proceedings surrounding Rose's disappearance. We're sending a team to search her London flat. Finn's farmhouse too.'

'What about the trainers?' Susie asked when she put down the phone.

'I forgot to ask.'

That was two hours ago. Since then journalists, anticipating another twist in the story, were congregating on the bridle path, and at least three television crews were on their way.

And here we are listening to Nat's confessionals as we prepare ourselves a hearty breakfast, she thinks miserably.

Why don't they care? She wants to scream at them to shut up, to think about Rose, do something positive. She grits her teeth. There's no sense in losing her temper. A helicopter whirrs overhead. She leans forward and looks up at the pale sky through the glass. The helicopter swoops down low and hovers over the nearby woodland, its flashlights focused on the undergrowth.

Lily shivers.

'Rose is a tough old bird. She'll be okay,' Susie says, putting her arm around her.

'I don't know. I've got a bad feeling about this.' It's as if a giant hand has plucked her from her boring, old life and planted her in the middle of a turbulent nightmare. A hopeless tangle of events set in motion by a man from beyond the grave.

'I think we should join in the hunt,' says Susie suddenly, squeezing Lily's hand.

'Thanks,' whispers Lily.

'Great idea,' says Fabian.

'What are we waiting for?' asks Nat.

'Let's go,' says Miles and turns off the hob.

They troop out of the house, the plan being to scour the verges. Lily carries an old wooden tennis racket, Fabian a broom handle, Nat a cricket bat, Miles a hoe he's found in the garage, and Susie a torch. They separate into two groups, the girls on one side of the road, the boys on the other. Two cars drive by in quick succession. The second slows down. The driver stares at them curiously before accelerating round the bend. Further up the road, two Alsatian dogs rush to the gate at the end of a short drive and jump in the air with deafening barks as they pass by. Above them the blades of the low-flying helicopter whirr loudly.

Beating a tentative path through the tangle of cow parsley, dandelions, nettles and celandines sprouting in amongst the long grass of the overgrown verges, takes time and progress is slow. The sun is out but the vegetation is soaked with last night's rain, and it isn't long before the legs of their jeans are sodden and sticking to their calves. As they round the next bend towards the wood, Lily catches sight of the Reverend Beeton walking his two Yorkshire terriers. He sees her and hurries over, his wavy, white hair, tousled, his face pink from his exertions. She acknowledges him with a slight wave of her hand.

'My dear girl. How are you?' The terriers rear up on their hind legs and dance around her shins, yapping. 'I owe you an apology. I should've come round again but I wasn't sure ...'

She bats the air with her hand. 'It doesn't matter. Really.'

On the other side of the road, the boys disappear round the bend ahead of them.

'If there's anything ...'

'Thank you. I will.'

He gestures at Susie's torch. 'Have you lost something?'

'Well—' begins Susie.

'Oh dear. Nothing too valuable I hope.'

'Actually ...'

Lily nudges her and pulls a face.

Susie shrugs. 'Hopefully not. And thank you for your concern, Reverend. You have a good day now.'

The reverend's face is covered with confusion. Susie treats him to her most brilliant smile. Appeased, he smiles back.

Around the next bend they see a group of policemen and women dressed in dark blue shirts, black jackets and trousers, with a couple of German Shepherd tracker dogs, straining on their leads.

Fabian rushes over to them. 'Would it be okay to join the hunt? Rose de Lisle is our friend.'

'Sure,' says one of the dog-handlers, a muscular-looking man in his thirties with wiry, steel-grey hair. 'We're about to split into two groups. Most of us are heading off towards the river, the rest will stay on the road.'

Lily doesn't want to leave the roadside, so she and Susie remain with the smaller of the two groups, while the boys join the larger river group. By now they've reached the edge of the woodland. A rural castellation defending the village from the threat of suburbia, it covers a vast area and is as dense as it is long. It'll take ages to search through it, she thinks. She glances at Susie already trampling through the waist-high undergrowth on its periphery, a sea of dying bluebells to her left. Every now and then her head disappears beneath the foliage as she ducks down to inspect something.

A young, talkative PC with a neat, blonde bob walks alongside her for a while. Her name is Heather Robinson and she's only been in the force a year. This is the first manhunt she's been on and she makes no secret of how shocked she is by the murders.

'Marshall thinks it's the work of two killers,' she says. 'But not everyone agrees with him. We were heckled by a group of reporters camped by the river earlier. They were goading us about the roasting our Guv'nor's going to get if we find another body. They'd love to be proved right. Having the press against him has been a nightmare for the Guv.'

'What do you think?' Lily asks, her eyes glued to the verge.

'It doesn't matter what I think. I just do the job I'm paid to do.'

'But you must have an opinion.'

PC Robinson smiles. 'Marshall is a bit of a legend. I was made up when I heard I was on his team.' She shakes her head, her smile evaporating. 'But I guess even the very best can make mistakes.'

'Look! Look what I've found.' Susie's voice is loud, almost a shriek as she points at a narrow strip of red material, caught on a low-lying bramble.

Rose's ribbon, torn, dirty and frayed, fluttering in the breeze.

One of the dog handlers, not far behind Susie, wades towards her. The German Shepherd sniffs the ribbon then careers forward, dragging the policeman further into the wood. PC Robinson dashes after him, shouting at Lily and Susie to remain where they are. But Lily can't wait. As the police trample through the bluebells, she follows in their tracks. The dog barks excitedly, straining on its leash, its tongue lolling out of the side of its mouth as it bounds deeper into the wood. It stops beside a large bush, tangled with brambles, and paws at the ground, whining. One of the policemen edges his way towards it. He leans down and parts the prickly foliage with his hands.

Lily screams when she sees the body. It is bloated and pierced with twigs and thorns. The left cheek rests on the ground. The exposed right cheek, covered in scratches, is swollen but turgid, the distended skin a cadaverous grey. It's a distorted version of the person it once was, unrecognisable, apart from the hair. The dark brown locks, straggly and wet, secured in a ragged ponytail, tied with the remnants of her scarlet ribbon. She is still wearing her crop-top, which is smeared with mud, and trainers on her feet. But her Lycra leggings have been removed. Circling the flesh of the slender neck is a fine, red mark. And staining the inside of her white, splayed thighs are two meandering rivers of blood, splattered with last night's rain.

39

Lily is perched on the edge of one of the cream sofas in the sitting room, next to Susie. They are wrapped in police blankets, cradling mugs of sweetened tea in trembling hands, which from time to time they attempt to drink. Lily's teeth are chattering. She can't get the image of Rose's semi-naked, bloated body out of her mind. The ragged ribbon, the blood. Did she owe Liam Smith money? Was she on coke too? It's my fault, she thinks. I should've tried harder to stop her going. She places the mug to her lips and tries to swallow a mouthful but she can't control her hands and it spills and dribbles down her chin.

There's a screech of brakes as a car skids to a stop in the drive. Seconds later, Marshall marches into the room, followed by a plain-clothed policeman, smaller and stouter than Marshall, with receding hair. The sooty bags under Marshall's eyes are puffy and the skin sags in overlapping folds, like a bloodhound. His linen jacket is more crumpled than ever and there are several hairs on his shoulders, along with traces of dandruff. He gesticulates to his colleague with a jerk of his head. 'I believe you've met DS Harry Mills.'

'Shall I make you some tea, Chief Inspector?' asks PC Robinson.

Marshall frowns with irritation and waves his hand dismissively as he turns his attention to the girls. 'I've come from the crime scene. I'm sorry you had to witness that. You shouldn't have been on the hunt,' he adds, shooting a look at the uniformed sergeant.

An ice-cold shiver ripples down Lily's spine. Rose is dead. She's seen it with her own eyes. She pictures her body lying naked under a plastic sheet on a shelf in the mortuary fridge, a buff identification tag tied round her big toe. She drums her forehead with her fists, fighting to banish images of Rose's last living moments to a sealed box in the very back of her mind. She hopes she didn't suffer too much. She hopes he was quick. She pictures the headline in tomorrow's papers. *Jogger Killer Strikes Again.* She hugs the blanket closer.

'So there's only one killer after all,' she says, thinking aloud.

Marshall exhales through his nose in a loud huff. 'Whoever killed Carly Stoner did not kill your husband.'

Unaware that she's spoken, Lily looks up in surprise.

'But he did kill Rose,' says Susie, putting down her mug. 'She was killed the same way.'

He clicks his tongue in irritation. 'It's too early to say but my gut feeling is that's what Rose's killer wants us to think.'

Lily cocks her head on one side and stares at Marshall, but he turns away and laces his fingers together then flexes them backwards at the joints until they crack. He's worried he's got it wrong, she thinks.

'We found Rose's trainers. Did she kill Adam?' asks Susie.

Lily sighs and shakes her head. Surely she doesn't believe that. Rose, kill Adam? It doesn't make sense.

Marshall turns round to face Susie and frowns. 'What?'

'Rose has been acting very weirdly. Like she's lost the plot or something. And I heard her arguing with Adam the night Carly Stoner was killed. You've got to admit, it makes sense.'

Marshall is working the muscle in his cheek furiously. He takes a deep breath, sucking up his anger. 'Look —' he begins.

The door to the sitting room swings open again, and a tall, fit, black detective, with closely cropped hair, dressed in a brown leather jacket and faded blue jeans, enters the room. He has an air of confidence about him, a triumphant expression on his face. He walks directly over to Marshall and whispers something in his ear.

Marshall's face unravels in surprise and the beginning of a smile settles on his lips. 'Send them off to forensics and request an urgent comparison with the footprint lifted from the crime scene.'

Susie catches Lily's eye. 'Rose's trainers?' she mouths.

Lily frowns.

'They've been cleaned,' says DI Hammond. 'Almost certainly in a washing machine.'

'Of course they have,' mutters Susie.

'Some blood may have soaked into the stitching,' says Marshall. 'It's still worth a shot. Where is he now?'

'At the station.'

'And the hotel is certain he didn't return before midnight?'

'Adamant.'

'So four hours remain unaccounted for.' Marshall runs his hands through his hair. 'And you found them in the boot of his Ferrari.'

Lily gasps, spilling more tea.

Susie leaps to her feet, her face alabaster white. 'What's happened? What are you talking about?'

'Fabian Stephens has been arrested. A pair of white Converse trainers has been found hidden beneath the spare wheel of his Ferrari, wrapped up in a plastic bag. The pattern of the right sole matches the footprint found at the murder scene.'

'But Fabian doesn't own any Converse trainers,' she says.

Marshall slaps the back of the sofa with the palms of his hands and glares at her, his blue eyes flashing. 'And you know that for a fact, do you?'

Susie springs back as if Marshall has hit her and not the furniture. She collapses back down onto the sofa, her mouth wavering at the edges.

DS Mills shoots the Detective Inspector a wary look. Marshall holds up his hands. 'I'm sorry.'

'But that means you think he killed Rose too,' says Lily.

'Stephens left the MIR in Easthaven at five-forty-five yesterday evening. Rose de Lisle's estimated time of death was between five-thirty and nine-thirty pm,' says DS Mills. 'So yes. It's entirely possible.'

Lily is lying on her bed. She has a splitting headache. She's trying but she can't think straight. They've been such a tight little group. Now they are falling like flies. The husband whom she blindly loved is dead. Rose, one of her closest friends, is dead also. And Fabian arrested. Is he really capable of murder? And if he is, what's his motive? She wills her mind to think. Rose had pissed them all off at work by squealing to the FSA. Adam argued with her. Delaney was angry enough to assault her. Is Fabian mad enough to kill her? Because whoever killed and raped Rose has to be insane. Her death was the work of a lunatic. It didn't make sense. Fabian isn't mad. And why, if he killed her, was he out searching for her? The police have got the wrong guy. They must have. What about Delaney? Are they questioning him again? Perhaps Delaney's wife lied to the police. Perhaps he came to Sussex and killed Adam after all. Perhaps he'd been angry enough with Rose for whistleblowing to seek her out and kill her too. Or are the press on the right track? Are the three murders the work of a serial killer? Was Rose simply in the wrong place at the wrong time? One thing Lily is sure of, Rose's death has rent their tightly knit little group apart. Is that the murderer's intention? Poor Rose. If only I'd stopped her from going.

And what about Finn? What's his role in all of this? Why did Adam have bird blood on his hands?

Downstairs in the hall she hears the muted voices of Danny Marshall, DI Hammond and Harry Mills. The front door opens and closes. A car engine fires and revs then accelerates down the drive as fast as it arrived. She groans and pounds the duvet with her fists. Adam's death has unleashed a Pandora's box of chaos. Would his lies have caught up with him if he were still alive? Did his life flash before his eyes as he lay dying by the river? Did he regret cheating on her and lying to her, undermining everything she believed her marriage, no, her life to be? He'd written her a note. He wanted to apologise. But for what? The chances are she'll never know the answers. What does any of it matter anyway? What does she care if she ends up in a box, six feet under? She already feels as if she is crumbling to nothing, her life an insignificant stain.

She turns her head to one side and thinks about Fabian locked up in a police cell. Do the trainers belong to him? She closes her eyes. Stars march across her retina in bold uniformed lines. Black, regular and five-pronged. The trademark of the All Star brand, the calling card of Adam's killer. Susie is adamant Fabian doesn't own a pair. Is that because she can't believe the man she loves is capable of murder? Or did someone else plant them in the boot of his car?

But who? Almost everyone she knows wears Converse trainers. Don't they?

She stares at the ceiling, at the cobwebs that have accumulated in the past week and which hang from the plaster in fine gossamer threads. Her mind drifts back to her thirtieth birthday party, the last time they'd all been together. That had been almost a month ago. They'd been a happy group back then, oblivious to their fate. Adam had given her earrings that he couldn't afford. Miles a silver bangle that had belonged to his grandmother. The ridiculous conclusion Nat had jumped to as he'd stormed into the room, colliding with the door and tripping on the laces of the scruffy trainers he always wore, whether he was dressed in black-tie, jeans or shorts.

She sits bolt upright. White Converse All Star trainers. Nat's trainers. He was moaning about losing them at Miles's lunch the other day. The pair of trainers DI Hammond found in Fabian's Ferrari. They must be.

Miles is slumped at the kitchen table. He's removed his spectacles and has buried his head in his folded arms. Nat is propped up against the wall of the kitchen, legs crossed, chewing his fingernails. Susie eyes him nervously. His hands are trembling so much he's having difficulty connecting his teeth to his nails. He's chosen the wrong day to jump on the wagon, she thinks, trudging over to the fridge. Too bad, I need a drink. She opens the door and pulls out an unopened bottle of wine. She places it into the fancy corkscrew on the wall and pulls down on the handle. The cork slides out with a squeak. Oblivious, Nat starts pacing again, shaking his head and muttering to himself. He's been doing that on and off since he arrived with Miles. It's driving her crazy.

Nat exhales through his nose in a loud snort. 'Why would Fabian want to kill Adam? And Rose for that matter? I don't get it.'

Susie fetches a glass out of the cupboard. She fills it to the brim and has a long satisfying swig. 'So you don't think he did it then?'

'It's incredibly unlikely, don't you think?'

'Yes, I do.'

'What about this man Lily's been seeing? How long has *that* been going on?'

Susie sighs. 'It was a knee-jerk reaction. They're friends, that's all.'

Nat stops pacing and runs his tongue over the edge of his chipped tooth. 'What do you think Miles?'

Miles raises his head. His eyes are red and his shoulders sag. These past few days he's been supporting just about everyone. She thinks perhaps he's finally run out of steam. Miles shrugs then reaches out for his spectacles but lowers his head again without putting them on.

Susie sips her wine. She knows there is nothing she can say to put things right. She is all burnt up inside. In the past hour the fragile framework of her life has shattered. Finding Rose's violated body was bad enough, but hearing Fabian has been arrested for both murders has pushed Susie to breaking point. She glances at Nat who's staring into nothingness, lost in thought.

'I'm going to see if Lily's all right,' he says suddenly.

Susie grunts. She knows how Lily feels about Nat. She knows she should be the one to go and find her. But her boyfriend has just been arrested for Lily's husband's murder. What could she possibly say or do to make her feel better? It's crazy. She's made love with the man. Loving, gentle, tender and caring, he wouldn't hurt a fly. She shudders. What kind of an animal stabs a woman between her legs? She slugs a large mouthful of wine and watches Nat hurrying out of the room. Lily will be fine. Nat is sober after all.

Lily is marching purposefully towards the door when Nat's florid face appears, swiftly followed by his body. She stops in her tracks and folds her arms. 'They're not Fabian's trainers are they?'

Nat tilts his head to one side as though he's a foreigner translating her words.

She steps towards him and jabs her index finger in his chest. 'They're *your* trainers, aren't they?'

Nat's blank reaction sits perfectly with his amnesia. But Lily is not going to let it lie. She has a point and she is going to ram it home. 'You lost them,' she says impatiently. 'Remember?'

'Yes, of course, but I'm absolutely certain I didn't leave them in Fabian's car.'

'Well maybe you left them at his house.'

'No. I definitely didn't. I haven't been round there in ages.'

'But they're white, right?'

Nat nods.

'Maybe you planted them in Fabian's car.'

'Stop it, Lily. I didn't put my trainers in Fabian's car.'

She narrows her eyes. 'I don't believe you.'

'Don't be silly. You're tired. Upset. We all are.' He reaches out to her.

'Don't touch me.'

Nat hops backwards as though he's trodden on a pin. 'Lily, for God's sake.'

Lily clenches her fists. 'Go on admit it.'

'Are you accusing me of murder?'

'Yes Nat. Yes I am,' she says, raising her fists, not scared any more.

Nat grabs her wrists. 'I didn't put my trainers in Fabian's car. Now get over it.'

'You're lying,' she hisses through gritted teeth.

'I know you're hurting and it's been a shit awful day but accusing me isn't helping.'

'Well it's helping me. That was a sneaky trick to pull.'

'Stop it,' cries Nat, tightening his grip.

Lily squirms, trying to free herself. 'Not until you tell me the truth.'

'I *am* telling you the truth, which is a whole lot more than you've been doing.'

'What's that supposed to mean?'

'Don't play the innocent. I've heard all about you and the sculptor. How could you?'

'That's rich coming from a cold-blooded killer.'

Nat's top lip curls back and he clenches his teeth. 'Shut the fuck up.'

The anger that has been threatening to spill over all day explodes out of Lily. She gathers up a mouthful of saliva and spits it at Nat, hitting him in the eye with a satisfying glob. Nat's face contorts with rage. He hurls Lily sideways through the air. She lands a good six feet away from him, her head colliding with the base of the bed. Stars fizz in front of her eyes but she can just about make out Nat hovering over her, his face incandescent.

'You bastard,' she yells.

Nat hooks his wrists under her armpits, yanks her to her feet and slams her against the wall so that her face is in line with his. 'Read my lips. I did not kill Adam or Rose.'

'What the hell are you doing?' asks Miles, rushing into the room. 'Put her down.'

Nat lowers her to the floor and turns to face Miles. 'She accused me of murdering Adam.'

Lily remains where she is, flat against the wall. Her head is throbbing, her brain straining against her skull, as if it's too big for the bony cavity. She clutches at her head and twists it angrily from side to side like a lid she can't unscrew.

'Lily, stop it.' Miles's disembodied voice drifts towards her. 'Stop it, you're scaring me.'

But she can't stop. She feels as though she is in the jaws of a crocodile, gasping for breath having survived the death roll, waiting to be eaten alive. She doesn't care what happens to her any more. She has run out of fight.

'You're having some kind of fit,' Miles says in a trembling voice. He pulls her away from the wall and tries to hug her, but she is rigid as a statue.

'I'm sorry. She said some awful things. I couldn't help myself,' says Nat.

'Mate. Lily's tired. She's upset. We'll talk about this later. I think it's probably time you left.'

'That's fine with me,' Nat says and storms out of the room, slamming the door behind him.

Miles levers Lily on to his shoulder. He staggers towards the bed, practically falling on top of her as he lowers her on to it, knocking the bottle of sleeping pills off the bedside table to the floor in the process. The pills rattle as the bottle hits the carpet. Miles bends down and retrieves them. 'I think you should take a couple of these,' he says, unscrewing the top.

Lily's nerves are shot to pieces. She's exhausted but she will not resort to pills. She shakes her head.

'Come on. You'll feel better after some sleep.'

'No,' she says, angrily. She wriggles across the bed and jumps out the other side.

Miles presses his lips together, his patience obviously waning. 'Lily! Please!'

'NO!' She dodges out the way and sprints to the window. Outside in the drive, his fists in two tight balls, Nat is storming down the drive with Susie in pursuit.

'Who is this Finn?' Miles asks eventually.

Lily's shoulders stiffen. 'He's a friend of mine.'

'Nat seems to think he's more than just a friend.'

'Well I can assure you he isn't. He's a liar and a fraud. Just like Adam.'

'You have to admit, it looks kind of odd.'

'Oh fuck off, Miles. I'll tell you what's odd. Adam was having an affair. He impregnated his mistress. In a flat I didn't know he owned. That's odd. I slept with Finn once, two nights ago, not that it's any of your business.'

Miles grimaces as though in pain. He clasps his hands behind his head. 'What you did was the same as Adam. I ... I ... thought you loved him.'

'I did love him. I loved him with all my heart. And look where that got me. What does it matter anyway? Adam didn't care about anyone but himself.' As she speaks her eyes settle on Adam's note by the side of her bed. A love note, written the day he died. She covers her cheeks with her hands.

'It matters to me,' says Miles.

But Lily doesn't hear him. She's thinking about the note.

'Do you love him?'

She snaps at Miles in irritation. 'What?'

'Finn. Do you love him?'

'Will you shut up about Finn?' She stamps her foot and turns her back to him and stares out the window, grinding her teeth. She doesn't want Miles there anymore. His compassion jars. She wants Susie to herself again. She feels fine with Susie. She feels dreadful now.

'I would feel much happier if you took a couple of these pills. You need a good night's sleep,' Miles continues, calmer now. 'We all do.'

'I'm fine.'

Directly below her, Lily watches Susie standing on the doorstep gazing down the empty drive. She wonders what she's thinking about. An escape route out of the asylum, perhaps. Susie pulls her mobile out of the back pocket of her jeans and frowns as she answers it. A rumble of thunder in the blackened sky overhead heralds the approach of a storm. As the first drops of rain begin to fall, Susie retreats inside.

Miles walks over and places a hand on Lily's shoulder. She can feel the warmth of his breath on her neck. 'Well, if you won't do it for me, at least do it for her. She could do with a break.'

She stares at the swollen raindrops exploding on to the drive like tiny water bombs. After a while, she sighs and holds out her open hand. Miles smiles briefly and drops two pills on her open palm.

'I'll get you some water,' he says, disappearing into the bathroom. Quickly, Lily shoves one in her pocket. The last thing she needs is to be drugged into senselessness. Miles returns and thrusts the glass at her. 'Well go on then.'

Lily pauses, not wanting to be rumbled.

The phone rings.

Before she can answer it, Miles grasps her arm. 'Leave it and take the goddamn pills!'

Rattled by his aggressive tone, she pops the single pill into her mouth and takes a swig of water. Satisfied, Miles relinquishes his hold. Lily reaches for the receiver. 'It might be Marshall.'

But it isn't. It's Nat.

'Please don't hang up,' he says. 'It's important. I've remembered where I left my trainers.'

Scowling, she thrusts the receiver at Miles.

'What now?' He listens to what Nat has to say, the muscles in his cheeks flickering. 'Where are you?'

He can't be far, thinks Lily. He only left five minutes ago.

'Shit!' Miles slams the phone on the bed. 'I have to go. Nat's about to do something stupid.'

'What? What's happened? Where did he leave them?'

But Miles has flung open the door and is already out of the room.

'Ouch!' squeals Susie from the landing. 'Careful.'

'Sorry, sorry.'

Lily rushes after him, passing Susie on the landing.

'What's got his goat?' Susie asks.

'Nat! He's going to do something stupid.' She tears down the stairs. 'Miles? Miles? Be careful, Miles.'

There's no reply. She runs into the kitchen. The sliding door is open. She dashes outside and round to the front of the house just in time to see his pale blue car exiting the drive.

She goes around the house through the open door into the kitchen, locks it behind her and walks into the hall.

'Did you accuse him of murdering Adam too?' asks Susie.

Lily stops dead, wounded by the unveiled sarcasm. 'What?'

'You really hurt Nat you know. He was concerned about you. He was trying to help.'

'But don't you see, Fabian is vindicated.'

Susie groans in frustration. 'Listen to yourself.'

'I'm sorry. Since when did you and Nat become so close?'

'And now Miles has run away.'

'He hasn't run away.' Lily yawns and slumps down on the bottom stair, incredibly tired all of a sudden. 'To be honest, I'm kind of pleased he's gone. He was beginning to get on my nerves.'

Susie slaps her forehead in frustration. 'You're paranoid, Lily. We've all been friends for years. Can't you see everybody's falling over themselves to help you?'

'Or maybe you're all too concerned with protecting one another to tell me the truth.'

Susie's eyes flash. 'What's do you mean by that? You think we're lying, is that it?'

Lily laces her hands round her neck and lowers her head.

Mistaking her silence for embarrassment, Susie emits an exasperated sigh. 'Miles was very upset to hear about your relationship with Finn. He asked me about it when Nat was upstairs with you. You can't blame him. Adam was his best friend.'

'Yes but his view of Adam must have changed these last few days. I know mine has.'

'But leaping into bed with a potential murderer!'

Lily flinches. 'I thought we'd been through this.'

'I expect you think Fabian is guilty too?'

She shakes her head. 'I don't know anything anymore.'

The silence that settles between them is heavy with unspoken words.

'The police rang,' says Susie flatly. 'They want to ask me some questions about Fabian.'

Lily cocks her head. Susie's anger suddenly makes sense. 'What do you mean? Surely they don't suspect you?'

'God knows. And to be honest, I'm way past caring. Marshall is making a total and utter hash of this whole investigation.'

Lily bites her lip but says nothing.

'Could I borrow your car?'

Stifling another yawn, Lily leans against the banisters and shuts her eyes. 'Sure. Why not?'

40

Labouring under the influence of the sleeping pill, Lily manages to navigate the stairs. She lists down the landing, colliding with the walls, until she reaches her bedroom where she collapses on to the bed. The rain clatters at the windows, rattling the glass in the frame but within seconds she is asleep.

The sun has gone down and a sickle moon as fine as a trimmed fingernail is dangling in the night sky. She can see it through the canopy of trees. It looks as sharp as a razor. Is the man in the moon a killer? Is it his habit to float down to earth on a moonbeam to kill errant humans with his lethal scythe? She notices a corpse standing a metre away from her, staring at her with its one good eye. A worm dangles from the other empty socket. Maggots crawl between the dry ribs of the abdomen, and a putrid length of decomposing gut spills free and swings uselessly like a frayed, disintegrating cable. Beneath the ribs the lungs pulse with life, but in the place where his heart should be is a rusted tin.

'You didn't love me,' she says. 'You couldn't. You're a heartless man.'

Adam straightens his remains and shrugs his dilapidated shoulders. 'Of course I loved you. Didn't you get my note?'

'Who killed you?' she asks, noticing the other figure for the first time, sitting cross-legged on a tree stump behind Adam's living carcass, muttering strange incantations. The stubs of two horns are clearly visible on either side of his head. His floppy hair has fallen over his eyes, but his fleshy lips are parted in an evil grin. She gasps, recognising him.

Adam's eye blinks rapidly. 'Don't worry, Lily, I'll protect you.'

He lunges at Finn with a blood-curdling yell. But Finn is too quick. He springs to his feet, seizes Adam's arm and throws him over his shoulder. Adam sprawls helplessly on the ground, his mouth full of dirt, several paces from where Finn stands laughing, clutching Adam's dismembered limb. A satanic glint in his dark demented eye, he beats Adam wildly about his head with the severed arm. There's a loud crack of splintering bone as Adam's humerus connects with his skull.

Lily wakes up shaking and drenched in sweat. It's a nightmare, she tells herself. It's not real. You fell asleep. The pill must have knocked you out.

She sits up, eyes darting around the room. Darkness has fallen like a magician's cloak. She glances at the alarm clock. Nine-thirteen. She's been asleep three hours. She pulls the duvet up to her chin. Neither Miles nor Susie has a key, which means she's still alone.

Scared now, Lily opens her eyes wide, her ears on full alert. The house seems to have come alive. The floorboards creak like old bones, the loose roof tiles chatter like teeth and the hot water in the cistern grumbles like an empty stomach. Lily thinks of Rose, of her violated, lifeless body, and her scarlet ribbon no longer sitting pretty on top of her perfectly pristine world.

Her palms sweating, she reaches for the handset lying beside her on the bed where Miles flung it earlier. She picks it up and dials his home. It rings and rings. After what seems an age the answerphone kicks in. Damn it, she thinks, where did I put my mobile. Her unease growing she decides the time has come to call Marshall. But his number is downstairs on the hall table.

Never mind, she tells herself, all you have to do is go downstairs and retrieve it. It's simple really. Nothing to it. Clutching the handset she gets out of bed and, without switching on the bedside lamp, tiptoes across the room.

She stops when she hears a tapping sound; a gentle rapping on the windowpane. Lily stiffens, and holds her breath. My imagination is playing tricks on me. It's the rain, she thinks, continuing towards the door. But she's barely taken two steps when the tapping starts up again. Louder and more rapid this time, more like a purposeful knock. Willing herself to remain calm, she tries to figure out the cause of the noise – the wisteria, maybe, being repeatedly blown against the window by the wind as it often is in a storm. No. It's too concise to be caused by a branch, too even and regular. Something is making the noise. It can't be a bird. Not at night. Unless it's an owl. Do owls do that? she wonders. Do they tap on windows?

The knocking is much louder now, like a human fist drumming the window. Lily's stomach lurches as though she's plummeted several floors in a lift. Terror takes hold in the middle of a breath and she swallows her saliva. She coughs and quickly covers her mouth to drown out the sound. Her heart is in overdrive. She thinks she might faint with fright. She breathes deeply, willing herself to remain conscious, trying to regain her composure. Perhaps it's Susie. Perhaps I didn't hear her knocking on the front door and she's found the ladder in the garage. Slowly, nervously, Lily walks to the window. She inches back the curtain. A face, partially obscured by a fringe of wet, straggly hair stares back.

Lily screams. She drops the curtain, runs out of the room and hurtles down the unlit landing, bumping into the wall. The phone flies from her hand, over the banisters. She hears the plastic casing smash as it hits the wooden floor. Crying now, she presses her back against the plaster and sidesteps down the landing until she reaches the door to Susie's room. She ducks inside and fumbles with the key. But her fingers are quaking so much she can't turn it. She tries again. There's a click as it rotates in the lock. Snatching noisy, spasmodic gulps of air, she turns around and leans against the door.

Be quiet. They'll hear you, she tells herself. Her heart booms in her chest, amplifying with each agonising beat, pounding in her ears, blocking out all other sounds. She slumps to the floor, her head in her hands, her imagination running riot. Gutless corpses, zombies with crazed expressions, axe-wielding murderers are coming at her from every angle. She hugs her arms around her knees and shakes her head to bring her mind in line. For about a minute she is fully in control of her entire self. But the sound of breaking glass puts an end to that.

It comes from her bedroom.

The intruder has broken in.

41

Sweat drips from Lily's body in icicles. Her body freezes rigid. Never mind fight or flight, she is paralysed. She wills herself to get up off the floor. With a monumental effort she hauls herself to her feet, only to be gripped by the instinct to flee. She unlocks the door and makes for the stairs but has barely grabbed the banister when the impostor, shrouded in darkness, intercepts her. She opens her mouth and screams.

'Lily, don't. It's me.'

She recognises the voice immediately. 'Finn.'

'I'm sorry. I tried knocking on the door but you didn't hear me. I guess I hadn't thought how frightening it would be if someone knocked on a window late at night.'

Please make it quick and painless, she thinks, not answering.

'And now you think I'm the fecking murderer. I'm right aren't I? You think you're in danger?'

'You–just–broke–into–into–my–house–and–I'm–scared.' Her chattering teeth make it impossible for her to explain.

'I had to see you.' He reaches out his hand.

She stumbles backwards. 'You could have phoned.'

'I don't know your home number and your mobile is switched off. I had to see you again. I thought you'd realise I'd try but I've blown it, haven't I?'

'What?'

'I love you, Lily.'

Those three words again. 'How did you get up to my window?'

'I climbed the wisteria.'

Lily shudders and makes a mental note to cut it down the next day, if she is still alive. 'I'm going to call the police.'

She dodges past Finn, flicks on the landing light then hurries downstairs. Treading over the debris of the broken handset, she picks up the other phone cradled in its base on the hall table and turns on the lamp. Finn follows but doesn't try and stop her. Rainwater is dripping off him. With his long wet hair, he cuts a pathetic figure. What if he's telling the truth? What if she is wrong about this?

'I was worried about you,' he says, as if he's reading her mind.

'But …' She makes an expansive gesture towards his wet form with her arms. She looks into his eyes, two deep, black fathomless pits, dark enough to contain a million secrets. Could he have killed Adam? Her heart screams *no* above a mind that says *maybe*. She stares at him, at his gorgeous mouth that's slightly parted. Trying manfully to keep the rising panic at bay she crosses the hall and turns the switch for the recessed ceiling lights.

It's awfully vain to think that Finn would kill for you, she thinks, shielding her eyes from the sudden brightness. He says he loves you but that doesn't mean he would kill for you.

'I was having a pint at my local with my sister, when Adam was killed.'

'Well that *was* lucky.'

'Lucky?'

'She's your sister, for God's sake. She'd lie for you.'

'Maybe she would if I'd asked but I wouldn't do that and she didn't. You can trust me.'

'After all the lies?' she asks, averting her eyes from his penetrating stare, pricked again by the far-reaching paranoia of her troubled mind.

'I didn't lie. I concealed the truth to protect you from more pain.'

'Because I'm a fragile, feeble little girl.'

'No, because I care.'

'What happened the night Adam died? Marshall said you had a fight with him.'

Finn casts his eyes upwards as though he's trying to make an important decision. 'I'll tell you exactly what happened.'

'Really?' Her question is loaded with sarcasm. 'No more secrets. That's what you said.'

'Adam was angry and busting for a fight when he barged into my studio. I recognised him but I couldn't place him. I'd no idea why he'd come or how he'd found me, until he shoved a mobile phone under my nose and commanded me to read the messages in the inbox. It was your phone Lily and they were messages from me. It was all the proof he needed we were having an affair.

'He was seething. Cursing and talking total shite. He called me every name under the sun. I explained that you and I were just friends but he wasn't having any of it. He told me I was a pathetic Casanova with balls for brains. He was centimetres away from me now. His face was crimson, his pupils dilated. I'd been working on a maquette and was standing behind it, having barely moved a muscle since he barged in. He picked it up and laughed as he pummelled the clay into a ball. He yelled as he hurled it at me, suddenly, from point blank range. I ducked. It missed me and hit the window instead, smashing the glass. Adam seemed hell bent on destroying the place. He swept his arm down the table, sending several sculptures flying. I told him to calm down and explained that the reason we'd become such good friends was because you had grown fond of my doves. That's when he noticed my tools. He picked up a knife and held it to my face. *Show me the doves,* he said. I thought about trying to disarm him but figured his anger had probably doubled his strength, so I led him to the dovecote. Archie was strutting around outside. Adam saw him, snatched him off the ground and, without any warning, rung his little neck. I yelled at the bastard but he just laughed. And then, as if killing the dove was not enough, he severed Archie's head with the knife.'

She gasps. What he's saying is horrible. Horrible. He's lying. He has to be. She wants him to stop. Only she'd seen the broken glass the night they'd made love. She'd lost her mobile. Archie had gone. And it explained why Adam had bird blood on his hands.

'I'm sorry but I promised to tell you the truth. I'm certain that Archie didn't suffer. He cried out in alarm but it happened quickly. That was when I lost it. I dived at Adam and tackled him to the ground. He dropped Archie's body and I wrenched the knife from him. I swore I'd kill him if he didn't leave. I didn't mean it. I was seething. It was an empty threat. But then I remembered the bruises on your arm that you'd tried to hide from me. I knew it was him who'd hurt you and I realised then that I hated this man. I wanted to drive over to your house, sweep you up in my arms and carry you away to safety. And who knows, I might have if my sister hadn't arrived at that moment. She recognised Adam immediately from all the times he'd viewed her flat. His sordid little secret out, he bolted. To his death as it turned out. I heard about it two days later on the television news, after I'd buried Archie's body beneath the lime tree. I was shocked. Horrified in fact. Seems I wasn't the only person who hated him. He was killed. I can't say I mourned his death. But it wasn't me who killed him.'

'I loved my husband. He was everything to me,' she whispers.

'I know. I understand that. I always have. That was why I never laid a finger on you, although I often dreamed of holding you in my arms and making love to you. I love you, Lily Green. I love you more than I thought it possible for one person to love another. Being around you, breathing in your beauty, I lose all sense of self.'

What's left of her heart, the little fragments that have not been broken by Adam, tug eagerly at their strings. Lily thinks of her future life, wrapped up in happiness, just Finn and her. But her wounds run too deep. She cannot, will not listen. 'And yet you lied to me. Twice.'

The phone she is still holding, rings. She almost drops it in surprise.

'Leave it,' implores Finn. 'Please.'

She turns her back and answers it. 'Hello.'

'Lily, it's Danny Marshall. Nathaniel Tyler's been found, stabbed, by the riverbank metres from where Adam was murdered.'

'What dead?'

'I don't know. The vicar was walking his dogs out late. He called an ambulance. He's not sure if he's still alive. The thing is, Nat called me earlier to tell me he'd remembered where he left his trainers.'

'Yes. Yes. He called me. Miles went to find him.' So Nat did do something stupid, she thinks as Marshall continues.

'—Very real danger.' There is a long, loud crackle as the line breaks up. 'Sit tight and don't open the door to ... The police are on their way ... concerned especially ... the evidence ... in the car ... attic ...'

'I can't hear you, you're breaking up.'

'—Hear me?'

'Not very well.'

The line goes dead.

'What's happened?' asks Finn.

Lily flinches. Marshall's news has rocked her sufficiently to forget about him. She replaces the receiver. 'It's Nat. He's been stabbed.'

'Jesus!'

Marshall's words *don't open the door* echo round her brain. Did Finn kill Nat before he came round here? Where is Miles? Did Finn kill him too? Bloody mobile phones.

'What did he say?' asks Finn.

Lily takes a deep breath and collects her thoughts. Marshall said that the evidence was stacking up. He mentioned a car and an attic, danger. Damn. Damn. Bloody mobile phones, cracking up just as Marshall was saying the killer's name. She's panicking now, breathing rapidly, shaking. If only she'd heard. Not that it will help her much if Finn is the killer.

'Are you okay?' Finn asks.

'Not really.'

'I'll get you a brandy. You're in shock.'

Alcohol might steady her nerves, she thinks. Besides he'll have to leave me alone to get it. 'There's a bottle in the larder in the kitchen.'

She waits in the hall for a moment, trying to formulate an escape plan. Susie has taken her car. She'll have to make a run for it in the rain. But Finn is fit. He'll catch up with her, no trouble. Wait a minute. Marshall told her the police were on their way. All she has to do is bide her time, act normally, endure the minutes until she's rescued. She takes another deep breath and follows Finn into the kitchen.

He hands her the tumbler of brandy he's holding. 'Please tell me what he said. I might be able to help.'

Trembling, she turns away to avoid his eyes. Her gaze flickers nervously round the room, at the clock on the wall with the large numbers, the Neff oven, the Dualit toaster, the maple block that ordinarily housed seven, black-handled Sabatier knives, only one of the slots is empty, she notices. Where is it?

'Did he warn you to keep away from me?' asks Finn eventually.

'Of course not,' she says, trying to assume a more confident poise, hand on hip.

'Lily, you're acting very strangely.'

Her armpits are damp with sweat. Droplets run down her back. Where is the knife?

'You believe I'm innocent don't you?'

And then she twigs. 'Do you own a pair of white Converse trainers?'

'What? Yes but I don't—'

Whatever it is he's about to say is drowned out by a loud hammering on the front door. The relief Lily experiences is indescribable. She sprints to the door, eager to reach the policeman before Finn. In a mindless reflex action caused by the belief she's about to be rescued, she forgets Marshall's words and opens the door.

42

'Miles!' exclaims Lily. He is standing on the doorstep in the pouring rain, soaking wet, his hands behind his back. Rods of water drip from his hair. Specks of rain dot his spectacles. 'I thought you'd gone to see ...'

Her voice tails off as she lowers her eyes. His pale blue jeans are muddy and splattered with blood. She covers her mouth with her hands to restrain her panic. She scans his face. His cheeks are ghostly white, gaunt as a cadaver and his brown puppy-dog eyes wear a haunted expression.

Slowly she lowers her hands. 'What have you done?'

Miles's lips part in unnatural smile as though someone is working him from behind. 'It's okay. Everything's going to be okay. I'm here. You're safe now.' He holds out a hand. Blood coats his palm in a fine, shiny veneer.

Her heart pumps loud and fast. 'What happened to your hand?'

'It's okay. I'm not hurt. I've come for you, Lily. I'm going to take care of you now.'

She stares at him not daring to believe the truth.

'I love you. I've always loved you. I loved you the moment I met you. And you've suffered, Lily, because I never had the courage to tell you.'

An icy shiver oscillates down her spine. 'This is madness, Miles. You're upset. You don't know what you're saying!'

Except at that moment Miles does not look deranged. He looks completely and utterly sane, like his usual self, in fact. Kind, reliable, honest Miles, standing in the rain, holding out a bloody hand to her as he confesses to a decade-long love.

A scream rises in her chest but she swallows it. 'What have you done?' she repeats, her voice hoarse.

'Come with me, Lily. You'll be safe with me. I'll take care of you. I promise.' He speaks with conviction, his eyes fixed on hers.

'Did you kill him?'

Miles says nothing.

'Did you kill Adam?' Her breath catches in her throat. 'And Rose. Did you kill her too?'

A shadow passes over his face. He blinks rapidly.

Lily's legs are shaking. Her head aches. She presses her fingers against her temples. 'Oh my God, Miles. I saw his body. I saw Rose's. What possessed you?'

'George.'

'George? What are you talking about?'

'She lied to you. She lied to all of us.' He's angry now, his voice a shout.

'She? Are you talking about Rose?'

Miles's left eye twitches uncontrollably. 'George is not the waiter's son. She lied about that.'

'She probably had her reasons,' Lily begins, staring at the bloody hand. Her mind reels. Why are you talking to him? He killed Rose. He killed Adam. His best friend. Adrenalin races through her arteries. She judders with the force.

'Oh, she had her reasons all right.'

He's still talking. Why won't he stop? She wants to put her fingers in her ears. But she can't move. She is frozen to the spot.

'Don't you see? The waiter isn't George's father.'

'Stop it, Miles.'

'Adam is. George is Adam's son.'

The arrow hits its target. She clutches her hands to her heart. 'No. Rose wouldn't do that. She wouldn't sleep with Adam. She's my friend.'

'She told me the other day, when I was cooking lunch. You heard me. I was furious with her.'

'No. You're lying.'

'It happened on the skiing holiday, in a cupboard, like she said.'

The waiter was left-handed. It was the only detail Rose could remember. Adam was left-handed too. Inside her trembling body Lily's blood runs cold. 'I don't believe you.'

But Miles isn't listening. 'It was one of the reasons he was so upset. She told him the night of your thirtieth birthday. He didn't believe her, of course, and was going to do a DNA test to prove she was lying.'

'But you didn't talk to him. You said—'

He leans closer until his nose is almost touching hers. 'You see Adam claimed he couldn't remember. That he was out–of–his–head drunk. But he can't have been that drunk, can he?' A triumphant smile hangs on his lips.

Lily turns her face away. 'No. It's not true. None of this is true.'

'You'd been going out, what, ten months by then?'

She wraps her arms around herself. She is light-headed. Nauseous. Weak. Frightened that she's about to fall over, she leans against the doorframe. 'Rose was about to tell me,' she whispers. 'I told you she wanted to talk to me. That's how you knew where she was.'

'Lily!'

At the sound of Finn's voice, Miles whips his other hand out from behind his back. Lily looks at the black handled Sabatier kitchen knife he's brandishing, smeared with dried blood.

Her knife.

Nat's blood.

Finn loops his arm around her waist and pulls her behind him just as Miles runs forward, letting out an anguished scream.

'You've ruined everything.' He slashes wildly with the knife, cutting Finn on the arm. Finn lunges at him and shoves. Miles topples backwards, out of the house and Finn slams the front door shut. He locks it and bolts it then leans against it, covering the wound in his upper arm with his hand. Blood seeps through his fingers, glistening red.

'For a moment I was under the illusion you were talking to the police,' he says breathlessly.

Lily is shaking her head.

'Friend of yours, is he?'

'I ... I ... I ... don't understand,' she says.

'I was hoping you'd be able to explain. I've never met the guy before.'

'Adam had a son,' she whispers.

But Finn doesn't hear her. 'I don't think he likes me all that much.'

'What are we going to do?' she asks weakly.

'Well that very much depends on what he does next. But right now I suggest we phone the police.'

Swallowing the bile that has risen in her throat, Lily runs to the phone on the hall table. With fumbling fingers she redials Marshall's number. The call goes straight to his voicemail. Her heart sinks so rapidly she feels dizzy. She slumps down on the bottom stair, defeated. 'Marshall's out of signal.'

'Dial 999! Quick!'

There's a resounding crash in the kitchen, the sound of broken glass clattering like hail on the tiles, and a crack as the brick, or whatever it is that Miles has hurled through the window, splits the door of one of the units. Lily leaps to her feet, dropping the phone in panic.

'Upstairs! We've got to hide,' says Finn. He shoves Lily towards the stairs. More glass shatters, the crystal shards skating across the kitchen floor, followed by the loud thud of the second brick. Gaining momentum, Lily reaches the landing and sprints towards her bedroom. As she reaches the door she steals a look over the banisters. Miles is taking the stairs two at a time, the knife in his hand. Finn shoulders her into the room. Sickened, terrified, Lily slams the door behind him. She tries to turn the key in the lock.

Finn barges her out the way. 'Let me.'

There's the sound of splintering wood and Miles's bloody fist appears through the top left hand panel of the door, missing Finn's shoulder by centimetres. Lily shrieks and runs to the other side of the bed.

'I'm going to barricade the door,' says Finn. His arm dripping blood, he charges over to the heavy, mahogany dressing table and heaves it across the floor. Blood rains down on the white carpet in crimson spots. Lily rushes to his side and helps him shove it into position, as bottles, ornaments and framed photographs fall to the floor.

'That should keep him out for a while,' says Finn. But Miles's fist breaks through the wood reappearing, this time, just above the height of the drawers. 'Then again, maybe not.'

He scans the room for other furniture to strengthen the blockade. He sees the slipper chair and levers it up on top of the dressing table. 'That'll do for starters.'

'And what about this?' Lily asks, sweeping her arm across the bedside table to remove the lamp. 'There are two of them.'

Finn picks up the other one and adds them to the pile. For a while all is quiet behind the door. He shoots Lily a reassuring smile. 'Hang in there.'

Lily nods dumbly.

But then there's a deafening roar from the landing as Miles runs at the door, ramming it with the full force of his weight.

'Lean against the dressing table!' instructs Finn.

But Miles's strength seems to have trebled. The door buckles and the furniture shifts slightly.

'The wisteria. It's our only chance,' says Finn.

Behind him the battered door inches open a fraction. Lily watches mesmerised.

'Come on,' says Finn, steering her to the window. He opens the frame but she hesitates for a second. 'Hang on to the sill and I'll hold on to your wrists until you find your footing. Then feel your way down with your feet.'

'But—'

Miles throws himself against the door again. One of the bedside tables wobbles precariously then topples off the pile. Its spindly leg snaps as it hits the floor.

'Do it, Lily!'

The furniture shifts inwards a bit more. There's a loud thump as the chair tumbles to the ground. Lily clambers out of the window. She clings to the sill. Finn holds on to her wrists, blood pouring from his wound down his arm and on to hers.

'Okay?'

Fuelled by fear, she lets go with one hand and grabs hold of one of the gnarled stems. Feeling her way with her feet and hands, she climbs awkwardly down. The rain thrashes her body like an icy whip but she's too preoccupied with trying to escape to notice, spurred on by the clamour in the room above. She reaches the safety of the drive by the time Finn's feet appear above her.

'Head to the Land Rover. And hurry. He's taking the stairs,' he says.

Lily strains her eyes in the inky blackness. The vehicle is parked in front of the garage, about four metres away. Finn jumps off the wisteria, landing cat-like on all fours. He springs to his feet, takes her hand and pulls her towards it. He opens the passenger door with his good arm and shoves Lily in then darts round to the driver's seat. He has the engine started before she's closed the door.

Miles morphs out of the shadows and takes a flying leap at the moving car. He runs up the bumper, on to the bonnet then flings himself at the windscreen, covering it with his spread-eagled body. Steering blind, Finn swerves and crashes into the giant horse chestnut tree. The massive jolt throws Miles to the ground by the driver's door. Finn crunches the gears into reverse but Miles is too quick. He springs to his feet, snatches at the handle and Finn's door swings open. He kicks out at Miles who sidesteps deftly out of the way. Lily watches in horror as, with a blood-curdling yell, Miles pitches forward and thrusts the knife into Finn's belly. Finn groans in agony. Flaunting a smile, a demonic glint in his eye, Miles draws out the bloodied blade and backs away.

An incredible surge of anger takes hold of her. Emboldened with rage she leaps out the car and around the bonnet. Miles raises the knife again but she dives at him, clasping his arm with both her hands.

'Drop the knife,' she shouts, shaking the limb as hard as she can.

Miles laughs. Taking Lily's wrists in his left hand he reels her in to his chest, bends down and kisses her on the cheek. Repulsed, she tries to wriggle free only to feel the cold edge of steel as he rests the flat side of the knife against her throat.

This is it. I'm going to die, she thinks. She feels nothing. No fear. No panic. Just a strange acceptance.

'Don't,' croaks Finn. His hands are clasped over the wound to his abdomen, which is haemorrhaging profusely, his T-shirt and jeans soaked in blood. 'You don't want to kill her.'

'What makes you say that?' asks Miles with a manic laugh.

'Because you love her,' rasps Finn. His face is a death mask. She knows she is losing him.

'Yes. But what's the point? She doesn't love me. She never did.' Miles rotates the knife, the sharp edge of the blade against her skin. 'And if *I* can't have her no one can.'

Locked in his painful embrace, she is a long way from understanding Miles's insanity. But she knows that he's way beyond caring about her, his mind and body possessed by a force outside his control. She can see it in his eyes, the satanic glint that focuses inward on his dark, obsessive fantasy.

'So kill me then. That way you'll have her all to yourself.' Finn's voice barely registers as a whisper. He slumps forward over the steering wheel.

'Great idea.' Miles sneers and lowers the bloody blade. He steps closer to Finn, dragging Lily with him and laughs as he raises the knife above his head to deliver the fatal blow.

'Miles, no!' she screams, twisting and writhing.

'Shut up!' he snaps. Tightening his grip around her chest, he squeezes the air out of her lungs.

'No,' she gasps. And in a last ditch attempt to draw Miles's attention away from Finn, she clamps her jaws around his forearm and bites hard.

'It's no use,' he says icily, aiming the knife at her chest. 'Enjoy this brief moment between life and death, Lily, because after I slip this blade between your gorgeous breasts, you *will* be mine.'

She feels a sharp stab of pain. Blue lights flash in front of her eyes. Sirens wail.

'STOP! ARMED POLICE!'

A shot is fired. She hears the muffled thud as the bullet reaches its target. And then she's falling backwards. There's a strident crack. Another shot.

Then nothing.

There is no soundtrack to her nightmare any more.

Only blood-drenched silence that slowly, seamlessly fades to black.

Epilogue

Lily comes to, panting. For a moment she thinks she is dead. But then the pain from her punctured shoulder kicks in and she remembers what has happened. Her body is cold and wet and unnaturally stiff. With difficulty she raises her head. Miles is lying face-up on the drive beside her; a growing pool of blood beside his head. His eyes behind his broken spectacles are staring sightlessly at the sky. The rictus smile of the psychotic murderer he's become still lingers on his lips. There's a small hole in his forehead, she notices, from the bullet which killed him. Beside his outstretched hand, pierced by the bullet from another shot, is the knife.

Shocked into senselessness she is vaguely aware of activity around her. Lying on the gravel, immobilised in the rain, soaked through to the skin, she feels as if she is shrinking into the earth. As the paramedics lift her on to a stretcher, she catches sight of Finn's body, slumped over the steering wheel, his blood running pink in the rainwater as it trickles to the ground. A blanket is thrown over her but she's aware of nothing else. Her mind and body are numb.

She is taken to hospital where the wound to her shoulder is cleaned, stitched and dressed. Pale and weak from the shock of her ordeal, she is hooked up to a saline drip and placed in a private room for the night. She doesn't object. Her brain has locked down. All she can see is the look in Miles's eyes as he raises the knife to kill Finn. He knows Finn is about to die but instead of triumph she can see only fear.

Perhaps that was the moment Miles faced his madness full on.

Later that night Marshall visits Lily. The sister in charge of her ward insists Lily is unfit for a police visit. But Lily begs her to let him in. She has too many questions to ask him. She knows she won't be able to rest until she has the answers. Fearing that to go against her patient's wishes would impede her recovery, the sister reluctantly agrees.

Danny Marshall's face is craggy and drawn, Lily notices as he sits down in the plastic chair beside her bed. He smiles ruefully at her, which relieves some of his facial tension and runs his hand through his greying hair.

'I'm sorry, Lily. We were a little too late.'

'Everybody loved Miles.' she begins, her voice tailing off.

'No,' he says, shaking his head. 'Everybody loved Adam.'

She nods and lowers her eyes. 'You always said there were two killers but I never guessed one of them was Miles.'

Marshall sighs and rubs his face. 'He was very convincing. And very clever. He covered his tracks. And he was lucky that Nat, Rose, Delaney, Finn and Fabian, particularly Fabian, had such strong motives. Fabian made a real meal of protecting Honor – disappearing like that, lying about her identity, her affair with Adam, following Adam down to Sussex to have it out with him. It was easy for Miles to frame him. We never suspected Miles, although we checked out his alibi. We visited the estate agents the day after Adam's death. There was no evidence his computer had been tampered with but when we pulled his office server apart we discovered he'd accessed it and tampered with the clock, altering the time from nineteen thirty-five to twenty thirty-five. He sent the emails to the server then reset the time. The recipient's inbox registered the arrival of the email seconds later, just as he had planned. It would have taken him a couple of minutes but more importantly it gave him the window he needed.'

Lily thought of Miles calmly cooking breakfast the morning after he killed Rose. 'He gave nothing away.'

'No,' He pauses for a second. 'The attic room at the top of his house was papered floor to ceiling with pictures of you Lily. It must have been a deep obsession.'

As the days pass she wonders how it could have turned out differently. What she could have done to prevent the course of events that led to Adam's death and the chaos and carnage that followed in its wake? How had she managed to miss the signs?

'None of us saw them,' Susie assures her. 'You mustn't blame yourself.'

'But the signs were there.'

'Well if they were, they were faint. I've been over it in my mind again and again, but I can't think of anything that incriminated him.'

'His overbearing protectiveness towards me. The stoical response he had to Adam's death. His anger towards Rose before lunch that day. His reaction when he discovered my relationship with Finn.'

'You are totally blameless in this. You must know that.'

She tells herself Susie is right. That she was nothing more than an innocent pawn in the complex game of chess that Miles's crazed mind was playing.

'Maybe I encouraged him.'

'You know that's not true.'

And she thinks of the expression on his face in the moments before he died; the look of a man jumping from a plane whose parachute has failed to open, knowing that he is freefalling to his death. And she tells herself again that Miles's heart was torn apart with madness, not love.

'Rest now, Lily. The nurse told me you need lots of sleep.'

But how can she sleep after all that she's been through?

The blade missed Nat's heart by centimetres but punctured a lung. The nurses at the hospital told him he's lucky to be alive, which of course he was. But with his two closest friends dead, luck was not an easy concept for him to understand. Like Lily, he blamed himself.

'I should have remembered where I left my trainers,' he tells her when she's well enough to visit him in his ward. 'Miles was wearing them that day. He told me he thought nothing of it at the time. He had no idea how conveniently they would cover his tracks. By the time I remembered I'd left them at his place the night after your party, it was too late.'

'I should have listened to you,' says Lily. 'I should have taken your call. I'm sorry.'

'I was in The Star when I rang you. I suggested to Miles we meet there for a drink and then I called Marshall. When Miles arrived, he seemed unnaturally wired and suggested we walk by the river. He seemed pretty desperate to talk. Confess, as it turned out,' he explains. 'I was a bit caught out by the knife.'

Lily listens as Nat relates the story of the life she shared with Adam as lived by Miles, at the dislocated truth that coursed beneath the surface of his demented story.

'Miles loved you, Lily,' continues Nat. 'He always did. Right from the moment he spoke to you the day you arrived at university. I knew it. Adam must have known it, even if he never admitted it. And he believed, as Adam did, that Rose was lying about George, but the damage had already been done. Adam slept with Rose, one of your closest friends, impregnated his mistress and hurt you beyond repair, the only girl he'd ever loved. His love for you drove him mad with hatred.'

She closes her eyes. Now at last she understands what was going on in Adam's life. Honor's pregnancy was the reality check he needed. Things had spiralled out of control. Work was going badly. Delaney had persuaded him to make money another way. He'd broken the law to cover his escalating debt. He was a suspect in a murder investigation. His mistress was pregnant. And now Rose was telling him he was George's dad. He didn't believe her but she was threatening to tell his wife. He would do a DNA test to silence her. But first he had to get the rest of his life in order.

He broke up with Honor. Put the flat on the market. Bought diamonds for his wife's thirtieth birthday and told Delaney he wanted out. The next step, to confess everything to the woman he loved. But when he got home, she wasn't there. He found her mobile and the text messages and, high on cocaine, went and had it out with Finn. And then he made his biggest mistake. He called Miles on his mobile. He wanted to talk, needed his advice. Miles already knew Adam was having an affair. He didn't like it. He knew about the cocaine. He didn't like that either. He knew about Delaney. Adam told him everything. He always had. But he didn't know Honor was pregnant and he didn't know about Rose.

'Rose, of course, was one step ahead,' explains Nat. 'She took some hair from Adam's hairbrush the night of the party and did the test which proved George was Adam's son. And because Adam hadn't believed her, she told Miles that day at lunch.'

We were childless, Lily thinks, because of me. Was that the driving force? Would things have turned out differently if I'd had a baby? Would it have stopped the rot?

Rose is cremated in London a week later. Lily is neither physically nor mentally up to the trip. The corridors of her fractured mind are dark and bleak. Her shoulder is still tender and supported by a sling. But she insists on going.

There are no red ribbons on Rose's coffin, although Lily half-expected there to be, just six brass handles and a spray of white lilies. Sitting in the front pew is a dark-haired boy, eight years old, flanked on either side by Rose's parents. George turns round once during the ceremony and looks Lily directly in the eye. He's just like his father, she thinks. How did she not notice that before? The grey stain of old tears meanders down his cheeks. He shows no signs of recognition and quickly turns away. A lump catches in her throat. He is just a boy, the son Adam did not know he had. She wants to scream at the injustice of it all. That Rose had the baby that she always longed for. Adam's baby. But she can't. George is an innocent child. His parents killed within a week of each other. An orphan. She watches in dislocated silence as Rose's bones and flesh are burnt to dust, her rosy, chocolate box world reduced to memories.

Adam is buried shortly afterwards. His funeral is a quiet ceremony attended by his family, Susie, Fabian, Nat and Lily. His mother, Ursula, a small but intimidating woman, sobs into a white embroidered handkerchief as her son's coffin is lowered into the ground. Henry, tall and indomitable, stands stiffly at one end of the open grave, his chin held high. Behind the stoic figure of their father, his sisters, holding hands, weep silently.

At the end of the service his parents approach the four friends who are standing, dry-eyed and faithless a few metres back, and thank them for coming. She wishes then with all her heart that she'd listened to her conscience and stayed away. She only came to satisfy any lingering doubt that she had dreamt the last few days. Reality has become a little shaky following the events of the past week. She thought by seeing his body lain to rest she might at last begin to accept it.

Time is a great healer. As the weeks pass Lily's nightmares begin to plague her less and less. She comes to comprehend the inevitability of what happened. That she was an innocent who got swept along, much like Finn Costello.

Carried away on a stretcher by the paramedics, she presumed Finn was dead. The wound to his abdomen was deep and he was bleeding to death. When Marshall visited her in her hospital bed with the news that, against all the odds, Finn had survived, she thought a miracle had occurred.

It was as though his life had risen from the ashes, like a phoenix.

It isn't easy for them trying to rebuild their lives. Like two battered soldiers invalided out of war, they both have to come to terms with what happened that day. The day the dove cried. And even though Finn was removed from the central conflict of the drama, it would be foolish of her to assume he's unaffected by it all. He lied to protect her, once upon a time, and in the end he almost died for her. Both of them will take time to mend, although she knows, for her, it will be harder. The mental bruises that Adam, Rose and Miles inflicted will take time to heal.

She sells Orchard House, moves away from Sussex and back to London. She is haunted by shadows but as the months pass, they begin to fade. She never stops thinking of Adam. She knows she loves him still. Will always love him, no matter what he did. He was the half that made her whole. Above all else that bothers her.

Finn waits, hoping that when she is ready she might love him too. He gives her time and space, never for a moment forcing the pace. It isn't until December that she feels strong enough to return to his farmhouse. It is a cold, crisp Christmas Eve, one that she will never forget, because it is the day she insists Finn marks Archie's grave with a small, white slab of alabaster stone.

The End

Acknowledgements

I would like to thank DCI Adam Hibbert and Inspector Adam Hayes of Sussex Police for their time and help in guiding me through the police procedures following a murder, and Leonardo Pereznieto for his invaluable insight into a sculptor's mind. I would also like to thank the RSPB for endeavouring to answer my slightly offbeat questions about doves. *Pigeons, Doves and Dovecotes* by M.D.L.Roberts and V.E.Gale, was a book I referred to time and time again.

To Victoria Pepe, my hardworking and enthusiastic editor, I give a huge thanks and also to Jenny Parrott for her support and guidance this past year.

Thank you to Adam Hayes, Simon Bottomley, Catherine Prendergast, Susie Horner, Rachel Angel, Lesley Frame, Fran Kazamia, Simon Allan and Libby Allan for reading the book in its various drafts, and to Kathleen Hinwood for her design expertise, and Helen Wheeler and Holly for their help with the marketing.

And finally a massive thank you to Simon for encouraging me to follow my dream, for believing in me and for his incredible patience every time my confidence deserts me, and to Holly and Sam for their love and support.

5110471R00167

Printed in Great Britain
by Amazon.co.uk, Ltd.,
Marston Gate.